ASCENDANT

THE ROYAL MARINE SPACE COMMANDOS
BOOK 3

JAMES EVANS

JON EVANS

Copyright © 2018 by James Evans & Jon Evans

Cover art by Christian Kallias Infinite Scifi

All rights reserved.

No part of this book may be reproduced in any form or by any electronic or mechanical means, including information storage and retrieval systems, without written permission from the author, except for the use of brief quotations in a book review.

❦ Created with Vellum

PROLOGUE

Atticus shrugged. "I don't know, Colour Jenkins, I imagine Lieutenant Warden thought you'd make good use of an ogre clone, given your combat experience."

Colour Sergeant Stephanie Jenkins muttered something under her breath and Atticus stifled a smile. There wasn't much he could do. He could hardly haul Warden over the coals for his assignment of clone body types.

"We'll be able to reassign some clones shortly, so if you want to be redeployed into a different model, I'm sure we can do that for you."

"Thank you, sir, much appreciated," Jenkins replied, the basso voice her clone produced somehow fitting her usually gruff demeanour.

"Now, it looks like we're approaching the Deathless base. Let's see if we can't turn this place into something useful, hmm?" Atticus said.

The base loomed ahead, still huge and impressive despite the devastation caused by Warden and his assault team during the attack on the so-called 'mothership'. With more Marines being deployed, they now had the bodies to make use of the base and recover more of the potentially useful equipment the Deathless had been forced to abandon. That meant getting to the base with a team to properly catalogue whatever Warden and Marine X hadn't turned to rubble.

More importantly, Atticus wanted to garrison the base before the Deathless colonists, who had landed only eight hundred kilometres to the southwest, could retake the site and settle back in. Warden had offered to lead the group, of course, but Atticus had overruled him and now led the mission himself.

Lieutenant Warden was now extremely busy with his new task: overseeing clone redeployment, work assignments and logistics. Warden had winced visibly when Atticus had given him the good news, but he hadn't complained. The job had to be done, and handling councillors' complaints about deploying Marines ahead of colonists or arguing with politicians about what types of clones to grow was just an unfortunate part of it. Atticus couldn't help grinning at the thought of Warden getting involved in local politics and dealing with the 'personalities'.

"And it'll look good on your resume, Tom," Atticus had said. "The general likes to see his officers taking on these sorts of responsibilities and while you get stuck in here, I can take A Troop on a nice, easy road trip." Warden hadn't been keen but they had talked it over and, by the time Atticus had left, the lieutenant was elbows deep into the detailed plans.

Which left Atticus out in the field, doing the job he loved. HQ claimed he had been a captain for too long, but they respected his lack of interest in promotion. If he had gone much higher in the ranks, he would have been stuck behind a desk for the rest of his career. There just weren't any large scale wars in this day and age, so nobody above the rank of captain saw any interesting action at all.

The troop carrier ground to a halt and bumped him out of his daydream. He went to crack his knuckles, then realised it wasn't going to work with the fingers of his Deathless officer clone. He pulled on his armoured gauntlets and ran a diagnostic check to confirm the power armour was functional.

Around him, the Marines were piling out of the enormous Deathless troop carrier and deploying across the plain. Colour Sergeant

Jenkins was in the van, leading a section forward at double-time to secure the area and take control of the remains of the gatehouse.

Behind the Marines, the civilians pulled up, their rovers hauling sleds to take back to Fort Widley anything of value that wasn't required to get the base up and running.

<Movement ahead> sent Jenkins.

<Confirmed?> Atticus checked his rifle, suddenly wary.

<Hold for confirmation> sent Jenkins, then a moment later, <Confirmed. Drones have Deathless troops in sight. Advancing to cover>

Atticus paused, watching the Marines fan out as Jenkins and her team, about two hundred metres ahead, sprinted for cover.

He turned to the civilians and waved at them, contacting their lead vehicle by HUD.

<Pull back, there are Deathless on site>

He found Sergeant Millar.

"Get Section 3 back there in the APC to babysit the civilians, in case there are any Deathless out here. I don't want an ambush."

Then he gathered up Section 2 and moved out with them, sprinting to catch up with Jenkins.

~

Atticus dove for cover as the head of the Marine next to him disintegrated under the impact of a railgun projectile.

"Railgun," he bellowed, and around him the Marines sought cover.

"Smoke out," he said, grabbing a grenade from his webbing and lobbing it forward. A cloud of concealing smoke spewed from the grenade, growing quickly as more grenades were thrown.

"Lance Corporal Mills, get me drone footage, I want to know where that sniper is," Atticus yelled as an enfilade clattered across the rocks they were sheltering behind.

Another railgun round boomed through the morning air, shattering a boulder and exposing the Marine who had taken shelter behind it. The trooper sprang forward, rifle returning fire as he bolted for cover. He almost made it but another round took him in the shoulder, spinning him around and separating his arm in a shower of blood.

"Bollocks to this — these rocks aren't as tough as they look. Jenkins, I need covering fire!" he shouted. "Keep moving."

<Sergeant Millar> sent Atticus, <get the cannon on the APC opened up around the gatehouse>

<Range is a bit extreme, sir, we pulled well back as ordered>

<I'm not interested in specifics, Sergeant, I only need to give them a reason to keep their heads down. Get it done>

<Roger that, sir> Sergeant Mills responded. The air was filled with fire from the Marines around Atticus, and then the cannon on the APC opened up too, rounds sparking off the foamcrete of the walls.

"Drone's up, sir," shouted Mills.

Atticus flipped to the drone's viewpoint, watching as the rounds suppressed the Deathless bastards. Time to move in three, two... one.

He sprinted out from behind the rock, rifle slung over his back as he wasn't planning to use it. Four hundred metres. Four hundred metres and the enemy had at least one railgun. If they kept their heads down, he might make it.

No such luck, he thought, as his leg went out from under him. Bugger. Damage reports flashed across his HUD, but he barely had time to register them as he crashed to the deck, throwing his arms out in front of him. He turned the dive into a forward roll and came up running, or at least stumbling quickly.

"You alright there, sir?" Jenkins asked.

"Just a scratch," Atticus replied jovially through gritted teeth, "but I wouldn't mind if someone could get those buggers to keep their heads down." He ran on, zig-zagging towards the wall.

"Roger that, sir. Come on, you lot — who wants to live forever?" Jenkins roared, rising to her feet and pounding after the captain. The enormous power armoured bulk of her ogre clone shook the ground as she sprinted forward, the shotgun in her hand pointed forward like a pistol. She fired at the top of the wall, where the enemy had to be, but the range was huge. The Deathless up there weren't immediately cowed and they returned a barrage of fire.

At two hundred metres, Atticus ordered an emergency cocktail of painkillers and stimulants from the suit's casualty support system. He put on a burst of speed as the pain lessened but the warning symbols were now blinking angrily in his HUD. He made it to a large rock and slid into cover, panting into his helmet for a few moments before righting himself.

The stimulants had kicked in now and he surged back to his feet, ignoring the alarms. Bullets ricocheted from the rock as he broke cover, sprinting forward as fire from his own team roared overhead. One hundred metres to go.

Atticus pulled a grapnel from his webbing as he ran and hooked the line to his harness as he drew closer to the wall. He switched direction again then took the shot as he fell under the shadow of the great wall. The grapnel looped over one of the foamcrete spikes that thrust out from the top of the wall and the winch yanked Atticus into the air even as he leapt at the wall.

He rose rapidly as the line was winched in. He pulled a flashbang from his webbing and lobbed it over the wall. It detonated as he neared the top of the wall. Then he dragged himself over the lip of the wall onto the parapet and unclipped from the line to free himself. As the grapnel swung free, Atticus unslung his rifle, shouldered it and fanned to the left.

Clear.

He turned right, rifle at the ready.

Contact.

Three rounds into the torso of a Deathless trooper still reeling from the grenade. Two more in the head of his mate.

Not his target though. He heard the railgun spit its lethal projectile again and wondered if he had lost another Marine to the brutal discharge. Fuck.

Where was the sniper? The bastard had to be here somewhere. Atticus pressed forward, his weapon kicking against his shoulder as he cut a bloody swathe through the Deathless troops.

Then he saw a flash from the roof of one of the buildings near the wall and heard the telltale sound of a railgun. He emptied his magazine towards the building and lobbed another grenade for good measure. He jogged back a few paces, swapped in a new magazine and slung his rifle. Then he turned to face the building, gritted his teeth and took a running jump.

Even as the power armour pushed him further than he could ever have jumped unaided, he knew he wasn't going to make it.

He wrapped his arms around his head and crashed through a window on a lower storey, rolling across the floor in a shower of glass and curses. Atticus staggered to his feet, shook himself free of the remains of the window then unslung his rifle and made for a staircase. The death knell of the railgun sang out again, and he yelled in frustration, taking the stairs four at a time.

The painkillers weren't doing much to suppress the punishment he was putting his leg through anymore and the 'scratch' burned like a red-hot poker. Well, like a bullet wound really, and he'd had lots of those. Never a red-hot poker, at least not to date, but it would surely be similar, wouldn't it?

The door to the roof was propped open, a sensible precaution if you wanted to get easily off the roof.

But not too smart if you're sniping at my Marines, you bastard, thought Atticus. He charged out onto the roof and ducked almost immediately as some cocky bugger tried to stab him with a glowing knife. Bloody hell, who gave these kids knives?

Atticus left the Deathless trooper with three ugly holes in his chest and throat, gurgling his last. The railgun fired again, revealing the sniper's location and Atticus crossed the roof as quickly as he could, one eye watching for any other jokers trying to stick things in his face.

He moved between two ventilation units and went left. The roof was clear, all along the wall. He swung quickly the other way, and saw the sniper was crouched near the wall.

But he wasn't aiming out over the wall — he was bringing his weapon to bear.

Atticus snarled and leapt. His rifle spat fire. The railgun boomed.

"Colour Jenkins, how goes it?" Atticus asked. She crouched down, her power armoured bulk casting a welcome shadow over him. Reaching out, she helped him remove his helmet. There was blood around his mouth and his face was creased with pain.

"They retreated, sir. The lasses and lads gave them a good seeing-to and they backed off. We lost a few, though, even after you put the railgun out of action. These ones are putting up a better fight than the others. They're more cunning, more resilient," Jenkins said, offering him a canteen. He shook his head and spat blood onto the roof.

"Maybe more experienced," Atticus suggested. "Where did they go?"

Jenkins shrugged, the gesture incongruous in her huge ogre clone. "Not sure, sir, they legged it to a dropship and took off before we could catch up and put it out of action."

"A dropship? They must be from the ship Warden scuttled. They only captured three of their dropships; we thought the fourth had gone down with the ship."

"Looks like it survived, sir. And I think they've been stripping the base. Not just today either. Lots of stuff is conspicuous by its absence. They must have their own Fort Widley somewhere," Jenkins said.

Atticus nodded, or at least tried to.

"You look a bit peaky, sir, if you don't mind me saying. Not that it's easy to tell with these Rupert clones," Jenkins said with a grin that didn't really hide her concern, "they all look the same to me."

"Har de har har, Colour Jenkins," said Atticus, blood dribbling down his chin. He tried to wipe it away but his arm wasn't working properly. "I do feel a little under the weather. I think I'll just lie here for a bit and get my second wind."

"Pretty sure you're missing a large chunk of your lung, sir. I don't think you'll be getting your second wind any time soon."

"Figure of speech, Jenkins," he whispered, "figure of speech."

"Sorry, sir. Any preference when we redeploy you?"

"Marine standard, please, and tell them you can go up to HMS *Albion* and have your pick too," Atticus said, voice almost inaudible as he coughed and spat out more blood.

Jenkins shook her head. "Actually, sir, I think I'll stick with this one for a while. It has its advantages and it looks like we aren't done with the Deathless on New Bristol yet." He nodded.

"No, Colour Sergeant, I think they'll be a thorn in our side…" he coughed once more and his head lolled to one side.

Jenkins sighed. It wasn't the clone that made the captain tough. Atticus held the record for the most deaths of any serving officer in the Royal Marine Space Commandos. Not because he was bad at it, far from it, but because he led from the front and didn't ask his Marines to do anything that he wouldn't do himself. She reached out and closed his alien-seeming eyes, whispered a short 'Fuck you' to the Deathless and stood up.

The base needed tidying up and the captain wouldn't thank her when he was redeployed if they had stood around all day just wailing and whining. She walked over to the side of the roof and bellowed down at the troop. "Right, you lot. The captain's dead!"

"Again?" some joker remarked.

"Yes, again, and just for that you can detail all the Deathless bodies and gather them up to be taken back to Fort Widley for recycling. I want this place checked for boobytraps before we let the civilians move in to requisition equipment and supplies. Load anything the colonists need and we don't onto the transports and haul it back to Fort Widley," said Jenkins.

"Are we falling back, Colour?" someone asked.

"No, we're bloody not. We're going to turn this mess into a forward operating base," Jenkins said, "and I want it operational before the Deathless come back." She paused, looking over her troops. "Get ready, ladies and gents. When the captain is back on his feet, we're going to war."

1

"Is that another new clone, Edward?" said General Bonneville, leaning close to peer at the image of Atticus.

"Yes, sir, fresh and clean, although not the outfit I requested."

"What happened to the old one?"

"Railgun round to the abdomen, sir, bled out before there was a chance to receive medical attention."

"Nasty. Was it at that Deathless colony?"

"No, sir. We have that under surveillance, but the colonists appear to be civilians and we haven't approached them yet. They're too far away to get there easily on the ground and we don't know what their anti-air capabilities are like yet, so we've not tried dropships for scouting. This was at the military outpost the Deathless had set up while we were there foraging for supplies. Unfortunately, so were they."

"The colonists?" Bonneville asked, clearly confused.

"No, sir. We think these were some of the original Deathless troopers from the initial invasion. Warden captured three dropships when he destroyed their capital ship but the fourth was assumed to have gone down with the ship. It seems some Deathless troopers got off the ship and have been in hiding ever since. They used the dropship to retreat from the base, so we're pretty sure that's the scenario."

"I see. So you have one colony town that needs to be kept in check and a roving band of Deathless you need to find."

"That's about the size of it, sir. We're not done here yet."

"I had hoped you might have room for a breather, but it appears not." Bonneville nodded and looked at something off-camera. "We need to reinforce you as soon as possible. If the Deathless come back, I don't want us caught with our pants down. The Navy is sending reinforcements for Vice Admiral Staines and I'm sending a full battalion to New Bristol for deployment as quickly as you can grow new clones."

"Yes, sir, that will be helpful. Who will take command, if you don't mind my asking?"

"Take command?" said Bonneville, frowning. "I'm not changing my lead coach halfway through the game, Atticus. You'll remain in charge, Lieutenant Colonel, and stick with the mission until it's done."

There was a pause while Atticus processed that, then a look of mild panic rushed across his face.

"With respect, sir, I'm not qualified to be bumped up so many ranks," he said, desperately seeking a way to avoid the promotion.

"If it were with respect, Atticus, you wouldn't presume to lecture me on the rules of battlefield promotions. I checked, and you're more than qualified. You passed all the requisite courses years ago, you have the necessary experience, and you have served as a captain for, let me see," the general looked at something, apparently flicking at a data slate.

Atticus forestalled him, "I know how long I've been a captain, sir, thank you."

"Quite. If you don't want me to remind you of the exact number of years, perhaps we could simply agree that it has been far more than any captain still in active service? You've been allowed to pass up promotion opportunities several times because of your distinguished service record and because we had plenty of alternatives more interested in advancement. I'm afraid we're now long past the point of being able to indulge your preferences, Edward. This isn't a democracy, and we're in a real shooting war for the first time in years. You're the man on the ground, you're already familiar with the enemy, you have more experience than any of our serving lieutenant colonels, and you have a good relationship with local government. I've already discussed this with the governor and she described the idea as 'capital', reporting also that she found you good to work with. Sorry, Lieutenant Colonel Atticus, but I really don't have a choice here," Bonneville said with a shrug that was just the right side of mildly apologetic with a touch of rank-pulling 'get over it' for good measure.

Atticus sighed resignedly as the general concluded his monologue. He'd had a good run. In fact, he was pretty sure he held the record for longest serving Royal Marine Space Commando captain since the corps had been renamed. The rank bump had been something he had avoided because it would mean stepping away from the frontline.

"Yes, sir. I understand and thank you for holding it off this long. I'll miss being on the frontline, though."

"Atticus, I don't think you quite understand. Neither you nor I have ever been on a frontline like this. This is the first serious war in centuries. It was bad enough when we thought they were the first alien contact but now it turns out they're the deadliest species known to man, namely *homo sapiens*. That's worse, in my book. Plus, their ancestors sound like they could very well have been total crackpots, which is probably not a good thing. You're still going to be very much on the leading and bleeding edge of this war unless it shifts away from New Bristol," Bonneville said.

"Understood, sir." Atticus brightened a little. Maybe promotion wouldn't be as bad as he had feared.

"On the other hand, they do seem to be startlingly incompetent, don't you think?"

"Yes, sir. More experienced, maybe. We have some ideas about that but no real evidence so far. We're hoping that Warden and

Cohen's plan to visit the enemy at NewPet will yield the necessary intelligence."

There was a pause while Bonneville thought about this. Then he nodded.

"Speaking of Warden, he'll need a bump as well. He's ready to be a captain, wouldn't you say?"

"Undoubtedly, sir."

"Good, because the mission profile that he and Cohen drafted will need at least a full company. I'm going to be sending you the best-qualified people I can to form your new command. They will be full companies from existing units, of course, so they're familiar with each other. Governor Denmead will act as my proxy for the promotion ceremony."

"I'd like to keep my existing command team if I may, sir."

"That's fine. You'll need additional personnel, of course. A battalion commander gets a whole bevy of adjutants and other buggers to follow them around. You'll get used to it. Just remember to delegate everything and trust your people to do their jobs. Check your roster, promote whomever you feel is qualified then let me know which gaps I need to fill. I'll try to send people you've worked with before to fill any positions necessary."

"We'll need to promote Jenkins and Milton," Atticus mused.

"Fine, just send me the list and I'll rubber-stamp the promotions. Over."

"Yes, sir. Out."

∽

The promotion ceremony had been brief, understated and yet somehow still excruciating for Atticus. Warden had practically fallen off his chair with laughter when he learned that Atticus was to be made up to lieutenant colonel. He had stopped laughing very quickly when Atticus had told him that he, too, was to be promoted.

They had then gone over the promotions for their teams. Colour Sergeant Jenkins was being made up to warrant officer and given the title of Colour Sergeant Major. Sergeant Milton would take Jenkin's spot as the new Colour Sergeant of Lympstone Company, which Warden was now taking over as captain.

Denmead had pushed the congratulations and back-slapping speech as far as she could without causing Atticus to blow his top. Her political acumen came to the fore as she expertly judged the fine line between embarrassing but entertaining pomp and a joke taken too far.

The crowd of colonists was suspiciously large, Atticus thought. He wondered which of his supposedly loyal troops had stitched him up there. There has been a lot of banners as well but nothing handmade, all good quality, professionally printed stuff.

The fireworks that went off at the end of the ceremony were evidently a surprise to Denmead as well as to everyone else. Atticus thought he sensed the hand of Marine X in that one.

The pièce de résistance had been the drone flyover by the children's militia pilots. The drones flew low, spewing red, white and blue smoke trails, and Atticus couldn't help but admire the ingenuity of it all, even as the prime suspects grinned uncontrollably and took photos.

After that, the embarrassed promotees were dragged off to a badly damaged but partly cleaned bar in Ashton for celebratory drinks.

"I swear, Fletcher, there's a perfectly intact piano upstairs," said Goodwin, pointing to the mezzanine floor that protruded from the remains of the wall.

"Can't be – look at this place, it's a bloody mess. Never mind New Bristol, it looks like Old Bristol on a Saturday night. There're no windows, the bar is shot full of holes and look, half the optics are missing!"

"Well, it is a war zone, you know."

"Yeah, but my point is, you can't play a broken piano."

"I can't play the piano even if it were in perfect working order, but you can," Goodwin pointed out, reasonably.

"Yeah, come on, Fletcher, give us a tune," Milton joined in the cajoling.

"Look," Fletcher said, turning and almost losing half her pint with the vigorous motion, "Sergeant Milton, sorry – Colour Milton – it's hard enough to play the piano in a standard RMSC clone, but it'll be damn near impossible in this hulking great brute of a thing."

"She has a point," conceded Milton, "but what's the worst that could happen? Maybe you'll be able to play loud enough to drown out Ten's – what did he call it? Some word which apparently means singing along to ancient music, without being in tune."

"Carry okey dokey, I think," slurred Fletcher.

"Yeah, anything's got to be better than him singing about getting postcards from chimpanzees for the third time," grumbled Goodwin.

Fletcher shook her head in defeat and trudged upstairs, slightly wobbly on her feet, her clone's huge bulk shaking loose dust with every step. The mezzanine curved out over the stage below with the grand piano positioned so the pianist could look out over the audience while the singer strutted their stuff below.

She sat down on the large bench, gingerly applying her substantial rump to the seat. Fortunately, it had a strong but elegant frame, built in an imitation art deco style. It was easy to produce such furniture with modern 3D printing techniques, so even a piano wouldn't have been too hard to make, although this one was no masterpiece. Still, it should be perfectly functional if the bomb damage to the bar-come-nightclub hadn't been too extreme.

Fletcher gave the ivories an experimental tinkle then, satisfied that the keyboard was working as expected, began to hammer out a rendition of that perennial favourite, "Over the Hills and Far Away". It drew immediate cheers and applause from the Royal Marine and civilian audience alike. Ten's drunken signing was soon drowned out entirely by other drunken people joining in on the familiar tune.

Once she realised the crowd was backing her, Fletcher grew much more enthusiastic. She stood up, pushing the stool back so that she could really give the piano a bashing with her clone's enormous fingers.

"Amazing that it's still in tune," yelled Milton to Goodwin over the noise of the singing.

"I don't like tuna sandwiches," Goodwin shouted back.

Eventually, even Ten began to sing along with Fletcher's music, his brief irritation replaced by the drunk's unshakeable belief that he could carry any tune. There were many things that Ten did well and with great showmanship; drunken singing was not one of them.

But they carried on, nonetheless, belting their way through the popular verses and even a few that were familiar to the Marines and, it seemed, Governor Denmead, but not to most of the colonists. When the last verse was done and the last key tinkled, the crowd chanted Fletcher's name.

Abashed, she walked to the front of the balcony and bowed flamboyantly, accepting the applause with as much grace as she could manage and all the elegance that her huge frame allowed. The crowd clapped enthusiastically as Ten gave his most extravagant courtly bow.

An ominous creak momentarily quieted the crowd as Ten straightened.

And then, with an almighty crash, the balcony carrying Fletcher and the piano broke free from its brutalised supports and crashed down onto the stage, right on top of the unfortunate Ten.

There was a moment of stunned silence as dust rose from the massive pile of rubble. Then Fletcher staggered out of the cloud of muck and onto the floor, covered in filth but otherwise unharmed.

"Encore!" someone shouted, and the Marines all fell about laughing.

2

Aboard *Albion*, the cloning bay was running at full capacity. All three troops of Warden's company were redeploying into Deathless clones in preparation for the voyage to the NewPet system, releasing a steady stream of standard RMSC bodies to be returned to storage, some a little more heavily abused than others.

The techs had made some adjustments to *Albion*'s equipment in order to handle the very large ogre clones and the strange body shapes of the harpies, but both were being processed, now that the bodies had been shuttled across from their storage bays on *Ascendant*.

"Plenty of meat aboard *Ascendant*," Cohen had reported once the inventory was complete, "but the equipment is setup for standard deployment of stored personalities, not a redeployment from a living body."

And that had meant either killing the Marines still running standard RMSC bodies – not an option – or moving the Deathless clones to *Albion* and adjusting the cloning bays to handle the larger frames. It had taken a while to thrash out the details, not to mention the time required to setup and secure the encrypted backup links that would save the Marines' personalities back to *Ascendant* if their bodies were killed in action, but everything was now up and running.

"Do you know anything about this guy?" said Beaufort, staring at a monitor reporting progress on the download of Penal Marine X to his new body. "I heard he was some sort of criminal."

Petty Officer Brin, the other cloning tech, looked up from his own monitor and sniffed. His younger colleague was often more curious than was good for her; this was one of those times.

"His name is listed as 'Marine X'," said Brin, looking back at his own monitor, "and you don't lose your naming rights without having done something very wrong."

"So how come he's here, then? Why bother shipping him out when he should be chilling somewhere on a base doing punishment duties?"

Brin said nothing for a moment. Then there was a ping from the monitor.

"None of our business," he said eventually, fiddling with the controls. "Let's just get them up and running and let the captain worry about whom we're deploying, yes?"

"Just seems weird," muttered Beaufort, checking the controls on her monitor as Brin leant over the clone he was preparing. "I mean, I didn't get shipped out when I got done for that stuff back on base – not that I actually did any of it," she added quickly.

Brin had heard it all before and tuned out as Beaufort whined away about the injustices of her career and the long list of slights and grievances that had culminated in her posting to *Albion*, still an Able Rating despite her years of service.

Then Brin's clone coughed and tried to sit up and Beaufort finally stopped talking.

"There you go, sir," said Brin, helping the clone to sit and swing his legs down to the ground. "Bound to be a little confusion just after redeployment but you're okay. Do you remember where you are?"

The clone looked around, blinking and flexing his fingers. Then he nodded.

"Yes," said Captain Warden, staring at his new fingers and marvelling at the way they moved, "I know where I am and what we're doing. Any problems during the transfer?"

"No, sir, smooth and easy, nothing at all of interest."

"Good, that's exactly how I like these things to go."

Then there was a cough from across the room and the other clone, the one Beaufort had been monitoring, came round.

"What the fuck!" it said, clearly angry and scrabbling at the edges of the slab on which it lay. "I mean, what the actual fuck!"

Warden and Brin turned to see the clone flopping around as Beaufort hurried over to help him sit up.

"Er, Marine X," said Beaufort nervously, hands hovering over the clone's arms as the technician tried to decide how best to help, or even if it was safe to help at all, "you've been deployed after your, er, death."

There was a moment of silence as Marine X focused on the technician and frowned, still trying to work out where he was and what the hell was going on.

"You're aboard *Albion*, sir," said Beaufort, "you, er, you were in an accident, sir. With a piano."

"Wait, what? Sorry, the ears on this thing aren't working properly, I could have sworn you said 'piano'."

"It's a most amusing tale, Marine X," said Warden, striving manfully to keep the grin from his face, "and I'm sure Milton will be keen to walk you through the video."

Marine X looked around then glanced down at his fingers.

"Death? So this was a straight deployment?"

"Yes, sir," said Beaufort, "straight into a Deathless clone, no problems," she went on, checking her monitor, "clean and easy, complete transference."

Marine X heaved himself upright and frowned. He peered at Warden, who was at the same height, then glanced down at his hands again.

"This seems a bit small for an ogre," he muttered, looking over the rest of his body, "shouldn't I be a bit, you know, taller?" he stared meaningfully at the unfortunate technician, who swallowed nervously and glanced at Warden.

The captain nodded encouragingly, utterly refusing to help her explain.

"Er, well, it's not exactly an ogre, sir," said Beaufort. "We didn't have one to hand so, er." She stopped as the frown deepened on Marine X's face. "Sorry."

"Not an ogre," said Marine X testily, taking a tentative step on what seemed to be very long and thin limbs. "So what is it?"

He flexed his arms and there was a sudden rush of air. Beaufort jumped quickly back as Marine X turned, trying to see what was going on behind him.

"What the hell? Have I got wings? Are these wings? What sort of shitty nonsense clone have you stuck me in?" he asked, turning back to the technician. Everyone ducked as his wings swept around the room again.

"It's a harpy, Marine X," said Warden, "one of the winged clones the Deathless use for scouting and sniping." He jumped clear as X turned again, wings still outstretched. "Maybe you could fold away your wings? They do rather fill the room."

Marine X frowned again and paused, standing quite still as he concentrated. Then there was a snap and his wings folded away neatly onto his back. He looked again at his thin, graceful legs and arms, unnaturally narrow hips and slim chest.

"I really wanted to play with an ogre clone," he murmured, his disappointment obvious. "They look like such a lot of fun."

Beaufort smiled nervously.

"But you'll be able to fly, sir," she blurted, trying to put a positive spin on the situation. Marine X glared at her, an expression so angry and hostile that Beaufort took half a step back.

"Marines," said X slowly as if explaining a new concept to a child, "fight on land and water. That's it. The only purpose of height is to fall from it as quickly as possible."

"Beaufort is right, though, sir," said Brin, "and that clone is a remarkable piece of engineering. The ogres are big and tough and surprisingly quick but these harpies are entirely another thing." Marine X looked at him and raised an eyebrow, unconvinced. "The bones are super-lightweight but engineered with titanium, so they're ridiculously strong. And the flight muscles are, weight for weight, about three times as strong as an ogre's."

"Okay, right, yes, could be useful," conceded Marine X. "Anything else I should know?"

"The lungs look hyper-efficient as well, and the synapse tests suggest the reflexes should be off-the-chart fast," said Brin, enthusiastic now that Marine X's hostility had receded somewhat, "and I think, even on the ground, you'll find it moves very quickly indeed. But you might need to eat quite a lot; that clone burns calories at a very high rate."

"Hmm," said Marine X thoughtfully, strutting around the cloning bay and looking at himself in the reflective surfaces of the machines. He flicked out his wings again and gave them a flap. "Does this mean I can break a man's arm with one blow of my wings?" He flicked them back in again.

Brin frowned, not really wanting to think about why Marine X might need to be able to do that.

"Maybe, but you might want to take it easy for a few days, just while you get used to it."

Marine X looked back at the technician as he pulled on the cut-down uniform the Deathless harpies used.

"Easy? Yeah, sure," he said, flexing his arms and popping out his wings again to give them an experimental flap. He pulled them back in and fixed Beaufort with a steady gaze.

"I'll take it," he said finally, "but put me in an ogre next time, right?"

The technician nodded furiously as Marine X and Captain Warden left the cloning bay.

"They're growing more clones on *Ascendant* at the moment," said Brin after the door had slid shut. "Better let them know about Marine X's preferences." Beaufort nodded and sat down at a terminal to compose a message. "Wouldn't want to be in your shoes if he gets deployed to a lizardman next time," said Brin, grinning evilly behind his colleague's back.

3

The temporary council chamber in the depths of Fort Widley had become, over the last week, considerably more permanent-looking and was now seriously crowded as the councillors filed in for the meeting. Restoration of the cloning bays to full capacity had coincided with the end of the fighting, allowing the casualties to be deployed and the colony to return to near strength.

"Yes, yes, settle down," said Governor Denmead as the councillors jostled for space and squeezed themselves onto the benches arrayed around the walls of the chamber. "I know this isn't ideal and yes, it's on the list of things to fix, but, just for now, we all have to do the best we can with what we have."

Eventually they settled and Johnson, Denmead's assistant, was able to bring the meeting to order.

"You've all had briefing packs, and I'm sure you've all digested them," said Denmead, knowing for a fact that some of the councillors had only been deployed to new bodies that morning and so were now trying to catch up with several weeks' worth of updates, "so I'm going to leap straight into the main topic." She nodded at Johnson, who flicked at his data slate until an image appeared on the new display screen at the end of the room. The councillors shuffled and craned their necks until they could all see the screen.

"This is the Deathless base where Captain Warden and his troop engaged the enemy about ten days ago and where Lieutenant Colonel Atticus," said Johnson, nodding to Atticus where he sat in a quiet corner, "fought a second engagement that required him to deploy to another new clone. These are new images from the micro-drones deployed over the base to keep an eye on things."

"And we've now set the AI to watch for enemy movement," said Atticus, his voice hissing slightly through the alien mouthparts of the Deathless Rupert clone, "so that we won't be surprised again by any mischief the remaining Deathless are plotting." He frowned, not entirely happy to again be wearing a Deathless clone rather than the standard RMSC body he had requested. Some mix-up at the cloning bay, Warden had said.

"As you can see," said Denmead, highlighting a section of the base and zooming in using her own slate, "this part isn't a static building, it's actually a spacecraft." She paused to allow the murmur of disquiet to drift away as the newer councillors gazed in awe at the images before them. "It's now clear that the sole role of this craft is to land on a planet and construct the defensive walls and principle habitation and manufacturing structures of a military operating base. Then it moves to a new location and repeats the process."

"In other words, it's a fully-automated base-building machine," said Atticus, "and we think that it had almost finished its work when we stumbled across it."

"Fully automated?" said Grimes with a challenging eyebrow raised almost to his hairline. "So you're telling us that there might be more of these things, more bases out there, spread across the face of the planet, ready to deploy Deathless troopers?" There was another round of uncomfortable murmuring from the assembled councillors. These were clearly questions they hadn't considered.

"No," said Atticus firmly, leaning forward slightly to better engage, or maybe intimidate, his audience. "Examination of the logs and files of *Ascendant* show that this craft was launched only fairly shortly before we found it and so had time to build only one base, namely that one," he finished, pointing at the screen.

Grimes nodded, a flash of relief showing on his normally inscrutable face. "Well, that's the first piece of good news we've had in a long time."

Atticus smiled. It made a pleasant change to get a positive response from Grimes, for once, who was normally dour and pessimistic.

"Sorry, excuse my ignorance," said one of the newer councillors, "but for those of us only recently restored to active duty, can you please give us a quick update on what's going on? What is *Ascendant*, for starters?"

Denmead and Atticus shared a look then she sighed. "This is all in the briefing pack, Len, but I know you've only been up for a few hours. *Ascendant* is a captured enemy starship, renamed by Vice Admiral Staines, whose fleet is currently in orbit around New Bristol. The enemy is descended from one of the lost Arks, *Koschei*, a Russian vessel populated by body hackers and ultra-liberals intent on pushing cloning technology as far as it would go in their search for functional immortality."

"And that's why...?" said Len, gesturing at Atticus's unusual body and grinning weakly.

"Yes, Len, that's why Lieutenant Colonel Atticus is wearing such an unusual clone. This one was seized from the Deathless and is, we believe, the model used by their officer classes. Look, there's a ton of detail in the background files, and I don't want to spend much more time on the subject, except to say that we are at war with a force that seems to be very much stronger and better resourced than we are, here, on New Bristol."

"I might add," said Atticus, "that current projections based on new data from *Ascendant* suggest that the Deathless may be more widespread and more capable than we had previously thought. All of this information has been relayed to the Admiralty in Sol, of course, and we expect further guidance as soon as they have had a chance to digest it all. Marine reinforcements are arriving as we speak and will be deployed as resources allow."

"In the meantime, though, we're on our own," said the governor.

"Thank you, Governor," said Len, sitting back in his chair, "I'll go through the briefing pack," he added, waving his data slate, "and see if there's anything I can do to help. I have experience in first-contact theory and encounter simulation, if that's any use."

"We're a little past the point of first contact," said Atticus grimly, "but the techs are doing a deal of planning and could always use some help."

"If we could just return to the topic at hand," said Denmead testily, shooting a glance at Atticus before treating the councillors to a somewhat warmer smile, "we wish to discuss the mothership and the plans we are now making for it."

"Of course, Governor," said Atticus, pulling out his own data slate and flicking at it with his long, alien fingers, "in brief, ladies and gentlemen, we wish to repair the mothership, repair the base to some degree and then use both for our own purposes. Our circumstances, as you may have noticed," he waved his hand at their surroundings, "are somewhat reduced. This vessel's fabricators are considerably more sophisticated than our own and we plan to use them to both rebuild Ashton and then to extend our own resource extraction efforts."

"In other words, we're going to return this vessel to service as quickly as possible and use it to build our way back to the habitable, desirable and pleasant colony that we had achieved before the Deathless arrived," said Denmead.

"That works for me," said Grimes, showing an unusual amount of enthusiasm, "but what did you mean by 'considerably more sophisticated'? Are we talking bigger structures, faster mechanisms or better materials?"

"All three, as far as we can tell," said Denmead, flicking at her slate so that the display showed close-up images of the inside of the base. "The damage done during Captain Warden's attack was considerable but then so was the effort expended. You've all seen the videos,

I expect, and if you haven't, you really should watch the one of the truck hitting the base wall."

She pulled another image onto the display. "You can see here, in this shot of the edge of the wrecked wall that circled the base, exactly how the wall was put together. We know that this was built in less than a week. What does that tell you, Mr Grimes?"

Grimes examined the image, then sat back.

"I'd need to see a sample to be sure," he said cautiously, "but it looks like it might be some sort of carbon nanotube-reinforced foamcrete."

"Catch," said Johnson, tossing a lump of rock across the table to Grimes.

"Yes, look," Grimes said excitedly, "you can see the distinctive patterning caused by the addition of the nanotubes to the foam mixture. Very clever, very advanced. We've got stuff like this back home, but it isn't used much because of the time it takes to make it and the difficulty of getting it to work. Theoretically, though, you could form it into pretty much any shape you want by spraying layers on top of each other, like you would with an old 3D printer, which means you can build fantastically strong and elegant structures easily and quickly."

"And we don't do that because...?" prompted Denmead.

"We don't do it because it's overkill," said Grimes. "This stuff is tough, granted, and you can build incredible structures with it, but it's expensive and difficult, and there's just no need, most of the time."

"But if the Deathless have worked out how to do it quickly...?"

"Well, yes. The whole base is made of this stuff? Then I would very much want to get a look at their machines, as would Smith, I think, and we'd want to deploy them as widely as possible across both New Bristol and the rest of the Commonwealth. This could be a game-changer for new colonies, asteroid mining and space habitat fabrication. Why, with this material, if you can make it fast enough, you might be able to build orbital megastructures..."

Grimes tailed off, lost to the conversation in a daydream of vast, star-sized orbital megastructures.

"And that's why we want you to help with this effort," said Atticus in an attempt to drag the conversation back, again, to the main topic. "We have some technical resources amongst the Marines but this is basically a civil engineering problem and it needs a civilian-led solution. That's where you come in," he said, looking at Grimes and Smith, "since you're the two people best placed to handle the technology and bring it online."

"And while you're doing that," said Denmead, on the principle that the best people to handle more work were those already loaded down with tasks, "we also need to get the ship flying again and then reprogram it to build useful villages, farms and outstations rather than the rather useless military-style bases it normally constructs."

She paused to look around the room.

"That makes sense, people, doesn't it? We repair the ship, move it to New Ashton, reconstruct what was destroyed and then deploy new fabricators to extend and improve our infrastructure, our civic spaces and our accommodation."

"And at the same time, we refurbish this base, which we're going to name HMS *Sultan* in honour of long-closed facilities on Earth, and set it up as a staging and training post for the Marines," said Atticus. "In the event of another invasion, we will already have a ready-made, fully militarised base of operations that should, with any luck, draw focus from the civilian areas."

"HMS *Sultan*, eh?" said Smith, sharing a glance with Grimes. "Well, I guess our first task is to get the local fabricators and manufacturing machines back on stream so that we can repair and rebuild. After that, Governor, Lieutenant Colonel, it'll be over to you."

"Very good, Mr Smith," said Denmead, sitting back in her chair and smiling benevolently at her councillors, "that will do very well indeed."

4

Captain Warden stood on the bridge of *Ascendant*, watching the panoramic forward view monitors as the last shuttle from *Albion* departed after dropping off its cargo of supplies.

"Flight control, report," Lieutenant Commander Cohen said, in the distinctive, clipped intonation of a bridge officer.

"Status green, sir. All shuttles have now cleared our vicinity and *Ascendant* is ready to depart."

Cohen nodded. "Navigation, set course for NewPet."

"Course confirmed; navigation ready."

"Helm, engage hyperspace drive," said Cohen.

The transition to hyperspace was smooth and controlled, like diving into cool water; real warships didn't jerk, shudder or creak as they did in cheap holo-shows. Once the drive was engaged, space simply folded beneath the ship and it vanished from normal space, moving through hyperspace in much the same way that the conventional engines would manoeuvre the ship in normal space.

The difference, of course, was the vast distance that could be quickly travelled in hyperspace. Unlike a wormhole, which allowed near instantaneous transmission of information, movement through hyperspace took time. Travelling at sub-light speed, the ship moved through the folds of hyperspace before exiting back into normal space at a distance that should have required them to travel faster than light.

Warden didn't pretend to understand the physics. In fact, hardly anyone in the universe understood how it all worked. All he needed to know was that that the effective rate of travel was many times lightspeed and that meant they could reach another system in weeks or even days, rather than centuries or millennia.

The fact that any wormhole larger than a pinprick would collapse without warning, at least with current technology, was both a blessing and a curse. Not being able to transfer ships meant that the Royal Navy couldn't deliver a ship instantly to a combat zone. The upside was that the enemy couldn't do that either, locking both sides into hyperspace or the slow vastness of real space.

Wormholes were still the arteries of modern life, allowing near instantaneous transmission of data across the vast reaches of spaces. Though the energy requirement was huge, any planet with sufficient power generation could easily allow its citizens to communicate through wormholes, sending messages to family or friends as if they were across the street rather than in another solar system.

"How long till we arrive?" asked Warden when the ship was comfortably underway.

"About two hundred and ten hours," said Cohen. Warden nodded thoughtfully. He was going to be busy. He now had a whole company to look after, and most of them were in fresh clones that were completely unfamiliar to them. They would need training if they were to use the clones to their full effect and they had fewer than nine days to get it done.

Warden excused himself from the bridge and went to see how Colour Milton was getting on with the setup of their training facilities.

∼

Warden entered the former mothership hangar from one of the upper balconies and looked out at the work Milton had done on their improvised training ground.

A wall of crates had been built on one side of the bay and bags of composite gel were being piled up as a backstop. That was the shooting range, positioned to ensure the rounds were not headed towards any of the access doors. You didn't want someone taking a shortcut through the range when they thought it wasn't in use; they couldn't afford to put more strain on the cloning bays.

The area to the side of the shooting range had been taped off to keep it clear of people and kit. On the other side of the hangar, mats had been laid out for unarmed combat practice, probably the most important training component for the newly deployed Marines. Martial arts, and even basic body movements such as throwing and catching a ball, were excellent ways to become accustomed to an unfamiliar clone model, and the RMSC had long experience in quickly getting their people ready for combat.

As Warden watched, a small flock of harpies flapped their way across the combat mats, gliding down from the balcony to land awkwardly on the floor. These were the clones that required the biggest adjustments. The different reflexes, muscle strength, even bone density, all played a part in throwing you off kilter.

The Marines seldom used winged troopers because they were just too specialised and while Ten had trained before in an RMSC clone with wings, it didn't compare favourably to this Deathless version. The harpy was lighter, faster and stronger than the RMSC equivalent, superior in every way, much though it pained Warden to admit it.

The practical difficulties of flight training, even in *Ascendant*'s immense hangar, were huge. About all they could do so far was climb up to a balcony and glide back down, flapping their wings a little to eke out as much distance as possible.

All the snipers and their spotters had been reassigned to harpies. With luck, deploying teams in winged bodies would help them reach otherwise inaccessible perches and allow them to target enemies they couldn't otherwise reach. The military advantages of being where the enemy didn't expect you were huge, since you could easily glide away from your perch once you were discovered.

"The problem will be food," Mueller had said when Warden had asked for his thoughts. "These clones are light and agile, but they have a high metabolic rate in order to deliver the energy required for the flight muscles. I estimate that they might chew, if you'll pardon the pun, through four to six thousand calories a day even if the wearer is only engaging in normal duties. If they fly, they might need six to eight thousand."

The other major downside was that the carrying capacity of the winged clones was much smaller than that of even the standard RMSC versions. Experiments had shown that a couple of days' food, a lightweight uniform and a primary weapon was about the limit that they could carry. The Deathless winged clones were superior and had lighter structures so they had a bit more leeway there, but they still needed calorie-dense food.

"And that means we're highly dependent on the lizardmen for any heavier weaponry," Marine X had said, "especially if we deploy our snipers for longer than a few hours. I recommend we use railguns, to conserve ammunition weight and increase effectiveness."

So deploying the harpies would require coordinated support from the lizardmen and, given their lack of armour, casualties were likely to be higher than amongst the beefier clones, if they were exposed to enemy fire. This meant they simply couldn't deploy them in forward roles in the same way they would usually do. The snipers and their spotters would have to restrict themselves to that function only, and stay off the front line.

Warden had asked Mueller to look at the available high-energy foodstuffs and try to come up with something better. He didn't want his sniper teams passing out on their perches from hunger and the standard chocolate protein bars still didn't add up to a pleasant meal. Despite the huge amount of sugar, they were more like chewing sweet cardboard than a chocolate bar.

Ten had sighed heavily during this conversation, looking somewhat miserable. Eventually, Warden had asked what was bothering him, and he'd confessed that the last time winged clones saw heavy use, there was a liquid diet that they were supplied. A pack of easily constituted energy supplements were added to their water supply and could be injected for a boost, should they need one in the field. He explained that this was particularly important when the wings were used to achieve lift, rather than just for gliding purposes.

"Why the long face then? That sounds like an easy solution. No pun intended," Warden had asked.

"Because the drink isn't like something you give kids or a soft drink you buy in a coffee shop. It tastes more like chemical plant runoff or essence of cabbage mixed in with dog food. It does not go down well and there's nothing you can add to it that will overpower the taste," Ten had replied.

"I've found it," Mueller said, excitedly, looking at his data slate. "Just as Marine X says, we can easily make enough of this with the food fabricators. Lots of supplementary vitamins and minerals, lots of energy and lots of electrolytes – which is probably what ruins the taste."

"Problem solved then," Warden said, though Ten didn't seem to agree.

In another area, Milton had a series of viewscreens and some chairs laid out as a classroom. She was going over HUD videos with the NCOs and lieutenants who now reported to Captain Warden.

Captain Warden. He still couldn't quite believe it. He hadn't expected a promotion for at least a couple of years but it seemed a shooting war had some career advantages. Nevertheless, professionally challenging and career-boosting though it was, he'd very much rather not be in a war against a group of Lost Ark malcontents with a fondness for genetic engineering and cutting-edge technology.

He moved to a ladder and slid down it, a handy trick he had taken the time to learn during his first posting aboard a Royal Navy ship. It saved a surprising amount of time but he'd seen more than one person cock it up and burn their hands or twist an ankle. Warden had taken the easy route to expertise; a conversation with a midshipman, a bottle of genuine gin from Earth and half an hour of supervised practice had given him the knack of it.

He smiled to himself as he remembered those simpler times aboard that first ship, back when his biggest concerns had been when he'd actually get to use his training in combat. Now that he had experienced combat, he was much more interested in ideas such as diplomacy and negotiation.

"Colour Milton, how are things going?"

"Fine, thank you, sir. I was just showing the replays from the attack on the base."

"Good, carry on, it looks like you're about to get to the good bits," said Warden.

Milton was showing the views from her own HUD and Warden's, not the mind-boggling video of Ten's exploits. Those files were kept strictly under wraps and even Lieutenant Colonel Atticus had avoided watching them.

"They're a bad example for impressionable boot-necks," Atticus had said, before comparing Ten's videos unfavourably to performance art made by adrenaline junkies whose only hobbies were ultra-extreme sports. "Just keep them out of the training programme." They would leak, of course, because these things always did, but the last thing anyone wanted was for young Marines to get the idea that Ten's behaviour was what was expected of them.

And so Milton had focused on the more normal videos so that the newly deployed Marines could see what the Deathless were like, how they responded under fire, how their weapons worked and how they moved and fought.

Warden stayed till the end of the base attack, through the distant music that signalled Ten's arrival, the enormous explosion of the dumper truck and the final assault on the mothership, which he supposed they should start calling a factory ship or something similar. He had wanted to bring it with them, in case they needed to deploy bases of their own, but the assessment of the civilian and Royal Navy teams had been that even with their combined efforts, it would take weeks to make the vessel space-worthy and even longer before it was fully operational again. It made more sense to leave it on New Bristol where, after only relatively minor repairs, it could do useful work while the techs laboured to bring it back to full capacity.

Instead, they would rely on the shuttles and dropships that *Ascendant* carried and hope none of the Deathless personnel at NewPet did a scan comprehensive enough to detect the absence of the enormous ship from its hangar. The jig would be up if they did, and they would have a devil of a time explaining the missing vessel if anyone got curious.

When Milton was done, Warden stood up to address the team.

"As you all know, this is an intelligence-gathering mission. We have no idea what we'll find when we get to NewPet. It could be an empty system, or it might be a convenient staging post on the way to more interesting places." He paused to look over the Marines. "But it could be a Naval base or even a civilian starbase. We're all in Deathless clones, and that's because we anticipate a need to infiltrate their facilities or to receive visitors to *Ascendant* in order to gather the kind of intelligence we need to support the Commonwealth."

There was a general murmur of surprise at that.

"Both those eventualities present significant challenges because, as you may have noticed from the signs around the ship, the Deathless speak their own language. It's not even Russian. They also have their own characters, presumably designed to be more efficient than either the Cyrillic or Latin character sets with which we're familiar. What we know about *Koschei* is that the founders of their group were all highly skilled academics, computer scientists, biologists, physicists and the like. They planned to improve on every aspect of their civilisation, and they didn't want to be constrained by any of the social mores or legal restrictions of the time.

"We don't know what we're going to find, so we're keeping our options open. If we find a target of opportunity, we may well launch an all-out assault, which could include a ground assault. If we were to find, for example, a vulnerable capital ship, we might attempt another capture, but havoc is not our primary objective. The goal is to gather as much intelligence as possible without giving much away in return.

"General Bonneville has sent some experts from the Puzzle Palace to join us, a team of language experts and lecturers from the staff training colleges on Earth. We will all receive some training on the rudiments of the Deathless language in case we have to bluff our way around their facilities on NewPet."

Hayes put her hand up. "Sir, won't we be using AI translation to handle most of this?"

"Yes, for ship-to-ship communication and anything over comms, that's the plan. If we have to go in person, though, and we think that's likely, the ability to take your helmet off and speak to someone could be the difference between success and failure. In addition, this is likely to be a long war, ladies and gentlemen, and even if a diplomatic solution is reached soon, we are going to need language skills in the long-term. We will be in the vanguard of that as the guinea pigs, which I'm sure you're all excited about."

"Will we be covering their written language as well?"

"Yes, that's part of the planned program, but time is short, so we'll focus on verbal skills. The HUD auto-translation of written language is automatic and the experts feel it's better than ninety per cent accurate, which should be good enough for our purposes."

"What's the balance going to be between combat training and this stuff?"

"You'll be pleased to hear that you'll be spending the bulk of your time on language skills, Lieutenant Hayes. You have two hours now to get in some concentrated physical training to familiarise yourselves with the clones. Those of you who have been using a Deathless clone for a while will be assisting with that until the first language classes start. I'm sending the training schedule to your HUD now. You will also note that we're going to be reviewing infiltration, stealth, sabotage and escape and evasion routines. I will be joining you for all this, so the pain will be shared. We have some excellent practical experts aboard for these aspects of mission prep."

"Who is doing the stealth training, Captain?" asked a suspicious Hayes.

"You will no doubt be delighted to hear that General Bonneville has decided that Marine X is best qualified to deliver a refresher course in creeping up on some poor sod and giving him the good news as quietly as possible." There was a chorus of groans until Warden raised his hand to quiet the audience. "Yes, I know he's a character, but he's also undeniably a Galaxy-class bastard when it comes to such matters, so you'd be wise to listen to his advice. I, for one, prefer to minimise the number of forced redeployments through which I have to go."

He paused to look around the team then nodded.

"Right, you all have PT to be getting on with. Try not to break anything; it won't get you out of language lessons."

5

"Coming up on NewPet, sir," came the message. Warden was in his quarters, reading again through his company's deployment list to commit to memory the details of which of his teams had been deployed into which clone types. Moving away from standard RMSC body designs brought a whole new set of challenges and opportunities.

"Very good, I'm on my way." He put down his data slate and swung himself off his bunk. Then he flicked the door controls and walked out, heading for the bridge.

"Sir," he said, nodding to Lieutenant Commander Cohen as he entered the bridge.

"Warden," acknowledged Cohen, nodding back, "we're close, re-entering normal space in," he paused to glance at the monitor and lick his lips, "forty-five seconds."

And then they would see what they would see. Nobody knew what sort of reception awaited them in NewPet. They didn't know what sort of forces might be arrayed against them or how the Deathless might react to their arrival. They didn't even know whether they would be noticed; it might be entirely normal for ships to make this journey or to arrive unannounced.

"I will confess to a certain, well, trepidation, Mr Warden," said Cohen as they watched the counter fall steadily towards zero, "there's a very real risk we'll give ourselves away in seconds and be shot to pieces before we achieve anything even vaguely useful."

It was ground they had covered several times during the voyage but without successfully formulating any plan more sophisticated than 'turn up, see what happens'. To Warden's mind, this was a somewhat lax approach, but he had reluctantly conceded that it was the best they could do with the information they had.

"There's a long naval tradition of formulating brilliant plans at the last minute," said Cohen, shifting uneasily in his seat, "although most of them also involved the commander losing some part of his anatomy, so I'm not keen to replicate the strategy entirely." He offered Warden a weak grin, then they both turned back to face the monitors as the countdown trickled towards zero.

"Three, two, one… and we're back to normal space," said Midshipman Martin from her unfamiliar lizardman clone.

For a few long minutes, nothing happened as the ship coasted towards the inner system where their nav-charts showed NewPet and the orbiting base it hosted.

Then a message flashed onto the monitor.

<<*Varpulis*. Proceed to dock bay six for refuelling and re-provisioning>>

The message was followed by a course that flashed up on the main display, a neat loop into the system to reach NewPet, which orbited its star at a little over a hundred and sixty million kilometres.

"At least the translation system is working," said Cohen with no small amount of relief, "acknowledge that, Midshipman Wood, and let's get that course laid in. No point hanging around."

"Yes, sir, acknowledging now."

"Course is laid in, sir, arrival in sixteen hours and thirty-seven minutes."

"Excellent, well done, everyone. Now, let's take a closer look at the planet, shall we? What can we see?"

The small science team had a well-equipped office and laboratory in the aft of the ship. They had rigged extra monitors on the bridge to provide video and audio feeds to Cohen and his team, just in case they found anything useful or interesting. It seemed that the architects of Deathless military vessels had made a serious effort to provide first-class research facilities to their scientists but hadn't thought it worthwhile to add a direct link to the bridge.

"The surface of the planet is rather green," came the voice of Chief Science Officer Mueller, who was down in what the crew had taken to calling 'the science pit', although it was really a very comfortable and well-equipped suite of rooms, "and we can see high concentrations of oxygen and nitrogen, so the atmosphere is probably breathable."

Warden frowned and shared a glance with Cohen.

"That sounds too good to be true, Mueller," he said. "What else can you tell us?"

"From this distance, not a great deal, I'm afraid. Once we're closer, I can give you a detailed breakdown of the composition of the atmosphere, thoughts on the florae and faunae, hi-res maps and topographical details of the surface and probably some indication of likely volcanic activity, but at the moment all we can really say is that it's likely to be wet in many places and that the gravity will be pretty similar to Earth's."

Warden nodded. All very interesting but it was clear that Mueller, whose normal posting was to lead a team of environmental and ecological research scientists based on *Albion*, had not been chosen for this mission because of his military background.

"And what about electromagnetic waves, Mueller?" asked Warden.

"Radios and such-like? Yes, plenty of those. Lots of activity all over the usual spectra and we can see lights on the night-side of the planet. All very normal." There was a pause. "I suppose that's the sort of thing you were interested in, Captain," said Mueller in a somewhat humbler voice. "Silly of me, sorry, I should have realised."

"Not to worry, Mr Mueller," said Warden, "but as soon as you know anything about the number of people on the planet, their locations, their technology..." he trailed off as Mueller nodded on the monitor, "anything you can tell us would be useful." Mueller nodded and killed the connection.

"I sometimes wonder if the Admiralty sends people like Mueller just to test the rest of us," Cohen mused, "but then we weren't really expecting this mission to be a shooting war."

The flight to the space station, which the crew had nicknamed 'Soyuz' for reasons that weren't entirely obvious to Warden, was uneventful to the point of extreme tedium. Warden slept a little, although his body didn't seem to need much rest, and checked his kit and armour. Then he found Cohen and Milton to talk about what they would do next.

"I'm not keen to dock with the space station," said Cohen, although they had known it might be necessary before they left New Bristol. "There are simply too many things that can go wrong, and once we're attached, breaking free may not be possible."

"We've already acknowledged the signal," pointed out Warden. "I'm not sure there's much else we can do."

"I know," said Cohen, "I know, but I don't have to like it. I'd just rather my first command didn't end with us all being captured by the enemy."

"Don't worry, you can always scuttle *Ascendant* if the worst comes to the worst," Warden said cheerfully.

Cohen glowered at him. "You Marines are always so bloody blasé about redeploying, aren't you?" Cohen said.

"Hazard of the job. You've got to look on the bright side of life, when you might step on a mine or take a railgun to the face at any moment," Warden said with a shrug. Cohen sighed and shook his head.

"How long will refuelling take?" Warden asked curiously.

"For a ship this size, we estimate that it might be anything from one to three hours," said Lieutenant Sierra, "but it's difficult to say for sure. Their documentation is unexpectedly lax in this area but from what we can tell, they mostly deliver fuel and raw materials through several high-pressure systems. That's one of the advantages of advanced fabricators; less need to load finished goods, although some of the weapon systems will be restocked by robots working on the outside of the ship."

"Lucky for us. If they had to bring everything in by hand they'd be sure to spot us."

"The bigger problem is the damage to the hull," said Cohen, bringing up an exterior shot of the hull that had been taken from *Albion* when they were re-supplying. "There's not a lot to see, thankfully, but if they do a close visual inspection or if dock six positions us in the wrong orientation –"

"They'll see the damage caused by the boarding pod," muttered Warden. "That hadn't occurred to me."

"Really? It's been causing me sleepless nights ever since we came up with this hare-brained scheme."

"But the hole was patched, wasn't it?" said Milton, nodding at the photo.

"It was, yes, but if their inspection is thorough, they'll probably spot the repairs and that might be enough for them to start asking awkward questions," said Sierra.

"And inspections are often very thorough and highly automated," said Cohen, "since nobody wants to fly in a ship whose hull has been dangerously ablated or where temporary repairs might not be able to handle combat stresses or that might be carrying space barnacles."

Warden thought about that for a moment. It did seem a reasonable fear. Then he frowned.

"Space barnacles?"

"Okay, no, I just made that up, but the point is that there are lots of things that could go wrong if the Deathless are any good as sailors."

Warden snorted. "Their soldiers haven't been much good so far. What's to say their sailors will be any different?"

Cohen raised an eyebrow at that but didn't have anything else to say on the matter. Milton also looked unconvinced, and rightly so; relying on an enemy's incompetence was a sure way to get caught out.

"Anyway," said Warden, moving swiftly onwards, "we need to worry about what we do while we're docked. If they notice the damage or realise we're not who we say we are, our only real option is to cut and run, right?"

Cohen nodded grimly. Nobody in the navy liked the idea of running from a fight, especially if it meant failing to complete their missions, and Warden could see that the thought sat poorly with the lieutenant commander.

"Let's work out what we're going to do with our sixty minutes," Warden said, skipping away from the idea of failure, "and how best to extract information from Soyuz while we're here."

"On that," said Lieutenant Sierra, "I have made some progress with our techs and we have have hacked together this." He pushed a small box across the surface of the table. "It's a backdoor, basically. You plug it into a network port like those ones," he pointed at the flat ports set into mouldings above the power outlets on the wall, "and that should give us a link into their systems."

Warden looked at the small box then raised an eyebrow and looked back at Sierra. "Just the one?"

"One should do the job, but we've got several. If we can install three, we'll have a reasonable chance of exfiltrating useful data." He saw Warden's skeptical expression and added, "We'll get a few more fabricated before you leave so you don't run out."

"What's the range?" asked Milton, picking up the box and waggling the cable. "And does it need power?"

"Battery powered, range about fifty metres, depending on what else is in the way. The best option is to use a data slate to dive straight in and rip out the files we need but if that's not possible, we'll try to pick up the signal from *Ascendant*, although that obviously only works while we're docked."

"Right," said Warden as Sierra passed over two more of the little boxes, "just walk us through the whole thing with that port over there," he said, gesturing at the wall, "and let's see if we can make it work."

~

And now they waited as the ship fired attitude thrusters to manoeuvre into the dock.

"Thirty seconds," said Midshipman Martin. Cohen and Sierra had retreated to the bridge leaving Warden and Milton just inside the main hatch with a full squad of armoured Marines waiting around the corner. They had raided *Ascendant*'s stores for Deathless uniforms that seemed appropriate for a space station, but the few images they had found in the computer or around the ship had been confusingly contradictory. They also had no clear understanding of the protocol for arrival at a space station.

"If there's an armed party waiting for us, sir," said Milton as the space station drifted gently closer, "then I'll see you on the other side and mine's a pint of stout."

"Really, Sergeant? I had you down as a fan of the old Port and lemon, if I'm honest."

"Only if it's a double, sir, or if Marine X is buying."

Warden frowned. "Marine X said something about a bet. I meant to ask earlier but…"

"Five seconds to dock," said Midshipman Martin.

"Maybe later, eh, sir?" said Milton, straightening her uniform.

There was a gentle clink and then a hiss of gas as the ship clamped itself to the space station and the cabin pressures equalised.

"Opening the doors," said Midshipman Martin, "and the best of luck to you all."

Warden stretched his neck, facing forward as the doors slid open, as tense as he'd ever been. Then the doors at the other end of the short corridor opened and he could finally see straight through into the station.

And there was nothing there. Nobody to greet them, no armed guards, no security that they could see of any type.

Warden stood there for a few moments. Then he sniffed and glanced at Milton. She shrugged and made an 'after you' gesture.

"Once more unto the breach," muttered Warden, stepping over the threshold and into the station. Milton followed and together they walked down the short corridor to a larger space, a reception room of some sort.

"Where is everybody?" murmured Milton as they turned into another corridor.

"Keep an eye out for a terminal," said Warden quietly, scanning everywhere for anything that might give them a clue as to what was going on, "or any sign of life."

At the end of the corridor, another door slid open and they suddenly stood in a huge space, a room at least a hundred metres across and full of Deathless soldiers. Milton twitched as if she wanted to draw a weapon. Warden frowned, eyes flicking as he counted, trying to estimate the number of troops that shuffled in lines from left to right, disappearing down a pair of corridors.

A minute later, most of the troops had gone and the room seemed even larger. It was scattered with chairs upon which a few soldiers lounged, kit bags at their feet. Most of the room was empty except for the eerie hum of the life-support systems.

"Staging post?" said Warden quietly. Milton nodded, not trusting herself to speak. "Those look like airport departure boards," said Warden, nodding towards the clusters of large monitors that were arranged above the doors that, now he came to look, were spaced at regular intervals along the walls.

"Feels like a military airport," observed Milton nervously, "and even less welcoming, if they work out who we are."

"You're right," said Warden, nodding as he glanced around. "Let's skirt the edges and see if we can find something useful, then get the hell out of here."

They strolled casually along the edge of the huge room, looking for an open terminal or an office where they could plug in to a network port. Fifty metres down, they found a quiet space with a dozen terminals.

"Perfect," muttered Warden as they slipped inside, "nobody around, network ports over there..." He pulled out one of Sierra's boxes and plugged it into a port. The techs had included self-adhesive tags on the back of the box, so Warden peeled away the releases and carefully stuck the box to the wall.

"Looks like it was meant to be there," said Milton as she fiddled with her data slate. "Yup, we're in. Translation system is mostly working, bit weird, but I can see some interesting things. Downloading now."

"More ports over here," said Warden, fitting a second box while Milton stared at her slate. "Right, that's done, let's try another room."

Warden followed Milton from the room only to see another officer clone walking towards them. The officer frowned, clearly confused to see someone leaving his office, then hurried on.

"Back, back," muttered Milton, turning to head back to *Ascendant*.

"Uh huh," said Warden, following. Behind them they heard the officer calling and moving quickly, hurrying after them.

"In here," hissed Milton, ducking into an empty side room. Warden followed, heart hammering and fingers twitching.

The room was long but only a few metres wide with a viewing port at the end. No other exits.

"Blades?" said Milton, fingering the handle of her dagger as she stood just inside the door. Warden looked around but couldn't see an alternative.

"Shit," he muttered. He hadn't planned to leave behind a pile of incriminating corpses.

Then the officer stepped into the room and looked at Warden, asking something that Warden's slate struggled to translate. The officer took another step forward, repeating his question, his hand falling to some sort of pistol at his waist.

Then Milton stepped forward and, with workmanlike calm, wrapped her arm around the Rupert's neck before neatly inserting her dagger into his throat. She stood there for a few seconds as the officer kicked, then dragged him into a corner and propped him against the wall.

"There, there," Milton said, patting his cheek. The corpse just sat there, eyes staring vacantly. "We'd better move, sir," she said. "If they track their officers, they'll already know something's wrong. We might only have seconds."

Warden nodded. He was fitting another of Sierra's boxes under the counter. "Almost done."

Milton looked around nervously, standing watch on the door. Her eyes were drawn to a monitor on one side which appeared to show a countdown and an external video feed.

"Looks like another incoming shuttle, sir," she hissed as Warden checked the box with his slate and triggered another download. "It's about to get really warm around here."

"Almost done, Sergeant," muttered Warden. Then he stood up and rammed the slate back into its case. "Right, let's go."

Milton slipped quickly through the door and Warden triggered the mechanism. The door slid closed behind him and they walked as nonchalantly as they could towards *Ascendant*'s corridor.

"This spy stuff is quite exciting," said Warden as the door to the departure lounge hissed closed. Milton just shook her head as she jogged down the corridor. She punched at the controls and the airlock door opened. Seconds later, she and Warden were back aboard *Ascendant*.

"Safe," she muttered, hands on her knees as she took deep, calming breaths.

"For some strange value of the word 'safe'," Warden said, "but a successful infiltration, I think."

"That was quick," said Cohen when Warden and Milton returned from their expedition. "I rather thought you'd be gone a lot longer."

"Things got a little sticky," said Warden, his post-infiltration high rapidly dissipating, "and we decided to make a quick exit."

Cohen raised quizzical eyebrows.

"A Rupert caught us, sir," elaborated Milton, "and we had to improvise."

"But we installed three boxes, and downloaded some things that might be interesting," said Warden, handing his slate to Sierra.

"I'll get these to the techs," said Sierra, taking Milton's slate as well, "and check on the comms links to the boxes." He disappeared and the others sat down.

"They're shuttling troops up from the planet," said Warden as the door closed behind Sierra, "and then shipping them out to other destinations. Looks like a staging post for troop deployments, which suggests that NewPet is a training ground as well as whatever else they're doing."

Cohen nodded thoughtfully. "We've seen flights to and from the surface and from the station to out of the system but no in-system traffic. I agree; it looks like a training location."

"But why here, sir?" asked Milton. "Why not train their troops at home and ship them out from there?"

Warden shrugged. "Deniability, maybe? Or something to do with space or terrain? Maybe their other planets are just too crowded." Then he frowned; that explanation was not at all appealing. "Either way, unless we learn something from our downloaded data, our next step is probably to visit the surface."

"I agree," said Cohen, standing up, "but let's give Sierra a few hours to see what he can find. You two look like you could do with a bit of time off."

"I'm sorry, Mr Mueller, but what are we looking at?" Cohen peered at the display at the end of the meeting room trying to work out why the Chief Science Officer had insisted on showing it to them.

"These are hi-res images of the planet's surface," said Mueller, speaking in the slow, calming tones of an indulgent father talking to a petulant child, "and we're looking at the northern hemisphere. As you can see, we have large islands and small continental masses, mostly covered with forest or jungle. The climate is predominantly damp and warm, which leads to what appear to be very large plant-like growths across all regions."

"Large plant-like growths?" asked Warden. "You mean the surface is covered in trees?"

"Not trees, no, because trees are a terrestrial species and won't have evolved here. And in any case, these florae are in excess of a hundred and fifty metres tall in some places, so are significantly taller than even the tallest trees on Earth."

"What else can you tell us, Mr Mueller?" asked Cohen, gently trying to prod the scientist back to the matter at hand.

"Well, the florae are very interesting, from a scientific perspective, but I suspect you'll be more concerned with the military bases and the trains."

There was a pause as if Mueller was waiting for confirmation to a question he hadn't really asked.

"Yes, Mr Mueller," said Warden eventually, "we would like to know about the military bases."

"Well, if we zoom in a little, the bases show up as clusters of dark spots in cleared areas surrounded by either desert or very low vegetation." He flicked at his data slate so that the main display zoomed in to show something that could be a base but could just as easily have been a cluster of buildings sitting astride a road. "These areas you can see all around the 'base' appear to have been cleared of major florae so that there is at least a two hundred metre open space between the edge of the forest and the buildings."

"That makes sense," said Warden, nodding along. "You see it in fortresses on Earth as well. They would build the walls, dig an encircling moat and hack back the vegetation so they could see approaching enemies."

"But what enemies would attack here, I wonder?" said Mueller. "As far as we know, the Deathless are the only people in the system. Could they be attacking themselves?"

Cohen shrugged and looked at Warden. "It's possible," he conceded, "but I don't think it's likely. They appear to operate as a single political entity, so going to war makes little sense."

"Indeed. So why build bases with defensive walls? And why clear the forest from those walls?" asked Mueller. There was another pause as Mueller waited for feedback.

"What is your theory, Mr Mueller?" asked Warden eventually, keen to finish the briefing before his clone reached its expiry date.

"Megafauna," said Mueller, beaming at the conference room, "giant animals of some sort, possibly like dinosaurs and dangerous enough to require counter-measures." There was a moment of stunned silence from the officers, then Cohen sniffed and leant forward.

"What are these dark lines, Mr Mueller?" he asked, moving swiftly on and pointing at the image. "Could they be roads?"

"No," said Mueller, somewhat deflated by the utter lack of interest in his megafauna theory, "they appear to be high-speed rail tracks of some sort, possibly maglev lines or maybe even an enclosed vacuum system. Either technology would be ideal for transporting troops and supplies between bases, but they're not really interesting from a scientific perspective."

"How many bases, Mr Mueller, and how extensive is their rail network?"

"Ah, you have an incisive military mind, Captain Warden. We've found thirty-two bases so far, spread right across the globe, all linked by high-speed lines, although some of them appear to run through tunnels or across the sea. The bases seem to be distributed across all climatic zones and, generally, they each link to two or three other bases, depending on their isolation."

"Isolation?" asked Cohen.

"Many of the bases are separated by one to two thousand kilometres but a few are more than three thousand kilometres from their nearest neighbours, making them very isolated indeed. Even with the best technology, it's difficult to see them being reached by rail in less than three to four hours."

"What about airports or landing strips?" said Milton, "Where are they?"

"There's a spaceport here," said Mueller, highlighting an area where three bases sat at the corners of a triangle with sides twelve hundred kilometres long, "but there are no landing strips or runways of any sort, as far as we can tell."

"And why might that be?" asked Warden quickly, having grown used to Mueller's dramatic pauses.

"We thought initially that it might be an atmospheric problem of some sort but that doesn't seem to be the case. The air is slightly thicker than Earth's but not so much as to inhibit flight or render the process dangerous. At the moment, our best guess is that it's something to do with the indigenous florae and faunae but beyond that, I'm afraid we really can't say. And it could just be that the Deathless don't like flying or prefer trains."

"Hmm," said Warden, "well, thank you, Mr Mueller, you've given us a whole lot of information to process." He looked at Milton and Cohen. "And I suppose our next task is to work out where we go from here."

6

"This is one of *Ascendant*'s tech specialists, Midshipman Emma Cornwell," said Goodwin, Warden's own technical expert, "we've been working on the data packages exfiltrated from Soyuz and using the hacking boxes to search for more stuff."

The briefing room was full. Cohen and his senior officers were there, along with Warden and his command team. Marine X was skulking towards the rear of the room having sneaked his way in despite not being on the attendee list. Warden might have asked him to leave but the penal Marine had a surprisingly wide set of knowledge and it was difficult to know when he might make a useful contribution to any particular discussion, assuming his attention could be kept on the matter at hand.

"The bandwidth is restricted by the distance and the structure of the space station, so the transfer rate is very low," said Midshipman Cornwell, "but all three boxes are still working and we're getting useful amounts of information."

And everything they'd found so far suggested, as Warden and Milton had seen, that large numbers of troops were being trained on the planet then shipped out of the system through Soyuz.

"We've been looking for documents that might describe the

broader Deathless strategy but that information is proving difficult to find. There are several systems to which we don't have access," said Goodwin, "which is frustrating. It looks like the Deathless data security measures are effective and well-implemented once you get beyond the public sections."

"What are we doing about that?" asked Cohen. "Do we have any way around their precautions?"

"Not yet, sir," said Cornwell. "We don't know how they'll react if we try to brute-force our way into their systems, so we've concentrated on getting anything we can reach without arousing suspicion."

"Their security is good, but it still relies on people doing what they're supposed to do," said Goodwin, "and as we know, the weakest parts of any system are the operators."

"And we found an encrypted package on one of the slates that we can't access but whose file name and metadata strongly suggest that we should try to get into it," said Cornwell.

"If we've got the file, surely we can just send it back to the Puzzle Palace and let the teams there crack it," said Warden, frowning. "They've got plenty of power, after all."

"We thought about that, sir, but we think the package has a security system that relies on a biometric reading. It's really sophisticated, which is one of the things that made us pay attention to it. Somebody dropped it into an insecure folder on their slate, which was probably something they shouldn't have done, but the encryption is so strong we'll never be able to crack it, at least not quickly enough for the information still to be useful."

"So how does the biometric system work?" asked Cohen.

Goodwin glanced at Cornwell, who grimaced.

"We're not certain, sir, but our theory is that the package contains DNA identifiers of individuals, or possibly clone classes, who can be given access to the file. That fits with what we can see in *Ascendant's* systems."

"You've seen the palm readers built into *Ascendant's* computers?" said Goodwin, "The clones have different palm prints and DNA markers, much like identical twins have different fingerprints, although in this case the differences are deliberately engineered rather than emerging spontaneously in the womb, obviously. We think that if we load the file into *Ascendant*'s computers, we then only need someone from the approved list to provide a palm print and a DNA sample – the palm readers have built-in DNA scanners – and we'll get access to the file."

There was a moment of silence as the room digested this news.

"Would such a palm also allow us through the network security?" Warden asked, leaning forward.

"Maybe, but only if the person had appropriate clearance," said Cornwell, "and none of the clones we've tried so far has been able to gain access to the file or to the secure parts of the network."

"What do we know about the clones' DNA?" asked Cohen. "Could we manipulate it to fake a way through the security measures?"

Cornwell shrugged and looked at Goodwin. "I think that's a question for CSO Mueller, sir."

All eyes turned to Chief Science Officer Mueller, who was staring at his data slate and muttering under his breath.

"Mr Mueller?" said Cohen. "Are you still with us?"

"Hmm, what?" Mueller, looked up from his slate. "Sorry, I was miles away."

"We were asking about Deathless clone DNA and its use within the biometric security system. Can we hack it?"

Now it was Mueller's turn to grimace.

"The security system appears to be keyed to specific DNA sequences but, obviously, the DNA of the clones is the same within each class. They're clones, after all, genetically identical," said Mueller, flicking an image from his slate to the room's main display, "so biometric security doesn't just work with every individual. We think that the Deathless insert additional markers for certain individuals when their personalities are deployed, which allows clones to be uniquely identified and provides those individuals with enhanced access to facilities, systems or information. They've got some pretty advanced genetic manipulation technologies, so it isn't too much of a stretch to imagine such a system."

"But can we hack it?" Cohen persisted. "Could we use their techniques to insert the appropriate DNA sequences to one of our own clones?"

"Ah, interesting question," said Mueller, "and I think, given the level of sophistication we've seen in the Deathless cloning suites and their general approach to DNA, that yes, this should be possible using the technology aboard *Ascendant*."

"Excellent," said Warden, "how soon can we do it?"

"I suppose the answer to that," said Mueller, "is that it depends how long it will take to determine which DNA markers to insert and where they need to go in the strand. Do we have that information?"

All eyes turned to Goodwin and Cornwell.

"Er, no," said Cornwell, "I mean, obviously there's some sort of version of the key embedded in the data package, but it'll be hashed with a one-way code. If we have a DNA string, we can test it against the encryption, but we can't take the encrypted information and decipher or reverse it to discover the required DNA strand."

There was a disappointed pause.

"And that means our best option is...?" asked Warden to the room at large.

"It means our only option," said Goodwin apologetically, "is to find an individual who already has the necessary clearance and both a DNA strand and a palm print referenced within the encrypted data package."

7

"Do you think delivery will be a problem?" asked Warden as he reviewed the plans for the landing on NewPet. The science briefing had broken up and now Warden, Cohen and Milton were in the commander's meeting room to discuss the next stage of the mission.

"No, it shouldn't be, we can send you down in a shuttle, or maybe in the dropship if you plan to take a large team," Cohen replied.

"I think this looks like a good spot," said Warden, "at least to start with. There are buildings but not much movement around them, so with any luck, we can have a nose around without being rumbled."

"Who are you taking?" Cohen asked.

"Just Goodwin. She can do the hacking while I snoop and watch her back."

"I think I should go with you, sir," Milton offered.

"No, I want to keep this as small as possible. I don't want an entire troop down there; that would only create more chances for someone to give the game away."

"But you need backup, sir. Two Marines on their own in an enemy camp when their closest allies are what, two hundred kilometres away? We won't be able to get to you if there's a problem."

"I'll have backup, Colour Milton, don't worry. I'm going to have Marine X on overwatch to help with our exfiltration, just in case something goes wrong." Milton nodded slowly, although it was clear she wasn't entirely happy.

"Where do you want to rendezvous for extraction?" Cohen asked.

"I think this," said Warden, pointing at a spot on the map, "is probably a good point for both pickup and drop-off."

"And your fallback in case the first RV is compromised?"

"It would be a hard slog through the jungle, but this area looks okay, doesn't it?"

Milton sniffed, clearly not at all keen on the plan. Cohen seemed less concerned.

"Shouldn't be a problem," said Cohen breezily, "it's a standard gravity world, predictable weather patterns, can't see any reason we might have an issue landing a shuttle at either point."

"Sir, I really wish you'd let someone else go," Milton said.

"It has to be me, I've been getting the highest scores in the language classes. I've got the best chance of bluffing our way out of trouble," Warden said with an apologetic shrug, although 'best chance' didn't necessarily mean very much.

"So, to be clear, you'll land here under cover of darkness, proceed to this small base and find a way in. Once inside, you'll extract any information you can in the hope it will tell us where the departing troops are being sent. If things go smoothly, your extraction point is here and if everything goes pear-shaped, we'll pick you up here instead," Cohen said, gesturing to the highlighted locations on the map displayed on the screen as he did.

Warden nodded. "That's the long and the short of it. Any objections?"

Cohen shook his head and Milton followed suit, somewhat reluctantly, a moment later.

"Then it's settled, we'll present the plan to Vice Admiral Staines and Lieutenant Colonel Atticus. Milton, can you brief Marine X, please, and make sure Lieutenant Hayes has her troop standing by, just in case we need ground support as a last resort."

"Yes, sir," the veteran NCO said, snapping a salute before leaving the war room.

Cohen waited until she'd left then asked Warden, "She doesn't seem all that happy about this. What happens if you're captured?"

Warden sighed. "That's part of the reason I want Marine X backing me up. His role is more difficult than I let on to Milton and I'm not convinced she'd go through with it if I asked her to."

The Navy man looked at him for a moment before light dawned. "How will he do it?"

"He'll be taking a railgun. If I'm captured, or Goodwin, Ten will put out our lights."

Cohen shuddered at the thought. The grim necessities of war had never seemed quite so personal.

~

"Cohen, Warden, what's the news from NewPet?" asked Vice Admiral Staines.

"We are transmitting our data now, sir. To summarise, there is a sizeable Deathless presence in the NewPet system. Upwards of sixty thousand personnel, as far as we can tell so far."

Staines was visibly taken aback by that news. "Sixty thousand? What the hell are they doing there? Is it a colony world?"

"No, sir," said Warden. "It appears to be entirely run by their military."

"My word. It must be a naval base. With sixty thousand you could support an enormous fleet."

"There are some ships here, sir, but not very many, nor the infrastructure to support a large ongoing fleet presence. There's a space station in orbit around NewPet itself that operates as some kind of transport hub, but the bulk of the personnel are on the planet itself. We think they have large camps down there and they're training troops, thousands of 'em," Cohen said.

Atticus chimed in, "What else do you have for us? I see from the report you've been on the station but already left it behind."

"We believe the Deathless are sending troops from here to other systems, not just New Bristol. They have a massive embarkation area in the Soyuz space station and there are multiple destinations listed, but their names translate to 'Target 1', 'Target 2' and so on. We don't know what those names mean in terms of locations in space, but we assume they are separate systems," explained Warden.

"Understood," said Atticus. "So you need authorisation for a change of mission profile, I assume?"

"Yes, sir, we want to carry out missions on NewPet itself and change our focus from general intelligence gathering to trying to answer the question of where they're sending those troops."

"We expect that this will be the point where the mission will go hot and we'll be discovered by the Deathless," Cohen added.

Atticus and Staines were silent for a few minutes while they reviewed the plan and Warden found himself chewing his lip nervously, like a student waiting for his essay to be read.

Finally, Atticus looked up at the camera. "Whose plan is this?"

"It's mine and Captain Warden's, sir," answered Cohen.

"It's a bit thin, chaps," commented Staines. "Are you sure you've been through it thoroughly?"

"We think we've got the foreseeable areas covered, Vice Admiral," answered Warden.

"What happens if your team is discovered?"

"We have a secondary extraction point in case the primary is rendered unviable during the course of the mission, sir."

"All well and good," said Staines, "but if you are discovered on the surface, that will also throw *Ascendant*'s loyalties into question, won't it?"

Cohen coughed and Warden gritted his teeth as the two men exchanged glances. The Vice Admiral was right; as soon as the Deathless found intruders on their planet, they would check for anomalies in recent shipping movements to find out how they reached the surface. *Ascendant*'s surprise arrival would be an obvious discrepancy that they were bound to investigate.

"My apologies, Vice Admiral," said Cohen. "I will prepare a

contingency plan in the event *Ascendant* is identified by the enemy during Captain Warden's mission."

"I also think we're missing an opportunity," said Atticus, flicking through the images that had been included in the data package. "If we're putting a team on the planet's surface, should we not also be gathering intelligence on the troop bases? That might be something that could be done while Warden is trying to locate an enemy officer who can open the encrypted files. There's a lot of activity on the planet and I, for one, want to know more about those troops and how they are being trained, not merely where they go once they finish their training."

Warden looked at the maps of the region and nodded.

"Yes, sir. I can add a second mission team to conduct surveillance on the Deathless troops while we infiltrate the target base and locate the information about their wider activities," Warden said, making notes on his data slate.

"Are you happy for us to proceed once we've made these changes, sirs?" Cohen asked hopefully.

Atticus and Staines muted their mics and had a short conversation before responding.

"We are agreed in principle that your mission should go ahead, gentlemen. That said, you need to make some changes to address the weaknesses we've discussed and although we recognise you are keen to get started, we want to see your revised plan before the mission is launched. We strongly suggest you sit down with your senior staff and that you take advice from the specialists and instructors that General Bonneville sent you. Present your plan as soon as you are ready and we will confirm authorisation if you've settled our doubts," said Vice Admiral Staines.

"Yes, sir, understood. We'll get right on it," Cohen confirmed.

"Remember," Staines leaned forward and wagged his finger to emphasise the point, "your priority is to find out where the Deathless are going and why, but bear in mind that a small amount of intelligence returned to HQ is a lot more useful than learning of a secret plan for galactic domination if you die before you can transmit the details. If at all possible, try to get out without them even knowing you were there."

"Yes, sir," said Cohen nodding, "we'll take every precaution."

"And we need to know more about the troops they're training, Warden," said Atticus, "so I want you to gather as much data as you can. If they've got tens of thousands of troops on NewPet, are they like the ones on New Bristol or are they from an entirely different batch? Make sure you record all unit insignia and get it to us for analysis."

"We'll include that in the mission profile, sir, and if we find anything actionable, we'll get it back to you. We won't let you down."

Cohen signed off and shut down the wormhole transmission.

"So, they didn't much like that, did they?"

"No, not one bit, but at least they supported the mission in principle, even if we did fuck up the first crack at the plan."

Cohen shrugged. "They were bound to find fault somewhere. I'm not happy about it but they have the experience and it's easy to criticise someone else's plan. Don't let it bother you, is my advice."

Warden grinned. "You're right, they are a lot older than us. They've probably done this to hundreds of junior officers. You reckon we can pull something workable out of this?"

Cohen shrugged. "No option, really. What's the worst that can happen?"

"Let's gather the team and see if we can't predict a few of the worst-case scenarios, eh?"

They went their separate ways, Cohen to gather his senior staff and Warden to go and find the Marines he wanted to hear from. Intelligence gathering operations were always tricky to plan, especially if you didn't know where to look.

An hour later they had re-worked the plan, thrashed out the details with the specialists and received at least grudging approval from Vice Admiral Staines. The plan was still thin but with so many unknowns, there wasn't much more they could do.

"You're sure about this?" asked Cohen as he watched the Marines prepping for their missions. "You don't want to take anyone else?" Warden was still taking only two people with him on the base infiltration mission: Goodwin to hack the Deathless computers and Marine X, who would be on overwatch to help them exfiltrate to one of the agreed rendezvous points.

The secondary mission would be led by Colour Sergeant Milton, who would take a small team to surveil the enemy training camps. They had found a location from which she could observe three camps that were placed close together.

"Or maybe it's just one large camp, slightly more spread out than the others," Milton had said. They had argued the point for a few minutes but nobody had been able to settle the question or even really explain why it was worth asking.

"What's the worst that can happen, sir?" said the irascible Marine X, grinning as he picked out weapons and supplies from *Ascendant*'s armoury.

Cohen glanced at the penal Marine but couldn't bring himself to answer. Milton did it for him, "You could come back with us, Ten?"

The criminal merely grinned, but Cohen thought the worst possible outcome was pretty obvious and he wasn't at all keen on Marine X's attitude, which smacked of the worst kind of amateur bravado. Why was a court-martialled Marine anywhere other than the brig anyway? He had never heard of such a deployment, but he'd checked the regulations and from what he could tell, it was above board, just very, very rare.

"I don't see an alternative," said Warden as he loaded magazines into his webbing. "I'm not all that keen on this plan myself, but do you see another way to get the information we need?"

Cohen shook his head. "It's a terrible risk," he said, "and not just to you."

Warden grinned and clapped him on the shoulder. "It'll be fine, you worry too much."

"And you don't worry enough," said Cohen, his face tight and grey, "but okay, yes." He held up his hands in resignation. "You're right, there's no other way. Just take care, will you?"

"Always. Don't worry, we'll be back before breakfast."

"Hah!" snorted Cohen. "Fine. We'll smoke you a kipper."

8

"This is shuttle *Gladstone*," said the pilot, Henry Smith. "Ready for launch."

"Acknowledged, *Gladstone*, thirty seconds."

The shuttle was small, designed for only a dozen passengers, but it still felt empty with only three Marines, even though both Warden and Goodwin were wearing power armour. Marine X sat opposite them, his thin frame dwarfed by his larger and more heavily armoured colleagues. Smith had volunteered for the mission and sat alone in the cockpit, the co-pilot's seat left vacant for this flight to reduce exposure.

<Another bet, Colour?> sent Marine X, head back and eyes closed as he relaxed in his seat.

<Why not? I'm on a winning streak. What did you have in mind?> she replied from the second shuttle, where she waited with her own small team.

<Weirdest alien encounter? It's a new planet, after all, and we've no idea what's down there. Could be some really freaky shit>

<Done, but if you lose, you pay up before the party starts, right? No more welching on your debts by getting yourself flattened>

Marine X grinned, his eyes still closed. It was a strange expression on his lightweight clone.

"Doors open," came the voice from *Ascendant*, "launch initiated."

"Acknowledged, *Ascendant*. Free-fall in ten seconds," said Smith over the internal comms system. "Right about now would be a good time to update your wills."

Ten snorted. "I'll leave it all to myself, can't imagine anyone else would want my stuff."

There was a bump as the shuttle was shunted to its launch point and then the artificial gravity disappeared as they moved free from *Ascendant*.

"Launched," said Smith needlessly, "firing attitude thrusters, nothing major, just some slow manoeuvring." They felt the slight jolt as the shuttle's engines fired briefly, shifting it away from *Ascendant* slowly at first but then more quickly as Smith tweaked their trajectory.

"How are we looking, *Ascendant*?"

"All good, *Gladstone*, no obvious signs of alarm, looks like you're in the clear."

"Acknowledged, *Ascendant*, and thanks. *Gladstone* out."

Warden, strapped securely into his seat, watched the video feed from Smith's monitors as they dropped quickly towards NewPet, heading for the nightside. Milton's shuttle followed just behind.

"Are you sure this will work, sir?" asked Goodwin nervously. "I mean, isn't it a bit risky?"

"Probably," said Warden, "but what other choice is there?"

They floated in silence for twenty minutes before Smith came back on the comms system.

"Re-entry begins," he said. "Hold on to your hats."

The shuttle bucked as NewPet's atmosphere began to make itself felt. Warden switched off the video feed and glanced at Goodwin, who looked somewhat uncomfortable. Warden grinned and Goodwin gave him a weak smile.

"Never really enjoyed this sort of thing, if I'm honest, sir," said the technician, hands clamped tight to the arms of her seat, "and I don't get how he does it."

Warden nodded and glanced at Marine X.

"I've given up trying to work out how he sleeps through these things. It's just a fact of life."

And Marine X snored lightly, utterly oblivious to everything around him.

~

"This is it," said Smith as the shuttle bumped down through the atmosphere. "Target forty kilometres ahead. The final approach will be bumpy and low, so get ready."

Even Marine X hadn't been able to sleep through the latter stages of their descent. They'd come down fast, much faster than a shuttle would have flown on a routine office transport flight, but now they were well within the atmosphere and dropping quickly, aiming for the relative safety of the hills.

"Two thousand metres," said Smith. "Sensors show nothing unusual, looking good so far."

The shuttle shot through the night sky, heading for the ground at a steep angle, aiming to get down and up again before the Soyuz was back overhead.

"One thousand metres, twenty kilometres out, still looking good."

"Just another walk in the park, sir," said Marine X, grinning. "Not sure what you were worried about."

Warden ignored him and focussed on the video feed from the front of the shuttle. The canopy was getting ever closer as Smith brought them down and began to level out in preparation for landing. Mueller had been right; the local plant-like organisms were huge, scraping into the sky like living towers, dwarfing anything he'd seen before.

"Four hundred metres," said Smith, "and I'll be looking for somewhere to land behind the hills over –" then he paused, and the shuttle lurched violently to one side then back the other way. Warden gripped the arms of his seat, all plans forgotten as the ship bucked violently.

"Are we hit?" he asked. "Is something shooting at us?"

"Negative," said Smith in a shocked voice, "not hit, but it was close. Shit, more of it, hold on."

The passengers watched the feed as Smith swerved violently, jinking the shuttle first one way then the other to avoid something that hung in the sky above the canopy.

"Taken some damage there, I'm afraid," said Smith as he brought the shuttle back to level flight. "Looks like there's some sort of nasty floating beastie out there."

"Is it serious? The damage?"

"Don't think so, sir, but I'll take a look when we're on the ground. Should have us down in a couple of minutes." The shuttle slowed further until it hovered just above the canopy. Then Smith took it gently down, easing it in amongst the giant plants and aiming for what looked like a clearing at ground level.

"Yeah, well, the ground's not quite as solid as I thought," conceded Smith as they stared at the shuttle.

All four of them were outside, standing on something that looked like a fallen tree trunk, staring at the shuttle as it sat in the mud, listing crazily.

"I think that's because you put it down in a fucking marsh," said Marine X, his sense of humour temporarily suppressed by having to slog through the muck with slimed wings to reach what passed for dry land around here. His thin uniform was soaked and covered in the stinking mess from the marsh, and he scraped ineffectually at his legs, trying to clean off the muck.

From here, they could see where the vines of the floating beasties, or 'gasbags' as Smith had christened them, had trailed over the port side of the shuttle. Whatever they were – and it wasn't at all clear – they had left blackened marks along the length of the hull.

"Let's get going," said Warden as Smith waded back to the shuttle and peered closely at the hull. "Anything you need, Smith?"

"No, sir, I think this is just surface damage, nothing serious. It looks like it's from an electrical discharge of some sort, though, so you might want to stay away from those gasbag things."

"Agreed. Good luck with the return flight, see you in a couple of days."

"Thanks, sir," said Smith, heading for the door. "Hope it goes well." And then he was gone, ducking into the shuttle and closing the door behind him. The three Marines watched as the shuttle lifted jerkily from the mud then crashed off through the foliage, climbing quickly out of sight.

Down here, beneath the canopy, the sudden quiet left by the shuttle's departure gradually filled with the chirrups and rustling noises of a rainforest. Not that anything sounded quite normal or familiar. The general oeuvre of a rainforest analogue was similar, though; the dank musk of the rotting vegetation, the close, humid atmosphere and the claustrophobic density of the canopy were strangely comforting.

"It's that way," said Warden, consulting his HUD and pointing, "about five kilometres. An hour, maybe, if we get moving."

Marine X picked up his kit, including the disassembled rail gun in the specially made carrying sack, and flicked out his wings. He gave an experimental flap, but the span was too great for flying in the dense jungle. He sighed, folded away his wings and slung his sack over his shoulder before following Warden and Goodwin.

Two hours of heavy slogging later, the three Marines lay on the ground at the edge of a low rise that overlooked their target base. The going had been tough, much tougher than they had expected, but they had eventually reached their target.

"There's not a lot going on down there," muttered Goodwin as she peered through her HUD, zoomed in so that she could scan the base, "hardly any lights, no movement that I can see."

"It's not exactly midday," said Marine X, who had sat up and was leaning against a tall plant-like thing, assembling the rail gun with his eyes closed, "maybe they're just asleep."

"Maybe," said Warden, fitting the suppressor to his rifle and checking the magazine, "but either way we need to get moving." His HUD had a countdown showing the time left until the sun began to rise. He glanced over at Marine X, who was running his hands over the rail gun, checking it over. "Ready, Marine X?"

"Yes, sir," he said, opening his eyes as he slotted a magazine into the gun, "good to go." Ten rolled over then arranged himself on the ground, gun trained on the base. The harpy's limbs fitted neatly around the rail gun's stock such that he was able to lie comfortably while cradling the weapon. "It's as if they were made for each other," Ten muttered as his hands rested naturally on the firing controls.

"Goodwin?"

"Yes, sir," said the tech, checking her own weapon then nodding in the gloom, "I'm ready."

"Here we go, then," said Warden, pushing himself upright and running in a low crouch across the open ground to the wall of the base. He stopped at the bottom as Goodwin joined him. The wall rose about them, ten metres high and topped with large spikes, just like the Deathless base on New Bristol.

"Familiar, eh?" said Warden, nodding at the spikes. Goodwin looked up and grinned in the dark. "And now we climb," said Warden, triggering the power armour's climbing feature. Spikes shot out of his fists and feet, and he kicked one foot into the foamcrete of the wall then levered himself up and rammed in his other foot. Goodwin followed suit and as Ten watched, the two Marines scaled the wall.

<What the hell do you think they put those spikes on their bases for? They're not much cop for stopping people getting in> Marine X sent, training his scope on the huge protrusions that curved out from the top of the wall.

<This really isn't the time> sent Warden, focusing on his climb.

<Maybe they're to keep out monsters> joked Goodwin as she heaved herself over the top of the wall and unslung her rifle.

<You're still clear> sent Marine X, <no sign of movement or alarm but I can't see beyond the wall>

<Acknowledged> sent Warden, unslinging his rifle as he joined Goodwin on the wall. And then they disappeared from sight as Marine X began scanning the walls and the roofs of the taller buildings, watching for anything that might present a threat to his commanding officer.

～

Warden and Goodwin crept along the wall, moving past cut-outs that were obviously firing points. Warden paused a few times to snap images and shoot a little video for later analysis; he couldn't imagine why a base on a Deathless planet would need firing points on its walls but maybe someone else would be able to figure it out later.

"Just like the base on New Bristol," muttered Goodwin, clearly wondering about the same features. "Made no sense there either."

At the end of the wall, a door opened into a gatehouse tower. Warden signalled Goodwin, counting down from three, then jerked open the door. Goodwin swept inside, HUD showing her every detail of the room beyond, rifle leading the way. Nothing.

They went down the stairs, searching everywhere for a terminal they could hack, but the tower was bare and empty.

"Not even seats," muttered Warden as they descended through a large room and down to ground level. A door opened out into the base's courtyard and after a moment to check for guards, they ghosted across the open space to the closest building.

"You see anything?"

"No, sir," whispered Goodwin, "everything's quiet out here."

"Too quiet," hissed Warden, "I don't like it." He reached for the door control and Goodwin stepped back, rifle raised. The door slid open and the interior lights flickered on, bathing the courtyard in a fan of white light.

"Shit," muttered Warden as Goodwin moved quickly into the

room, checking for anything that might be an alarm. The door slid silently shut behind them, leaving them in what appeared to be a boot room of some sort, although the benches were covered in dust and lockers were empty, their doors hanging open.

"Where the fuck is everybody?" murmured Warden as they moved across the room to the next door. Goodwin touched the controls and the door slid open. Beyond, another room, much larger and festooned with monitors and control desks.

"Some sort of control centre?" asked Warden as they swept the room for enemy soldiers. Goodwin nodded, closing the door behind them before moving away to check the other side of the room.

"Clear," she said eventually, standing up from her crouch and lowering her weapon, "and these desks are covered in dust, sir. Looks like they haven't been touched in weeks."

"Or longer," agreed Warden, shouldering his weapon and peering at one of the dormant terminals, "but that works for us, right?"

"Indeed." Goodwin fished out one of Sierra's hacking boxes and plugged it into a network port. Then she pulled out a data slate, connected to the box and began to flick through the contents of the network. While she worked, Warden inspected the rest of the room. There was a staircase in the corner leading up to another floor, but the rooms above were as empty and forgotten as the rest of the base. He came back down and sat on a chair near where Goodwin was working.

\<Anything moving?\> he sent.

\<There's something large crashing around in the jungle. Nothing near the base\> sent Marine X.

\<Nothing to see here\> sent Warden \<hacking now\>

"I don't like this, Goodwin. It's unnatural."

Goodwin grunted but didn't look up from her work or answer, and Warden pulled out his own slate to check for messages or updates from Cohen. Nothing. Apart from the lack of Deathless at this base, it seemed that things were going to plan.

∼

"That's about it, sir," said Goodwin, pushing back from the desk and setting down her slate, "there's a load of information here but I don't think it's going to be very useful. If you want to know about leave protocols or the arrangements of supplies and local troop movements, we're sorted. For anything else, we still need access to the secure network." She paused to rub her eyes. "Or that encrypted file. I just have a feeling we might find something in that."

"Bugger," said Warden, stretching his neck, "I'd hoped to get some answers here."

"Sorry, sir, no answers," said Goodwin, packing away her kit, "but there is this." She flicked around on her slate until she brought up a map of the area, then she zoomed in until the screen showed their current location and the stretch of land to the west. She offered the slate to Warden.

"What am I looking at?"

"We're here," said Goodwin needlessly, pointing at the pale blue dot that pulsed gently on the map, "and this is the secondary target, the base of unknown use about fifteen kilometres to the west." She took the slate back and flicked over to a translated document. "And this is a list of the people currently in that base. I think we might find answers there," said Goodwin, returning the slate to Warden, "because all the guests on the roster are officers and there's a load of servants of some kind, civilians maybe, but basically cooks and masseurs and suchlike, plus a small garrison."

"Interesting," said Warden, flicking through the list, "and I think we've found a likely target," he said, tapping on a name to bring up a detailed profile of one of the current residents.

<Some... things are starting to stir out here> sent Marine X, intruding on Warden's musing, <it might be a really good idea to get moving>

<Acknowledged> sent Warden, <we're on our way>

"Right," said Warden, turning to Goodwin, "let's get out of here. I'm not sure I want to know what might be out there that could make Ten nervous, do you?"

9

Milton watched as the shuttle headed away from the bases, back the way they had come. The team had disembarked in a small river gully and they had a good ten kilometres to cover before they reached their observation point.

Fortunately, it was a clear night and, with the low light vision their HUDs provided, it felt almost like daylight. A night hike like this would be a nightmare without that level of visibility but the power armour also meant it was hard to twist an ankle. Nigh on impossible, really. They would be fine.

The only wrinkle they might reasonably encounter would be an enemy exercise. With three bases in their line of sight, the butte they were aiming for was an obvious landmark and Milton thought the probability that they might meet Deathless trainees on a night exercise was alarmingly high.

"Keep your eyes open," said Milton as her team arranged themselves. "I don't trust these Deathless bastards to be safely tucked up in their beds."

As they began their yomp to the top of the butte, she thought about options for falling back but there really weren't that many. And the bet with Ten about unusual wildlife was starting to look like it might have been a bad idea; there wasn't much of anything moving up here in this arid environment.

NewPet was turning out to be a planet of strange contrasts. This area was rocky with relatively little vegetation, so dry it bordered on being outright dessert. But less than two hundred kilometres to the north, where Warden had deployed with Ten and Goodwin, there was a lush forest that was the local equivalent of a jungle. A long mountain range ran east-west to separate the two zones, keeping the rain clouds from moving south into the arid regions.

Even at night, high up on the ridge, it was warm. Milton was soon grateful for the power armour's cooling systems as they trekked along the ridge that led to the butte where they planned to make their base for the next few days. Up here, there were only a few small shrub-like things and the occasional taller tree-like plant clinging to the lifeless rock or scraping a living from the dusty soil. During the day, this place would be battered by the sun and she had made sure that everyone had brought extra water rations. They would need to take care to avoid overheating or dehydrating, even with the automated water reclamation and cooling systems built into their suits.

The need to maintain secrecy and avoid prying eyes meant that their route was less than optimal. Even in the powered suits, it took almost three hours to cross the ten kilometres to the base of the butte and another half an hour to climb the cliff face. Once at the top, they had the luxury of a relatively flat plateau and several hours to make camp before dawn rolled around and the sun began baking the rock again.

Marine Cooke found a dip near the northern edge which must have been worn away by an ancient riverbed before the butte formed. It was deep and gently curved, and the tenacious plants of the region had established their dominion along the edges where fractures in the rock allowed them to put down roots.

"It's as good a spot as any," murmured Milton, looking around the ancient riverbed. "Let's get settled in."

The Marines moved swiftly to erect their campsite. The riverbed was covered with rolls of graphene-based, nano-weave camouflage supported by carbon-fibre rods and tied off to some of the larger shrubs. The favourable geography meant that the spot was much more spacious than some of the observation points Milton had set up in the past. Making sure their priorities were straight, she left her team to get a brew on while she and Marine Harrington went to check their views of each of the three camps.

During the night they would use passive night vision cameras to record the activity in each camp. They would continue during the day but would also use the Mark 1 eyeball and the binocular features of their HUDs to evaluate the enemy.

Milton and Marine Cooke identified three likely spots for the daytime observations and noted them on their HUD tactical maps before they returned to the camp for a brew. Then the whole team worked to place cameras and tiny passive sensors around the butte; some would warn if Deathless troopers approached on foot or in some sort of ground vehicle, some were designed to monitor air traffic. The rest of the equipment was aimed at the Deathless camps and the training grounds that surrounded them, recording everything they saw.

"It's a big camp," muttered Marine Cooke as they reviewed the feeds from the night vision cameras, "bigger than any I've ever seen."

Milton grunted her agreement. The camps were bigger than any she had seen as well but they still represented only a fraction of the troops on NewPet. Whatever the Deathless were doing here, it looked intensive and well-organised.

"Do you think they're copying our methods, Colour?" asked Cooke, chewing at his nails.

Milton looked sideways at him and frowned. The basic training for a new Commando was two full years and that only included normal operations with brief tasters of a range of specialisms to allow individual aptitudes to be assessed. The sheer variety of equipment and operational scenarios a Royal Marine could expect to encounter in their first five years of service meant that even this level of training wasn't always enough. And officers did a further year of intensive courses after earning their green beret.

"I certainly hope not," said Milton, worried by the idea now that Cooke had raised the possibility, "let's just focus on gathering information." Anything they could discover would be useful to the analysts on *Ascendant* but the material would also be sent back to the Puzzle Palace on Earth to be pored over in detail by experts who would extract every last morsel of intelligence from it.

Could the Deathless be replicating the Marines' own training programmes? It was a frightening thought.

The officers and the governor were certainly in awe of the Deathless' ability to produce bases, equipment and armaments far more rapidly than their own manufactories. The Deathless kit, including the power armour she was wearing, was excellent and often technologically superior to their own.

But to Milton, it seemed that only the Deathless' training and experience were letting them down. Maybe that was enough to explain the existence of NewPet and its camps. How long had the planet been in use? The Deathless were industrious bastards and she wouldn't have put it past them to have built all this in the last few months.

The best-case scenario was that the planet had long been settled and that the Deathless troops who had invaded New Bristol had been their best recruits, graduates of this training facility. If that were the case, whatever the Deathless were doing here probably wasn't all that effective.

But Milton didn't think that was likely.

Still, it would be dawn before they were able to get a proper look at the camps in action, and all Milton could do at the moment was speculate about their plans and capabilities. Time to finish their prep and get some shuteye before the Deathless surfaced in the morning.

Milton's few hours of restless sleep in the warm air of an alien planet were ended by an insistent haptic alarm that woke her just before dawn. An order to the suit's med suite furnished her with a cocktail of mild stimulants that cleared the last vestiges of sleep from her brain, like drinking the galaxy's strongest coffee. Harrington, who had been on sentry duty, returned to the campsite, gave a brief report, then took the reverse cocktail and fell immediately asleep.

Milton checked that each Marine was appropriately concealed under their individual camo nets, then joined Cooke to get an early look at the westerly base. There was a wide crevice in the cliff where it looked like a giant claw had gripped the edge of the butte and gouged out a notch as wide as three people, making it a great place for an observation point. A couple of shrubs used the shade of the notch to eke out a living, and all the Marines had done was sling another camouflage net over the top of the crevice to conceal their presence. It wasn't quite tall enough to stand up in but you could lay down and look through the shrubs or rise to a crouch to move about, and two people could fit easily side-by-side.

Cooke was already there, staring down at the base.

"What have I missed?" asked Milton as she wriggled into place, her armour grinding away at the ground. She wouldn't have fancied being here without power armour, especially as the Marines had nothing to use as padding between them and the rocks. The shrubs they were forced to squirm their way past to get a clear line of sight were covered in vicious spines that would not have made for a good day for an unsuspecting Marine in standard fatigues and body armour.

"Looks like they're just getting up," said Cooke, stretching his neck. "They're not the earliest of risers."

Milton grunted and settled down to watch.

Twenty minutes later, the sunrise was in full swing and it looked like it was going to be another day in paradise, if by paradise you meant a sun-drenched hell-hole a score of light years from the nearest gin and tonic.

A movement barely seen from the corner of Milton's eye caught her attention and she twisted her body to get a closer look. Something was crawling out from a crack in the rock, woken by the first rays of the sun. It made a beeline for a small shrub in front of her, where a fat little creature was happily chewing the leaves, itself an ugly cross between a slug and a beetle.

The thing that had drawn her attention had a long, sinuous body made of banded segments that made it look a little like a shower hose. Hundreds of tiny legs propelled it rapidly towards the bush and, when it reached its target, it reared up and slammed its head down into the abdomen of the slug bug. Milton and Cooke watched in horrified fascination as the creature's mandibles clamped down on the unfortunate prey.

"Ten won't have seen anything like this," she muttered, making sure she had good quality images of the thing as it fed, "no way he'll win this bet now." She'd call him later with the good news.

"Looks like a giant millipede," murmured Cooke, "if millipedes were the thickness of my, er," he paused and glanced at Milton, "my arm and grew to be two metres long. Fucking horrible, whatever it is."

Milton couldn't help agreeing, especially when the thing began to spew some kind of greenish liquid onto the slug bug, which writhed in agony as its flesh liquefied under the onslaught of the toxin the mega-millipede exuded.

"Gross," muttered Cooke, now thoroughly distracted from the job at hand.

Milton reached slowly across her webbing as the horror show went on. A moment later she sighted along the barrel of her pistol and put two rounds in the head and upper body of the millipede, sending it careening off the top of the plateau, dissolving dinner still twitching in its mouth.

Cooke gave her a startled look.

"What?" asked Milton, "That was disgusting to watch. And I had the suppressor on, so they won't have heard it down there. Besides," she added with a smug grin, "that's definitely going to win me my bet with Ten."

Marine Cooke nodded in agreement; the scene had been morbidly fascinating but it was enough to make you lose your lunch. That nasty wee beastie wasn't going to be missed.

'Down there', as Milton had put it, was Camp West, as the Marines had imaginatively named it, and it turned out to be for motorised ground vehicle training. Milton and Cooke watched, somewhat bored, as the troops rose, went through their morning ablutions and breakfast, then broke up into teams to practise vehicle drills.

The first couple of cycles were vaguely interesting. The Deathless would start behind a line, get into one of their enormous APCs, drive a hundred metres then pile out into a combat-ready defensive position. Rinse and repeat, ad nauseam while instructors strutted about shouting orders and berating anyone who moved too slowly or stood in the wrong position.

Milton didn't need to understand their language or even be able to hear them speak to know they were getting a bollocking. *Are your boots tied together? No? Then why aren't you running? You call that running? My sofa is faster on its feet! Did you mean to drop that rifle or was it improvisational theatre?* She grinned, glad that she was now firmly on the giving side of that relationship.

Then a message came in from Warden. She scanned through it in her HUD, the details flashing before her eyes.

"Looks like the captain hasn't found what he was looking for," muttered Milton. Cooke said nothing, still watching the enemy troopers training with their vehicles. "They're relocating to another base to try to kidnap an enemy officer."

That got Cooke's attention. He shifted a little to look at Milton. "That's a bit risky, isn't it, Colour?"

"Very," said Milton, grinding her teeth, "but if anyone can pull it off, it's those three."

"Three? I thought he was with Goodwin?"

"And Marine X. He's on overwatch, keeping the captain and Goodwin safe."

Cooke shuddered. "Rather them than me," he said with feeling, "that guy gives me the creeps."

Milton grunted and went back to reviewing Warden's message. Cooke's feelings about Ten could wait, although she made a mental note to find out if any of the other Marines had similar reservations.

Warden's message went on to say that their secondary target had a maglev station so the backup extraction plan should still work. Milton digested that then composed an update on the situation on the butte, which was luxurious by comparison since all they had to do was sit around all day and look at things, not yomp through dense jungle.

After two hours of watching vehicles drive back and forth, though, she had to admit that even 'luxury' could get boring and that she needed to move on. At least she was able to move around and get a little variety; Cooke had to stay here and watch this base all day. Maybe she'd swap the whole team around in a couple of hours so that they took turns observing different camps. It might help them to stay fresh, and there was no need to tell them she was just helping them cope with the boredom of the duty.

The second observation point overlooking Camp North was not nearly so comfortable. They'd had to dig into the loose topsoil near the cliff face to carve out a shallow foxhole, which meant lying prone and wriggling forward under a low camouflage net to peer over the edge of the cliff face. It was vertiginous, cramped and windy with nowhere to move to get comfortable. Moving out from under the camouflage to stretch your legs wasn't a good idea and if they had raised the net any further, it would have changed the profile of the butte. An observant Deathless trooper interested in landscapes might notice, even from the plains, that the top of the enormous and distinctive rock had changed its skyline.

Milton squeezed herself into the foxhole alongside Marine Watson and peered out over the camp.

Camp North was all about shooting ranges. The whole thing. Come to sunny Camp North and spend all day, every day, shooting an exciting variety of weapons until you can actually hit the targets. The brochure would have made it sound exciting, but for most people, static range shooting was only fun for the first hour or two. The people who continued to find range shooting engaging after half a day tended to become snipers, since patience and an inability to suffer from the boredom of repetitive action were key traits in sharp-shooting. Detailed knowledge of wind and gravity could be trained into someone but if they didn't have the natural ability and the right personality, they probably weren't going to be great snipers. It was the truly dedicated, detail-oriented obsessives that you wanted on your team.

"Anything interesting?" asked Milton.

"They're burning through a lot of ammo," replied Watson. "The shooting is continuous and they're cycling their people."

As Milton watched, it became clear that the Deathless had no qualms about giving their troops as much ammunition as they needed to learn to shoot straight. There were at least a dozen gun ranges of various designs, as well as grenade emplacements and buildings that looked like they might be killing rooms simulating urban environments.

"Just make sure you're recording everything," said Milton, "and see if you can learn anything about their accuracy." She paused, watching a squad practising with railguns on a range that the HUD measured at five hundred and twenty metres. "Especially those fuckers," she said, tagging the snipers in the HUD for Watson to see, "they're a bit of a worry."

But it was Camp East that most worried Milton. Something about the camp had seemed wrong, even at first sight, but she hadn't been able to figure out exactly what.

In the observation post, she found Lance Corporal Bailey and her spotter, Parker, sitting in a scoop-like depression on the edge of the cliff. There were shrubs along the front edge of the coop and room for four or five people to sit and move around. The Marines had strung a camouflage net between the tops of the shrubs at the front and the wall at the back so that it wouldn't be visible from the ground as a disruption in the profile of the cliff.

There was even room to stand, just about, and the Marines had improvised seats from some of the flatter rocks to make this by far the most comfortable of the three observation posts.

"Morning," said Milton, stepping carefully into the scoop and crouching down. Bailey and Parker barely moved, testament to their ability to ignore distractions. "What's new and exciting?"

Parker shifted and glanced over his shoulder.

"Morning, Colour," he said, and it was clear from the tone of his voice that he, too, was worried by Camp East. "We've been watching them put their recruits through their paces. Look." Parker dropped a couple of flags into the HUD and Milton looked down on the camp.

"What am I look..." she began. Then she froze, seeing it for the first time, and shivering with recognition.

Parker had flagged a section of the camp that had been laid out as an extensive assault course. There were dozens of platoons on the course, hundreds of troops in total, all being put through their paces first thing in the morning.

"It gets worse," muttered Bailey, flagging an entirely separate course where a large squad practised in power armour. Even from here, they could see the telltale signs of live fire being used to acclimatise the troops to the sound of bullets flying over their heads.

"Well, bugger," said Milton quietly, because now it was obvious what had worried her about Camp East; it looked exactly like the first training camp she had ever attended, all those years before, when she had first signed up. She shivered.

"And look there," said Parker, flagging a group that stood along the edge of the assault course, watching, "we think they're the instructors and that they're taking notes on recruits' performance, evaluating them."

Milton nodded and brought her HUD to bear. The instructors had data slates and were clearly assigning ratings to the individual troops. Exactly as happened on the Commando course.

"Keep an eye on that for me," she said unnecessarily, trying to cover her mounting feelings of disquiet, "we need to know what they're doing."

She watched the power armoured recruits as they completed their assault course. When they reached the end, they climbed a high wall then ran down a steep hill on the other side. Rifles at the ready, they advanced to a firing position and emptied their clips into the targets at the end of the range. As each recruit cleared their magazine, they raised their rifle. Within a few seconds, every rifle was held high and, even from here, Milton could see triumph in the way they stood.

Then a team of instructors, also in power armour, popped up on either side of the jubilant troops. They advanced and fired immediately, rounds clattering from the armour of the shocked recruits, who quickly began to panic. Some curled up into balls, some sought cover or dove to the ground, others ran.

Milton gave a sickly grin. It was certainly an intense introduction to live fire and obviously a complete surprise for the recruits. It was over in moments and whatever ammunition had been used didn't seem to have penetrated the recruits' armour.

The instructors strutted around, calming their recruits. Then they lined them up and gave what looked a stern lecture, probably explaining in small words why using all your ammunition when you didn't know what was coming next was a bad idea.

"Brutal," she murmured, although it was undeniably a dramatic exercise. "Did you get that?"

"Yup, safe and sound," replied Bailey.

Milton wondered if something similar would be added to the training programme for the bootnecks after the Puzzle Palace saw the video. The exercise was harsh and tough, but the intention was clearly to teach the recruits a lesson in ammunition conservation and force them to focus on the limits of their armour's protective abilities.

They had not yet seen any surveillance drones, but Milton still checked the skies before heading back to the main campsite to review the information they had collected. Then she issued new orders to the team and set a countdown timer to get them cycling between the observation posts.

"And now we wait," she murmured to herself, replaying the video of the assault course and trying not to worry too much about the possible implications.

10

The jungle proved to be as thick and unaccommodating as Mueller had warned. Their yomp from the drop point to the first target looked like a beach-side promenade compared to the virgin jungle through which they now trekked. Beneath the canopy, it was gloomy even at midday, and a continuous spatter of falling water meant that Marine X was soaked within minutes of re-entering the jungle.

"Fifteen kilometres through this could take a while," muttered Ten as they hacked their way through the vegetation and around the trunks of the vast plants whose leaves formed the light-blocking top canopy. Goodwin grunted, pushing past saplings and diving through bushes, her power armour making light work of the plant life as she led the way.

And then Goodwin stumbled out onto a wide track that ran dead straight and due west, heading in almost exactly the direction they wanted to travel. The three Marines stood in the middle of the track and peered suspiciously first one way and then the other, looking along a wide green tunnel of trampled undergrowth that stretched as far as they could see before disappearing under the green gloom.

"What the hell did this?" muttered Warden, kicking at the bushy plants that had been crushed and flattened against the jungle floor. "Look at the way this is all churned up; it looks like a herd stampeded through here."

"Well, if it was a stampede, they won't be back, will they?" asked Ten, stretching his wings and giving a gentle flap. Even fully extended, he couldn't reach the edges of the tunnel. "It's going the right way and it'll be a hell of a lot easier to follow this path than to keep pushing our way through the jungle."

Warden hesitated, suspicious. "I don't like it," he said eventually. "What if the things that caused the stampede in the first place are still on the trail?"

"Don't worry, sir," said Ten in a reassuring tone. "I won't let the nasty monsters get you."

Warden gave him a flat look but the penal Marine had already turned back to the tunnel and was staring at the marks on the ground.

"What kind of thing do you think made these prints, eh?" he asked, focussing on something towards the edge of the tunnel. "I mean, they don't look like hooves, more like toeless feet of some kind. Really big feet from lots of beasties, but footprints nonetheless."

"Let's just keep our minds on the job, Marine X, and see where this damned tunnel takes us."

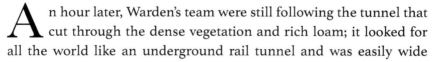

An hour later, Warden's team were still following the tunnel that cut through the dense vegetation and rich loam; it looked for all the world like an underground rail tunnel and was easily wide enough for two trains.

Even after they had travelled six kilometres, it still headed west as if following a line set down by some ancient cartographer. The tunnel showed no sign of coming to an end, and Warden had begun to wonder if it would carry them all the way to their second target. That was a worry, though, because, for all its convenience, it suggested that the Deathless had made the tunnel. They had assumed a herd of animals made it, but now he was considering other possibilities.

A little further on, the tunnel changed direction slightly to curve around a huge trunk. A series of scrapes and gouges ran around the side of the tree as if a massive vehicle had been driven too close and had rubbed against the bark, scraping loose the weird blue-flowered moss-like stuff that clung to every vertical surface.

"A tank of some sort?" suggested Ten, frowning. Then he shrugged, not really all that interested in solving the problem. Warden stared at the marks a little longer then shook his head. This wasn't a puzzle they were going to solve anytime soon.

Ten was first to feel it, a slight rumbling in the ground. He lifted his head and stared back down the tunnel, looking east. Around them, the jungle had grown quieter, as if all the nearby beasties had fallen still. For a long moment, Ten stood and stared as Warden and Goodwin loped off down the tunnel, heading west.

Then, his sense of unease growing, he turned and charged after them.

"I think we need to get off the road," he said when he caught up a few moments later, "and I think we need to get off right now." Warden looked at him, searching for evidence of a joke, but then he too felt the rumbling.

"You feel that?" he asked.

Ten nodded. His lighter clone was more sensitive to vibration and whatever was making the drumming was getting rapidly closer. Even Goodwin, in her heavier lizardman clone and wearing power armour, could feel the earth rumbling.

"Umm. Yup. Yup, yup, yup," Warden said as the ground began to vibrate beneath them and an ominous sound that was reminiscent of a high-pitched cement mixer overlaid with the pounding thunder of stampeding creatures. "Move. Now. Move, move, move!"

They sprinted along the tunnel, looking for an easy way into the undergrowth.

"There!" shouted Goodwin, pointing at a warped tree at the side of the tunnel. She jumped as she reached it, grabbing vines that hung from the upper branches and beginning to climb as quickly as possible. Warden and Ten followed her, and they moved swiftly into the lower branches.

"Fuck me, would you look at that," Ten said. The forest floor was visibly shaking, rippling the water pooled on the flattened ground of the tunnel. A few hundred metres down the tunnel, the trees at either side were shaking as something brushed and trampled past them.

They had been perched in the tree for only a moment before the rainforest divulged its secret. An enormous armoured beast thundered along the tunnel. Its segmented body undulated as hundreds of thick legs pounded the jungle floor. It was as tall as a house and it moved with frightening speed. As it ran, the spines on its flanks cut through the vegetation as if they were salad leaves and scraped chunks from the trunks of the larger trees. The thing's head, easily the size of a medium tank, was a nightmare of mandibles, antennae and jet black eyes.

It slowed as it drew nearer, the antennae twitching back and forth as if it searched for something. What the hell did this thing eat? Warden glanced at Ten, whose winged form prohibited power armour and meant he alone was not completely sealed inside an airtight suit. Could this behemoth smell Ten's sweet, tender, Deathless clone-flesh, maybe?

"Stay very, very quiet," Ten hissed, stating the bleeding obvious. Warden had to remind himself not to hold his breath as they waited to see what the hellish creature would do.

"Hey, Ten, I think I've won the bet," Milton said cheerfully over the comms.

"Really?" Ten whispered.

"You won't believe this thing; it's the biggest insect you've ever seen. Well, arthropod, I think, strictly speaking. Horrible beasty, long and wriggly, the mouth on this thing is straight out of some cheesy horror holo-vid."

"You don't say," hissed Ten as the giant monster lowered its head to the ground, snuffling back and forth across the tunnel. "Long and wriggly?"

Warden glared at Ten, chopping his hand across his throat in the universal gesture of 'shut the fuck up'.

"Oh yeah, this thing was huge, two metres long, easily. Had to shoot it to get rid of it. No way you're going to beat it."

<I'll buy a barrel of gin for the company if I can't beat it, but right now we're a little bit busy. Take a picture for me, eh?>

<Roger that. Pictures to follow. Looking forward to the cocktails, Ten>

<Yeah, me too, if we make it out of this>

Warden chewed his lip as they waited. He had imagined all sorts of ways the mission could fail – capture by the Deathless, *Ascendant* blown out of orbit, Goodwin unable to hack the information, shuttle shot down on their way back to *Ascendant* – but he hadn't considered the possibility of being eaten by a hundred-ton nasty.

And then suddenly its head reared up and it screamed, a great cry that went on and on, like a meth-crazed foghorn. Then it began to move again, gathering speed until it was charging along the tunnel, passing by the three Marines fast enough that they could feel the wind rush past them. The stench of the thing surpassed even the ever-present scents of the rotting vegetation on the forest floor. A hundred metres long or more, it went on until, abruptly, it had passed.

They waited in the trees until they could no longer hear it screaming as it barreled down the tunnel, nor feel the vibrations from its passage. As the rest of the jungle began to come back to life, they climbed gingerly down from their platform in the canopy and stepped back into the tunnel, peering both ways. Then Marine X sniffed, gagged for a moment from the stink it left and spat on the on the floor.

"That was unexpected," he said, a masterful piece of understatement. "How do they turn around?"

Warden looked at him then grunted, utterly disinterested in the question, and set off along the tunnel, yomping away in the long, loping strides of the power armour.

Goodwin quickly followed but Marine X stood for a moment longer, looking at the tracks and thinking about how a train-sized monster might use a network of tunnels in the undergrowth. Then he sighed and began running. The sooner they were out of this jungle, the better.

Warden called a halt only a little way further along the track. The tunnel had opened out into a wide clearing where a second tunnel crossed the first. Two hundred metres across and heavily trampled, it was clear that the monsters were doing more than turning around in the clearing.

"What do you think they eat?" said Goodwin as the Marines stood in the crossroads. Warden and Ten looked at him, and Goodwin shrugged. "Just wondered. I mean, it's not like we've seen much in the way of game, is it, and something with huge jaws that moves at that sort of speed isn't likely to be a herbivore."

Warden shuffled uneasily. "I think I would have preferred you not to verbalise that thought," he said, scanning the tunnels and jungle uneasily.

"At least we're only four kilometres from the target," said Marine X, checking his HUD, "another hour and we'll be there, and then we'll see what's going on." He took a swallow from his water flask then unwrapped another energy bar. "Maybe there's some sort of monster buffet at the end of the tunnel."

Warden shook his head, finished his own snack and stretched his neck. "Let's keep moving. I want to get set up well before dusk."

They pushed on until they reached the end of the tunnel and the edge of the jungle. The valley had been clear-cut; massive tree stumps could be seen across the expanse between the jungle and the base. The buildings stood right in the middle of the valley, surrounded by nothing but low shrubs and crawling vines.

The colossal plants of the jungle marched no closer than the edge of the valley, reaching over a hundred metres above the low ridge and heavily hung with great leaves and trailing vines. The animal calls and sounds that had been a near constant accompaniment so far had died down and, for the first time, the jungle seemed subdued, quiet and ominous.

A maglev line emerged from the forest a kilometre away, dropping to a station near the base before rising again to head back out of the valley. Beyond the pylons that supported the line as it approached the base, the valley fell steeply away so that the base seemed to perch at the end of the world.

"There must be another base to the north," said Warden, checking the plans that Mueller had provided, "but there wasn't anything on the map."

"More gasbags," said Goodwin, peering out across the clearing towards the base. The walls were over two hundred metres away, ten metres tall and topped with the familiar curved spikes. Above the canopy, at the head of the valley where a small river dropped from the hills, a flock of the floating creatures hung in the air, seemingly tethered to the plants.

"Like jellyfish back home," said Marine X, "but with electrically charged tentacles instead of venomous barbs," he went on, remembering the scorch marks on the outside of the shuttle. "Nasty."

"I don't recall ever seeing a zeppelin-sized jellyfish floating above the treetops back home but yeah, just like that," Goodwin replied.

As they watched, the vines on one of the nearer gasbags jerked and shook then began to retract slowly. The Marines watched, open-mouthed, as a large animal was dragged up towards the underside of the floating body. Then it disappeared, stuffed into a huge maw that opened to receive its gift. The empty vines fell back to the forest canopy, and the gasbag hung there, giving no sign that it had just consumed a creature the size of a cow.

Ten cleared his throat, breaking the silence. "The locals are a bit unfriendly," he observed.

"Maybe that's why the Deathless didn't settle here," said Goodwin. Then she paused and frowned as another thought struck. "I wonder what those cow things eat?"

Marine X glared at the tech and shifted uncomfortably.

"We need a higher vantage point for the surveillance kit," said Warden eventually, "to give us a view down across the base. This ridge isn't high enough, not with those bloody walls in the way." Marine X looked at his commander then glanced at the nearest plants before finally looking at the Gasbags.

Then he sighed and rummaged in his bag for a remote camera kit. He stuck it to his webbing and looked up at the tree.

"Maybe there's a convenient branch with a clear view," he said unenthusiastically. "I guess I'd better have a look, right?"

"Probably for the best," agreed Warden. "You're the lightest, there's less chance of you falling, and if you do, it won't matter."

"Yeah, I do have wings, I suppose."

"Wings, right, I'd forgotten about those," Warden replied with a smirk.

Ten's eyes narrowed and he pursed his lips, then he cocked his head and looked hopefully at Goodwin, just in case the tech was keen to place the camera.

"Don't look at me," Goodwin said quickly, raising her arms, "this armour isn't really suited for climbing trees."

Marine X narrowed his eyes to slits but said nothing more. He checked his blades then shuffled back from their viewing spot and circled around to the far side of the nearest tree. Then he crouched and sprang, leaping several metres straight up and landing on the trunk, fists gripping the fibrous growths on the surface. He paused to look once more at Warden and Goodwin, but they just waved cheerfully and went back to watching the base.

"Fuckers," muttered Ten as he began to climb, checking for gasbag vines with every reach and hold.

Seventy metres up, with the greenery showing little sign of thinning, he found a thick branch that poked into the valley, overhanging the edge of the ridge. He stepped out onto the metre-wide branch and gave an experimental jump. It barely moved, so he walked gingerly out, towards the open air of the valley, working his way around the numerous branches that speared out in all directions.

"That'll bloody do," he said quietly. The branch had narrowed quickly and was now getting distinctly bouncy, even with Ten's lightweight body. He unpacked the camera, a tiny remote unit with a zoom lens and wide-spectrum sensitivity. A proper Gucci bit of gear, far better than the stuff they were usually issued.

The kit included a telescopic carbon-fibre mounting pole. Ten fitted the camera then began unshipping the pole, raising the camera cautiously towards the top of the canopy. As it reached the top, he switched to his HUD and stared out through the camera's lens.

"Slowly, slowly," he muttered, focusing on his task. The feed showed the undersides of huge leaves and the thin, spiny lengths of the topmost branches. Then the last spiny leaf was brushed away, and the camera burst out into the open space above the trees. Ten had a moment of vertigo as the camera's focus shifted rapidly and adjusted to the changing light. Then it settled to show a clear view across the jungle to the base. He switched away from the camera feed, rammed the end of the monopole into the trunk and checked it was secure.

<You seeing this?> he sent to Warden and Goodwin.

<Yes>

<On my way back> sent Ten, edging back along the branch.

On the ground, Warden and Goodwin both keyed into the feed. The camera had a long view across the valley and into the base. They couldn't see everything that was going on in the base, but by zooming and panning around, they could build a pretty good picture of the Deathless activity.

The problem was that Warden didn't like the picture he was seeing.

"Any good?" said Marine X, when he re-joined them a few minutes later.

"The feed is good," said Warden, "but I don't think we'll get in and out quietly." He paused to flick some captured stills to his slate then showed them to Goodwin and Marine X.

"Apart from the walls, the killing ground all around the outside of the base, the maglev station for rapid reinforcement and the wall-mounted cannons, this looks very straightforward."

"The cannons might be for the gasbags, sir," said Goodwin, "you know, to keep them from hunting inside the compound."

Warden switched his HUD to zoom out to the gasbag and then back to the walls, inspecting the cannons.

"Maybe," he conceded, "but the bits I really don't like are the towers," he said, flicking back to the remote camera feed and focusing on one of the four tall towers that held high watch positions above the base. "We might sneak in under their gaze, but they're going to make exfiltration really bloody difficult if things get noisy."

They spent a few minutes scanning the base and reviewing the feed from the camera, but nobody could see a way to avoid the towers.

"How many Deathless are in there, do you think?" asked Warden.

"If those two long buildings are barracks or apartments of some sort, maybe thirty bunks, then another fifty or so in the guard houses over there," said Marine X, panning around with the camera and flagging the buildings in his HUD. "That looks like some sort of conference facility and there's a big open area that might be a parade or exercise ground, and maybe a rec room?"

"Maybe eighty to a hundred then, in total," said Warden, grimacing. "I don't like our odds."

"There's a shitload of Ruperts down there," observed Marine X, "far more than any normal base, I'd say. And I can't see any specialists. No ogres or harpies, just lizardmen and Ruperts."

Warden frowned. "So this is what, exactly? A training campus?"

Marine X shrugged. "Could be they've erected an officers' stately pleasure dome," he said, grinning, "you know, somewhere they go for a bit of a jolly." Warden raised an eyebrow. "Or a retreat, maybe, where the brass meet to set strategy." Warden looked at him strangely, and Marine X frowned. "What?" he asked. "We have them at home, why not here?"

That was news to Warden, but he nodded, remembering that the well-preserved Penal Marine had acquired a wealth of training and obscure knowledge over his decades of service. How he knew about the habits of the most senior officers was a question for another day.

"An officer's retreat, then," said Warden quietly, "set far enough from the other bases to ensure privacy but still connected to the maglev network for convenience. Sounds ideal for what we need, I just wish it wasn't so bloody large. I would have preferred a nice, modest hunting lodge, to be honest. And at least there's no sign of a runway or a landing pad."

"Wouldn't want to fly too near the surface, sir," pointed out Goodwin, "not if you thought there might be gasbags floating around. Rail makes sense."

"And the maglev lines are on stilts because those giant millipede things might disrupt the trains," mused Warden.

"Nah," said Marine X, "I reckon it's just easier to sink piles to hold up the rail than it is to clear the ground and build on it. But there might be other megafauna, herds of giant herbivores maybe, that we haven't seen yet. Wouldn't want them sitting on the track as you were speeding along at three hundred kilometres per hour."

"Millipede shish kebab," murmured Goodwin in a rare moment of humour.

"Anyway," said Warden, dragging the conversation back to the matter at hand, "the point is that there are lots of them down there, they've probably got guards in the towers, and we've got to sneak right in there to grab one of their top brass. That's not something we can do quietly."

Goodwin nodded and Marine X, absorbed in the feed from the remote camera, merely grunted. Warden sat and thought for a few minutes, trying to see a way to do it.

"Nope, sooner or later it'll get hot," he said eventually. "It only needs one of those guards to sound an alarm or to get off a decent shot as we're retreating across the killing ground, and this whole thing will have been for naught."

He looked at Marine X and Goodwin. "I'm going to call in Milton and her team. Goodwin, you and I will infiltrate as planned. You'll run overwatch, Ten, and we'll have Milton to back us up when things go pear-shaped. Then we'll all head to the secondary extraction point."

Marine X flicked up his HUD. "Risky, very risky," he said, grinning, "but I like it."

11

"Come on, look lively," said Milton. Warden's orders had made it clear that time was of the essence, so now the camp was a hotbed of activity as the team packed away their gear and tidied the site.

"Leave no traces behind, people," said Milton as she folded down her own gear and stowed it in her pack. Bailey and Parker, lacking power armour and its advanced processing facilities, were bagging their solid waste for exfiltration along with the rest of the gear they'd brought for the two-day reconnaissance. Watson had drawn the short straw and was now packing bags of solid waste into his pack, carefully checking that each was properly sealed and surrounded by soft, non-piercing objects.

Had they been in the jungle, Milton might have risked burying the solid waste and trusting to the vegetation to hide both the evidence of digging and any lingering smells. Up here, with only dusty rock and thin soil, there was no option but to bag the crap and take it with them. Nobody's favourite job, but Warden had been clear: the enemy was to learn nothing from the site.

And so it was being scoured. Once they had finished, all the enemy would learn – if they ever came to look – was that someone had been up here for a while.

The observation posts were dismantled as well, all traces carefully removed, every stone and plant checked to make sure it looked natural, untouched. As each post was dismantled, Milton checked for any signs they might have left behind, but her team were professionals and she found nothing that would indicate they had once been there.

In fact, the only thing they left behind was the body of the millipede thing that Milton had shot. She looked at it as it baked in the sun then decided that as there was no practical way to hide it or take it with them. Their only option was to leave it where it lay. Besides, it had been shot with a Deathless pistol so even if the body was found and examined, the enemy would learn nothing about the Marines.

"That's looking good, people," said Milton as she completed her last round of inspections and the Marines shouldered their packs, "but we've got a long way to go and a short time to get there, so let's get moving."

It was still light when they left the site, which meant travelling less quickly than Milton would have liked and taking extra care with the route to ensure they stayed out of sight. Progress was slow, but they couldn't afford to be silhouetted against a skyline or spotted by a passing aircraft, not that the Deathless seemed to find much use for aircraft.

Bailey and Parker took the lead, scouting ahead to find the best route and checking for Deathless troopers and vehicles. The harpy clones made excellent scouts and even though they flew only a few metres off the ground, they were able to make much faster progress than the rest of the team.

Every five hundred metres, Bailey would halt and take up overwatch, scanning the sky for signs of enemy movement while Milton and the rest of the reconnaissance team yomped on. When they had almost caught up, Bailey and Parker would push on to their next overwatch point, searching continuously for signs of the enemy.

Slow and steady wins the race, thought Milton. With bases on every side of the butte, they would be easily surrounded if the Deathless discovered them.

The sun had just finished setting when Bailey sounded the alarm.

<Freeze> Bailey broadcast to the team, the command flashing an urgent red across their HUDs.

There was no cover, just the rocks and contours of the ridge, so the team crouched motionless on the ground, trusting their dust-coloured armour to hide them from hostile eyes.

<Problem?> sent Milton.

<Movement in Camp East>

<Do you have eyes on?>

<Just about – feed open now> confirmed Bailey.

Milton switched her HUD to show the world from Bailey's perspective. Down in the camp, vehicles were moving out, their headlights shining in the dim light. Bailey tagged them in her HUD, which showed the vehicles moving at fifty kilometres per hour. Considering the terrain and the complete lack of roads, that was dangerously fast.

<Where are they going?> Milton asked.

<Not sure, Colour. They're heading roughly east but can't tell why or what they doing>

<Roger that> Milton replied, wondering what the hell was going on. Had they been discovered or was this merely a night exercise?

She flipped to an overhead map display and extrapolated the current path of the small convoy. They planned to board the maglev train just past the point where the ridge curved a little to the northeast. There was a long tunnel passing through the hills, the Deathless having simply dug straight through to maintain a fast line rather than go around or over the hills, and the station that seemed to serve the camps was on the northern side of the tunnel.

That was where Milton and her team needed to be; then it was a clear shot to the rendezvous with Captain Warden. They were still almost ten kilometres out, though. The Deathless convoy could be coming up into the hills between them and the station. If they'd detected them, it would be logical to get ahead of them and either set up an ambush or force them back up towards the butte and the other camps.

"There's nothing on the map," muttered Milton, tracking the convoy's likely path, "so they must be heading to the station." The more she thought about it, the more likely it seemed. If they had planned an ambush, they would have been driving with night vision rather than headlights, which surely even the Deathless knew would be a giveaway. The troops she'd been watching in Camp East seemed to be disturbingly competent and she couldn't imagine them making such an easily avoided error.

<We have to assume they're going for the station. We need to pick up the pace and see what happens. Bailey, Parker, get to an overwatch point for the station as quickly and quietly as you can. The rest of us will follow as quickly as possible. Notify us of any major changes> Milton ordered.

<Roger that, Colour> Bailey confirmed. Milton could just make them out in the distance as they unfurled their wings and ran forward, gliding along the line of the ridge, as low to the ground as possible. They should reach the station in about ten minutes, depending on the wind and altitude.

At daylight pace, Milton and her team could expect to take an hour to complete their yomp to the station, but the power armour did have some advantages.

"Switch to full night-vision mode," she ordered as her HUD scanned and mapped the terrain ahead, laying down an amber route for her to follow. "Stay close and look sharp. And if this takes us more than thirty minutes, I'll have you all doing drills until you spew pavement pizza, understood?" Milton looked around at her small team then nodded and broke into a loping run, following the route her HUD overlaid onto the ground in front of her. They might not reach the station before the Deathless, but she was damned if she would give them time to prepare an ambush.

∼

<B>ad</B> news, Colour Milton> Bailey sent.

<Busy hoofing it, Bailey, we don't all have wings. What's up?>

<We've reached overwatch position and you have less than twelve minutes to make it to the train>

<We'll get the next one>

<Negative, Colour. There's an illuminated sign on the platform and maintenance on the line after this train; the next one isn't for another twelve hours>

<Buggery bollocks! Get a fucking shift on! If we don't make that train, we'll miss the RV with the captain and that means we won't get picked up by *Ascendant*. We are not getting stuck on this shithole>

<Permission to use stims, Colour?> requested Harrington.

Milton thought quickly as she huffed into the rebreather of her helmet, which sucked away her moist breath and condensed the water out of the air before returning it to her reservoir.

<Confirmed> she sent, issuing the order to the team and authorising their suits to dispense stimulants, increase the oxygen supply and deliver a cocktail of mild painkillers and anti-inflammatories.

<Dial up the servos> she sent, tweaking her own suit's settings so that she could run faster. It would cut the operational time of the suits' batteries in half, but they needed to reach their train more than they needed the power reserves.

The Marines accelerated, hurtling through the night, pushing their clones to the very edge of their design envelope. Even in the suits, there were risks, especially over terrain as rocky and broken as this. More than once Milton stumbled or missed her footing or found that the ground was sloping up rather than down. Their night vision gear was excellent, but it was easy to misinterpret, especially at speed, and there were limits to what the power armour could do to protect them.

Worse, they had no clear idea what the extra oxygen might do to the Deathless clones they wore. Their standard RMSC clones were better at handling oxygen than their biological bodies, but it could still do funny things to their minds. And while the painkillers were great for hiding the ache of sore limbs, they also cut the feedback loops that prevented small injuries from getting more serious.

Own it, thought Milton as she ran, teeth gritted, *fucking own it and push through it.*

Run or fail. Catch the train or get left behind on an alien planet and commit a very thorough form of suicide in order to protect the mission.

The Marines ran for all they were worth.

<Bailey. We need a solid plan to get straight on that train> sent Milton.

<Working on it. Those soldiers from Camp East are standing ready to board the train. Looks like they're going in our direction>

<Then we still need that plan, Bailey, and it better be a bloody good one>

A minute later, Bailey came back on.

<Sending a new route. Faster>

<That's fucking close to the edge>

<Only way you'll get here in time, Colour>

<Roger that> sent Milton, <changing course>

The new course took them far closer to the edge of the ridge. If there was anyone down there, all they needed to do was look up and they'd see the four Marines pounding along for all they were worth, illuminated by the stars that shone brightly through the clean air. And who knew how much noise they might be making as they steamed across the rocky slope? Sound did funny things in the desert at night.

No point panicking though, thought Milton. *Just put one foot in front of the other until you're finished.*

Jenkins stumbled when a small boulder slipped as his foot landed on it, and he almost went down, face first. Rebecca Watson was just close enough to grab his webbing and haul him up short before he could break his head open. Milton was bringing up the rear, and she reached down and grabbed him under the left shoulder, helping him to stand and get moving again.

<Four minutes, Colour>

<I bet these bastards have the only trains anywhere that bloody run on time> sent Milton, cursing to herself as she ran.

<Yeah, looks that way, Colour Sergeant. We clocked it as it approached the other side of the ridge. It's below the ridgeline now, but the HUD estimates its speed will put it in the station at the time shown on the platform sign. You have no slack> Bailey responded.

<So what's the boarding plan?>

"Say that again, Parker?" Milton hissed incredulously. They had made it to the rendezvous point about sixty seconds before the train was due to depart.

"There are Deathless in all the carriages that aren't still in the tunnel," said Parker apologetically, speaking quickly, "so we have to wait until the train moves off then get on an empty carriage. It's okay, I checked; there are four more carriages."

"No," Milton seethed, "it is most definitely not okay, Parker. Have you ever seen a maglev accelerate out of a station? They do not hang about. You want us to jump onto a moving maglev train and get ourselves attached to it before the wind shear yanks us off?"

"Well, I don't want to do it either, Colour Sergeant," Parker protested, "but there's not much choice. Oh, and you're going to have to hold on to me and Bailey because without power armour we probably won't be able to keep a grip." He grinned weakly and raised his thing, graceful hand.

"Oh spiffing, this just gets better and better."

"Sorry, Colour," Parker glanced at the train, "but there isn't time for us to get into the carriages at the back and the tunnel is too tight for us to crawl down it and get ready. Even if we did, we'd be clomping our boots all over the roof of one of the carriages with Deathless in it. On the plus side, the station isn't manned, so we can get right up to the lip of the tunnel ready to jump onto the second carriage. All at once of course, or it'll be too late."

"Fuck, fuck, fuckity fuck, fuck," Milton spat, "bollocks to it, we don't have a choice, do we?" She paused, chewing at her lip but there was no other way and she knew it. "Let's give it a go. This night can't get much worse, anyway."

"That's the spirit, Colour Sergeant," Bailey said with a broad grin. Easy for her to say, of course; she and Parker had wings to get them out of trouble if it all went wrong.

The team shuffled to the lip of the tunnel. Parker was right – it was less than a metre above the roof of the maglev carriages, and there was no way they could get in without giving themselves away.

"I think we just need to drop onto the second carriage. Better to have an empty carriage between the Deathless and us, yes?"

"Agreed. At least this thing is wide enough that we don't have to do it one by one. Three abreast, folks," said Milton, more confident now that the decision had been made, "and get your carabiners ready so that we can rig ourselves together. This is going to be a punishing ride. Once we're aboard, we'll be on this thing for a few hours before we get to the rendezvous with Captain Warden."

Below them, a whining noise indicated the maglev train was about to depart the station and that the time for talking was over. Milton checked her gear was securely strapped and that the rest of the team were in place.

Then they leapt.

The train was moving under them as Milton landed on the carriage roof. She heard the rest of the team land a few metres behind her and it sounded like they were down safely. Now, if she could just hold on to the edge of the carriage for a few hours, everything would be rosy.

"Sergeant!" Bailey shouted into the comms channel. "You seem to be hanging off the side of the train!"

"Thank you, Bailey, I hadn't noticed," she said sarcastically through gritted teeth as she gripped the rail at the edge of the carriage roof, "and it's 'Colour Milton'."

"I'm on my way, hang on," Bailey said, "you know, in case you weren't doing that already."

"Hadn't planned on letting go," hissed Milton as the train accelerated.

Bailey swooped in low and grabbed a rail at the side of the carriage to bring herself to a sharp stop. With her wings for lift, it was easy for her to get back up on the roof of the train. Milton, on the other hand, was clinging for dear life to the edge of the carriage with one hand while she tried very hard not to loosen her grip.

Then the train began to bank to the left, which would have been helpful if Milton had been on the right side, but a fifteen-degree tilt left her dangling in thin air, over at least a thirty-metre drop. With the train now travelling at over a hundred kilometres an hour and still accelerating rapidly, this was not helpful. Even the power armour wouldn't save her if she fell off at this speed but the bigger risk was someone in a leading carriage looking back and spotting her.

"I'm here, Sergeant!" Bailey said.

"If you tell me to hang on or take your hand, I will end you, Bailey."

"No, that would be stupid. If I have to tell you to hang on, why would I want you in charge? You'd be too stupid to live and if you could get your spare hand to me, you'd pull yourself up," Bailey replied as she busied herself with something.

"Good to know. Do you have anything useful to say?"

"Yes, I plan to say, 'Attach this carabiner to your webbing so we can haul you up'. Just prepping the line."

Thirty seconds later, the aforementioned article dropped over the side of the carriage, and Milton was able to grab it on the third try with her dangling left hand. She clipped it on to her shoulder straps and checked they were still tight.

"You've got a live one here," she shouted, left hand clutching at the line above the carabiner, just in case, "reel me in."

The line went taut as the Marines pulled her up the side of the carriage. She scrambled onto the roof and took a few seconds for a breather. Then, as the train pushed past a hundred and fifty kilometres an hour, she checked that the team was roped together and clamped to the roof.

A few minutes later, the train returned to an even keel and began to accelerate to maximum speed. Bailey and Parker were squeezed between Jenkins and Harrington in their power armour, with Milton at the front to take the brunt of the wind and Watson at the rear. They had used their climbing claws to give them extra grip, and each Marine was clipped to two others by a short length of cord and a carabiner.

The battering from the wind was severe and they squirmed and adjusted their positions until each had found the lowest possible profile to minimise the drag. Now, all they could do was cling on for dear life. This was going to be a gruelling couple of hours.

Milton cast her mind back to the Commando course, the final milestone of the Royal Marine Space Commandos training programme. Centuries before, the course had been only a week long but now, with all the extra combat roles the Marines faced, it took a full month with only a few precious 'rest' days between the various tests of endurance and confidence. The location had shifted as well, with the second half of the course now taking place on the harsh terrain of Mars rather than the relatively friendly Devonshire countryside.

Now, tied to the roof of an enemy train as it rattled across an alien planet at over four hundred kilometres an hour, Milton compared it to the last gruelling training week on Mars and decided it merited only 'challenging'. Then she chuckled as she remembered the weeks of paperwork and administration that had followed the earning of her Green Beret, and she downgraded her evaluation of the wind rushing past her to 'bracing'.

12

For Warden's small team, dusk took a very long time to fall. They lay at the edge of the jungle, one sleeping, one on guard, one watching the Deathless base, all waiting for the sun to sink below the horizon.

Marine X assembled and checked his railgun while the light was still good, tweaking the sights and making sure that they were set to take account of the light breeze. Then he propped it against the trunk of the tree and settled down to wait.

At dusk, a train rocketed across the valley and drew to a halt at the station on the edge of the compound.

"Sixty-five seconds," said Warden as the train pulled away again, "a few on, a few off, maybe." He shrugged. They hadn't found a timetable in their stolen data cache, so it was impossible to say when the next train might arrive, where it might come from or what it might be carrying.

All they knew for certain was that Milton and her crew were riding a train at that moment, inbound at something like four hundred kilometres an hour, all clinging to the outside of the carriages.

"Rather her than me," Ten had said when Warden described what

Milton's team were having to do. "What if there are tunnels or carriage scrapers or something? What if the train runs through a station and someone sees them?"

But nobody had been able to come up with a better idea and it seemed to be working, so far. Milton's last report had said they were making good progress and that she had a newfound respect for tumbleweeds.

Across the valley, the train finally slipped from view and a flock of something that looked like large, leathery birds flapped its way across the compound before disappearing over the trees.

"That's our entry point," said Warden after watching the video of the train arriving and pulling away several times, "we'll wait for full night, creep down, infiltrate the station and then go in from there."

Around the Marines, the nightlife was starting to emerge from the jungle, and the calls and noises were growing louder, more insistent.

"Why through the station, sir?" asked Goodwin, watching the video again in her HUD.

"Whatever the walls guard against, it's not people," said Warden, "so they probably don't have guards in the station, and they might not even lock the doors. It would fit with their previous performance."

Goodwin nodded but looked doubtful.

"And this is our target," said Warden, sharing an image from the files they had liberated earlier in the day, "he's got the right rank and job title and, with any luck, he'll get us into the secure spaces."

Goodwin nodded again but still looked sceptical. Sneaking around was something they were all happy to do, but kidnapping enemy officers was just a little too much like spying, and it didn't sit within the tech's comfort zone.

"It'll be alright, Goodwin," said Marine X cheerfully. "What could possibly go wrong?"

∽

"That's late enough," said Warden eventually, one eye on the clock and the other paying attention to the base. Activity had died down an hour before, and now the compound was silent and still. They had plotted a route to the base that took them around the side of the valley to the maglev lines. "And then we just follow the pylons. Easy, and no chance of being spotted."

"It'll take a while," said Marine X doubtfully. "Hacking through the jungle in the dark won't be a lot of fun."

"Two hours," said Warden, "possibly a little more, but no chance of getting lost."

Marine X nodded, almost invisible under the thin starlight that penetrated the canopy.

"Milton's hours away, but by the time we get out, she should be pretty much here," Warden went on. He paused to check his kit again then he looked at Goodwin.

"Ready, sir," said the tech.

"I'm going to edge around the top of the valley, find somewhere with better visibility of the rail," said Marine X as he loaded his rail gun and re-checked the mechanism, hands moving quickly and confidently despite the dark.

Warden nodded to him, checked his rifle and webbing one last time, then he set out along the edge of the valley, following the route they had mapped out earlier in the day and that now pulsed dully in his HUD. The jungle was thick and progress, as Marine X had predicted, was slow. It took more than an hour to reach the first of the tall foamcrete stilts that supported the maglev line.

"That's our marker," said Warden. Goodwin nodded and followed him down the slope at the edge of the valley. Tracking the maglev rail took them across the valley, where the jungle's greenery was already trying to reclaim the open ground. They reached a small river, not much more than a stream, that flowed under the maglev line before diving into the deeper valley beyond.

An hour later, they had crept across the river and over the mangled remains of the local foliage so that they were only a hundred metres from the maglev station. The rail, ten metres above their heads, flew on towards the station as Warden and Goodwin advanced in its shadow, all the way to the train station.

The fifty-metre long train platform stood on more foamcrete stilts, an elegant structure that Warden might have considered architecturally interesting in other circumstances. At the back of the station, a short walkway led to the wall and then into the compound. From the ground, they couldn't see enough to spot movement, but there were no sounds from above, only the distant animal calls of the jungle.

Then there was some sort of animal alarm call from the jungle, far off down the valley, a high-pitched screaming cacophony that split the night air. Warden and Goodwin looked around, trying to spot the source of the problem, but even the HUDs couldn't resolve the details of the jungle where Marine X was hiding.

<Problem?> sent Warden, crouched behind a foamcrete stilt.

<Space monkeys> came the reply, <dealing>

"What the fuck?" breathed Goodwin.

Warden shrugged, the gesture almost invisible without the vision-enhancing capabilities of the HUDs.

<We're at the station> sent Warden. <Are we clear to ascend?>

<Hold, still dealing> came the reply. Warden frowned. Marine X was rarely unreliable.

Warden squatted down, resting his back against a foamcrete stilt. Goodwin scanned the area then she too settled down to wait.

"What the hell is going on?" muttered Warden after they had been waiting for a few minutes.

<Update, Marine X> he sent, marking the message urgent.

There was no reply, and Warden was beginning to fear that something untoward might have happened to the Penal Marine.

"This is taking too long," he said after giving Ten another ten minutes. "We have to get going." He gestured at the stilt, preparing to climb. Goodwin nodded, shifting so that she could see the platform and cover the captain.

Warden took a deep breath and began to heave himself up the

foamcrete support. The clone was well-suited to this sort of activity and the power armour made it all seem easy. In seconds, he was at the top and sliding silently over the parapet and into the station.

He scanned left and right, rifle at the ready, checking for Deathless sentries or other staff. Satisfied, he signalled Goodwin.

<We're in the station, all clear> sent Warden. <Are you ready?>

<Still dealing> sent Marine X, <give me a minute>

<No time for jokes, Marine X. Are you ready?>

There was no reply. For twenty long minutes, Warden and Goodwin crouched in the shelter of the station. Warden switched from the remote camera video feed to the HUD's night vision, alternately scanning the compound and the local area then staring out towards the jungle where Marine X was supposed to be providing overwatch.

Warden was in the process of composing a forceful note and a formal reprimand when Marine X finally responded.

<Sorry, space monkeys. All sorted now>

Warden and Goodwin shared a look.

<Save the excuses, Marine X, we'll talk about this later> sent Warden, <just get to your position>

<Almost there> came the response. Then a few minutes later, <In position. Good visibility, I see you. No movement in the compound, guard towers quiet and dark>

<Copy that> sent Warden. He stood slowly, stretching his cramped muscles, then he and Goodwin began moving, heading to the back of the station and the raised walkway that would take them into the compound.

<Station clear, no signs of security> sent Warden as he and Goodwin moved quietly along the walkway. At the far end, a steel door barred their way. Goodwin searched in vain for a control pad that would allow them access before they noticed the handle recessed into the face of the door. Warden stood back, rifle raised, as Goodwin pulled gently on the handle and the door slid on silent runners into the wall.

<Door unlocked> sent Warden as he stepped over the threshold,

Goodwin following. The room beyond was empty, dark and windowless but large enough to hold a company as they waited for a train to arrive. Ahead, a door led out towards the compound; to the right, a second door led somewhere else.

Warden shook his head, marvelling at the total lack of security. Had he ever been on a base that lacked even basic mechanical locks and guards? But then why lock doors on a planet where your nearest neighbours were over a thousand kilometres away? Bloody amateurs, they weren't much better than space pirates, only with a lot more ships and people.

Goodwin slid the door closed, and they stood for a moment, checking their surroundings and waiting to see if they had triggered silent alarms.

<No sign of activity> sent Marine X. <Looks like they're all asleep>

Warden nodded and signalled towards the door that led out into the compound. Goodwin sidled over and touched the control. The door slid back, and a gust of warm air flowed into the room, carrying with it the smells of the base and the jungle. Outside, a wide stairway led down to the ground where foamcrete paths were laid between the buildings.

"We're allowed to be here, remember?" said Warden quietly, shouldering his weapon and standing up straight. Goodwin looked at him for a moment then nodded and shouldered her own rifle. "But keep your pistol ready." Warden held up his hand to show a suppressed pistol, then he strolled casually down the stairs and into the compound, not quite whistling but definitely walking with a jaunty air.

Goodwin waited a few seconds then followed, her own pistol hanging at her side. They had mapped a route to the most likely residential block, and now all Warden had to do was follow the trail displayed in his HUD. A few minutes of stealthy walking took them around the edge of the compound and to a long, low building that seemed to be a series of apartments overlooking the parade ground.

"Looks like a holiday camp," muttered Goodwin, frowning.

But a holiday camp designed by military minds rather than fun-loving architects or anyone who had ever been on an actual holiday. The paths were all straight and neat, and the buildings were plain and utilitarian, unadorned squares and oblongs of bare, unpainted foamcrete.

Even the imported plants – bushes and small trees that were clearly descended from Earth originals – were arranged neatly but without imagination, as if the whole compound had been laid out with function as the only principle worth following. Warden felt that it gave the whole scene a strange, unfriendly feel, like old bases back home where the joy had been sucked out of everything by bureaucrats and pen-pushers.

"Pretty shitty holiday," he whispered, making for the long low building that they'd pegged as the officers' quarters.

The path took them straight there, lit by bright, overhead lights on simple galvanised steel supports.

"Look for nameplates," hissed Warden, checking the apartment doors. They hadn't found a layout plan that showed room allocations and their target could be behind any one of these doors.

"Nothing," whispered Goodwin, "just a number."

"Shit, nothing on these ones either," murmured Warden. "Well, that's a bugger." Neither of them said anything for a few seconds, then Warden shrugged. "I guess we just take whoever's in the biggest room, then." Goodwin nodded and pointed at a large apartment set slightly away from the others at the end of the row.

Warden nodded and switched from his pistol to the suppressed rifle. Then they padded down the row of apartments towards the one at the end.

"Keep an eye on that tower," muttered Warden as they moved beyond the shelter of the apartments and back into the open space between buildings. He stopped by the door, checking that Goodwin was in place, then reached for the opening control.

<Movement on the tower> sent Marine X as Warden's hand brushed the control, <changing guard, maybe>

"Bugger," muttered Warden as the door slid open. The lights were off inside but the HUD gave them excellent night vision, and nothing seemed to be moving. He slipped into the room, and Goodwin followed, tapping the door control so that it slid shut behind them.

The room was large but sparsely furnished. A pair of sofas were arranged in front of a large display that hung on the wall. A desk and chair sat against another wall.

"Grab that," hissed Warden, pointing at a small computer of some sort that sat on the desk. Goodwin sidled over and picked it up, slipping it into her pack. She slung the pack over her back and turned back, collecting her rifle as she went. Then there was a bang and a crash as she caught a desk lamp with his arm and knocked it flying.

Goodwin stared in horror for a moment then both Marines swung round to look at the other door, the one they assumed opened into some sort of bedroom. From beyond the door, there came the sounds of stealthy movement.

Warden flicked his finger, gesturing to Goodwin to get out of sight. Then he moved the other way, trying to get close to the bedroom door. He was about halfway there, with Goodwin still moving the other way, when the door opened, and a Rupert clad only in light trousers stepped out into the room.

There was a moment of quiet surprise as they all stared at each other, then the Rupert said something, head turning to look at Warden, whose clone was essentially identical. The HUDs translated but the mangled text didn't help much.

<Who the sexual act is you? I will call the guards who are covered in blood!>

Then Goodwin smacked the Rupert in the head with the butt of her rifle and knocked him unconscious.

<Target acquired> sent Warden. <Beginning exfiltration>

<Hold> sent Marine X, <movement, two lizardmen heading your way>

"Shit," muttered Warden. He looked around then moved so that he was standing in front of the door. "Grab him," he said quietly to Goodwin, "and get ready to move."

<Two coming your way, no shot, under cover>

Warden readied his rifle as Goodwin picked up the unconscious

Deathless officer. The power armour made light work of the job as Goodwin slung the clone over her shoulder and drew her pistol. She nodded at Warden.

Then there was a knock at the door, and a question was asked in the Deathless language. Warden and Goodwin froze, still and silent, then the question came again, louder and with more insistent knocking.

There was a pause then came the gentle chime of the lock and the door slid open. A surprised lizardman stood on the threshold wearing only a light uniform. Then Warden shot him, his suppressed rifle spitting three times to punch neat holes in the clone's chest.

<Contact> sent Goodwin as the captain moved, looking for the second lizardman before the first had really processed the fact that he had been shot. Warden leapt forward, grabbed the stunned Deathless by his shirt and dragged him into the room. The clone collapsed across the floor and his partner, only now realising that something was wrong, yelled and made a grab for his pistol as he dived away.

Warden let loose a short burst but wasn't sure he hit anything. He stepped quickly over the threshold of the apartment then ducked back as the Deathless clone fired three quick rounds from his pistol.

<The guard towers are awake> sent Marine X, <eyes down for a full house. Firing>

"Move," shouted Warden, their chances for a quiet escape had been comprehensively blown by the lizardman, who had shuffled around the edge of the building away from the Marines and was yelling for all it was worth, "fast as you can, please."

Goodwin needed no further encouragement. She moved quickly across the apartment, sleeping Rupert on his shoulder, and followed the captain out onto the veranda.

Warden's rifle spat again but the lizardman had gone, ducking away into the gloom beyond the apartments as around them the compound began to show signs of life.

"Time to go," said Warden, leading the way. They retraced their steps, heading back to the station. A door opened ahead of them, and another Rupert stepped out, pistol in hand. Warden shot him several times from near point-blank range then pushed the corpse off the doorframe and back into the apartment.

<Stop> sent Marine X and Warden skidded to a halt just before the end of the apartment block. There was a whistle of a passing railgun round then the unpleasant fleshy sound of muscle and bone being torn apart and the familiar crack of equipment falling onto foamcrete.

<Check right> sent Marine X.

Warden poked his head around the corner to see two lizardman corpses, both with rifles but neither wearing power armour, laid out on the path.

"Come on," he said, waving Goodwin forward and hurrying for the steps.

<Firing> sent Marine X again. <Targeting guard towers>

Warden jogged towards the steps, rifle swinging every way as he tried to cover all approaches. A pair of lizardmen came around a corner, and the captain fired a quick burst in their direction, sending them scurrying for cover but not doing any real damage. They were almost at the steps when a guard on one of the towers started shooting.

They ducked back into cover, unable to see exactly where the shooting was coming from, and Warden switched out his magazines. He raised his head cautiously above the steps and then whipped it back down as rounds pinged off the foamcrete, altogether too close for comfort.

<We're pinned> he sent. <Can you help?>

<He's firing from the western guard tower but he's out of sight> sent Marine X. <I'll put one close and see if I can keep him down>

<Roger, ready to move>

Warden edged away, rifle ready, Goodwin behind him.

<Go now> sent Marine X. Warden came up firing, aiming in the rough direction of the tower and hoping they'd done enough to keep the Deathless guard down.

They hadn't. Two rounds went past Warden's head then a third pinged off his shoulder, knocking him around. Goodwin charged past, the Rupert still slumped over her shoulder, as more rounds rained down. Warden fired again, no better aimed than his last burst, and surged up the steps pushing Goodwin before him.

They dived in through the open door and sprawled across the floor of the large waiting room.

<More coming> sent Marine X, <move now>

Goodwin swore under her breath as she forced herself back to her feet and picked up the unconscious Rupert. Warden grabbed his rifle, punched in a new magazine and pushed himself upright.

"Gah!" he said, staggering sideways. He caught himself on a seat and managed to stay upright by holding the back of it. "I've been shot," he said quietly, faintly outraged by the very idea, "in the leg."

Goodwin spun around and peered at Warden's leg, eyes slightly wild behind her HUD.

"Walk it off, sir," she hissed, "we have to go!"

Warden nodded and hobbled after Goodwin, putting as little weight on his injured leg as he could.

<Captain Warden's hit> sent Goodwin. <Flesh wound only but it's going to slow us down>

<Keep bloody moving> came the reply, <straight across the walkway then drop down on the far side>

<Acknowledged> sent Goodwin, shaking his shoulders to resettle the Rupert. "Come on, sir," she said, gesturing urgently to Warden. The captain hopped and staggered across the waiting room as Goodwin fired her pistol at the unseen shapes lurking on the station steps.

Warden yanked the door handle, but this time the door didn't budge. He pulled it again as Goodwin emptied her pistol at their pursuers.

"The door won't open," he hissed through gritted teeth. Goodwin looked at him as he heaved again, putting his whole weight on the handle. Nothing happened. Then he noticed the keypad beside the door and cursed; it looked like the Deathless did sometimes lock their doors, even if there was nobody else on the planet.

"Shit," said Goodwin, "let me take a look." She dropped the

Rupert to the floor and peered at the control as Warden stepped away. "Base is locked-down," she muttered, "no way to open this from here." Warden boggled at her. "Sorry, sir, we're trapped."

Warden looked around wildly, desperately searching for a way out.

"That way, through that door," he said, edging along the room, his back against the wall as his leg dripped a trail of blood.

"Seriously?" said Goodwin, slamming a new magazine into her pistol before heaving the Rupert back onto her shoulder. "What's that way?"

"No fucking clue," said Warden through gritted teeth, "but we can't stay here."

He heaved the door open just as a pair of black objects sailed over the threshold from the stairs and clattered over the floor.

"Grenades," warned Goodwin, stumbling to the door. There was an almighty bang and a huge flash of bright light and both Marines were punched through the door and onto the narrow balcony that overlooked the compound.

<Can't see you> sent Marine X, <can't see much of anything moving>

Warden heaved himself back to his feet, shaking his head to clear the fuzz in his brain.

"Get up," he yelled at Goodwin, who was on her knees. The tech shook her head and pushed herself to her feet, settling her rifle across her shoulder. "Pick him up, get onto the roof," said Warden, louder than he needed.

Goodwin shook her head again but grabbed the Rupert, armoured hands slipping on the clone's now blood-slicked skin.

"Just get up there," said Warden, aiming his rifle across the waiting room then firing two quick bursts as a squad of lizardmen tried to storm the door. Behind him, Goodwin managed to get the injured Rupert onto her back and struggled up onto the rail that ran around the veranda. The top of the wall was only a few feet above the roof of the waiting room, but Goodwin was never going to reach it with the Rupert on her back.

"You'll have to pass him up to me, sir," said Goodwin. Warden swore and glanced up. Goodwin was right; there was no way either of them could climb to the wall with the Rupert on their back. He nodded, fired another quick burst at the doorway, then slung his rifle.

Goodwin dropped the Rupert into his arms and Warden staggered slightly, his wounded leg protesting mightily.

Unburdened, Goodwin simply reached up to the wall and heaved herself up. Then she lay flat and reached back down for the Rupert. Warden stood up and lifted the clone as high as he could, holding out its arm so that Goodwin could grab it and heave it up alongside her on the wall.

"Shit," murmured Goodwin as shots rang out and bullets pinged off the foamcrete wall, "we're a bit exposed here, sir."

Warden nodded and fired a last burst at the lizardmen clustering around the door.

"Get down there," he said, pointing over the wall. "I'll drop him down to you."

Goodwin looked surprised for a moment then nodded and slid over the wall, lowering herself as far as she could go before dropping and trusting that the armour would protect her.

Warden slung his rifle and heaved himself up onto the wall. He peered over the edge but couldn't see Goodwin in the gloom. More rounds bounced from the foamcrete on the wall as the guard in the tower opened up again, letting rip in a long, sustained burst.

"Fuck this for a game of soldiers," muttered Warden. He pushed the Deathless officer off the wall in the hope that Goodwin would catch him, slid a little further along then rolled himself over, intending to hang and drop in a controlled way, just as Goodwin had done.

A round struck the foamcrete sending shards rattling across Warden's faceplate. He flinched as he rolled and another round hit him in the shoulder, knocking him back. One hand scrabbled desperately for the edge of the wall and then he was over, bouncing off the wall as he fell to the ground.

13

<A *scendant*, this is Marine X>

The message flashed up on the main monitor in the bridge and Cohen frowned in annoyance.

"How is he doing that?" he asked the room in general. Before anyone could answer, there were more messages.

<Be warned that Captain Warden and Marine Goodwin are in the Deathless compound. The enemy is aware of their presence>

"Oh," muttered Cohen, "that might make things a bit more interesting."

He turned to check his other monitors. Nothing moving nearby, nothing showing on the long-range passive scanners.

"Launch the dropship," he said, settling into his chair and checking the mission timer on the principal monitor, "get it clear and lined up for the extraction." He paused to check the status of the near-space sensors again then nodded to himself. Warden might have made a mess of the extraction on NewPet but, up here, everything seemed to be going very well indeed.

"Message from Soyuz," said Midshipman Wood, the communications officer, "translating and putting it on the forward monitor."

. . .

<<*Varpulis*. Dock at gate six immediately.>>

"Well, that's not good," muttered Cohen. "I guess that means they're on to us as well." He stared at the message for a moment, pondering his response. "Send this please, Mr Wood: 'Docking gear being serviced. Full function in six hours. Will dock once repairs are complete.'"

"Translating," said Wood, "and sending."

Cohen focused on his breathing as he watched the monitor. He just needed to win a few more hours for Warden's team to complete their mission. Once they were safely back on *Ascendant*, he could relax.

<<*Varpulis*. Remain in current orbit. Prepare to be boarded by warship *Posvist*.>>

They all stared at the message for a few seconds. Then Cohen cleared his throat.

"Time to go to work, ladies and gentlemen," he announced. "Give me an update on the dropship."

There was a pause then Midshipman Jackson said, "Dropship is on the rails, launching in twenty seconds, clear for us to manoeuvre in fifty seconds."

"Good, thank you, Jackson. Mr Wood, another message if you please. 'Acknowledged, *Varpulis* standing ready.'" He paused while Wood sent the message.

"Dropship has launched, clear in thirty seconds," reported Jackson.

"Helm, get ready to move. Navigation, how far to the closest body of any size?"

"Helm ready, sir," said Martin.

"The second planet's orbit is about twenty million kilometres in towards the sun, sir," said Midshipman Martin, "but it's sixty degrees ahead."

"Too far to be useful, then," said Cohen, "so plot a course that will take us directly away from Soyuz and prep for high-G manoeuvres as soon as the dropship is clear."

"Aye, sir, preparing," said Midshipman Martin, her hands flicking over the controls.

"And let's find that warship, please. I'd like to know where she is before we break cover."

"Scanning, sir, nothing showing up at the moment," said Wood, peering at the scanners. Then, "I think I've found her, sir. Drone scans are showing a large ship near Soyuz, manoeuvring away from the station." The drones had been left behind when *Ascendant* had left Soyuz, a dozen tiny machines watching the station and relaying back images and information.

"If she's by the station, we've got, what, maybe five minutes before she has line of sight?" said Lieutenant White, Cohen's XO. "Do we fight?" he added quietly.

Cohen closed his eyes for a moment, considering the question. Then he took a deep breath and blew it out slowly, remembering how Admiral Staines had behaved and acted during the battle over New Bristol. This was his first combat command, and out here, far from home, there was nobody to hear him scream. He grinned briefly, then forced himself to focus on the monitor.

"One on one? Let's see what she does before we make any decisions," said Cohen in a low voice.

"Dropship clear in fifteen seconds," said Jackson, as calm and disinterested as if he were announcing the late running of a train.

"A blip on the scans, sir," said Wood, popping images onto one of the main monitors, "looks like a second warship, similar size to *Posvist*, coming around the planet in the other direction."

"Sneaky," muttered Cohen as he inspected the images, "very sneaky." He turned to White. "Discretion today, I think." White nodded his agreement. "We'll jink out a little, get some distance, then head off at a tangent and try to lose them." White nodded again; a solid, if risky, plan.

"Take us to action stations, Mr MacCaibe," said Cohen.

"Sir," acknowledged Midshipman MacCaibe, punching the command. A klaxon rang out and the bridge crew's seats reconfigured automatically for high-G combat manoeuvres.

"Dropship is clear," said Jackson.

"Spin us around, Ms Martin," said White, "and sound the warning for high-G manoeuvres."

"Acknowledged," said Martin, punching the ten-second warning and triggering the attitudinal thrusters. The ship rotated smoothly, like a swan gliding across a pond, until her engines faced the planet. "Manoeuvre complete."

Cohen watched the monitors as crew stations reported their readiness. He drummed his fingers on the arm of his chair for a tense thirty seconds as the crew raced to secure their areas and themselves. After what seemed like hours, the counter hit one hundred per cent and Cohen nodded.

"And away we go, please, Ms Martin."

"Acknowledged," she said, sounding the high-G klaxon again, "sixty-five-second maximum power firing of the main engines in three, two, one." She punched the control, and the ship shot forward, pressing the command crew into their flight chairs and making every simple movement ten times as difficult.

All eyes turned to the display to watch the timer tick slowly down to zero.

"Main burn complete," said Martin eventually. The release of pressure as the engines switched off was like being gifted with a super-power that allowed easy use of arms and hands.

"Let's launch a few drones, Mr White," said Cohen, "just in case they try to follow us."

White made the arrangements, dispersing a dozen of the tiny machines in a random pattern, some to float in the wake of *Ascendant*, others to move outward in an ever-growing sphere.

"Spin us around to ninety degrees from the orbital plane, Ms

Martin, and sound the warning for high-G burn in ninety seconds," said Cohen, watching the monitors on which the positions of the *Posvist* and the second warship were plotted.

"Low-G manoeuvres in three, two, one," said Martin before triggering the controls. The attitudinal thrusters fired and the ship span, no more than a gentle push compared to the massive compression of the main engines. "Manoeuvre complete."

"It's going to be close," said White, watching the monitors and reviewing the course that Cohen was planning, "we'll have to trim the burn to stay out of view."

Cohen nodded.

"Twenty-five seconds on the main engines please, Ms Martin, full power."

"Acknowledged," said Martin, sounding the high-G klaxon again, "firing in three, two, one." The acceleration pressed them into their couches as the main engines pushed them at right-angles to their trajectory. There was a pause before Martin said, "End of burn in three, two, one."

"Enemy vessels still out of sight around NewPet," said White.

"Everything off," said Cohen, "we'll run dark for a few minutes then see where things stand."

"Active sensors offline," reported MacCaibe, "passive sensors only, weapons powered-down."

"Running lights and transponder off," said Martin.

"Better hope there isn't a friendly-fire beacon," said White, "or this is going to be the shortest escape attempt in history."

"How long till the enemy comes out from behind the planet?" asked Cohen, peering at the monitors.

"*Posvist* will be out in just over thirty seconds, sir," said Wood, "the other ship in maybe fifteen minutes."

"A quick flare of the starboard and aft attitudinal thrusters please, Ms Martin," said Cohen, "just enough to give us a gentle tumbling roll."

"Firing thrusters," said Martin, "thrusters fired for a half-second burn, our roll is stable at one revolution every ninety minutes."

"Just like an asteroid," murmured White, eyebrows raised.

"Exactly so," said Cohen, "it won't fool everyone but they've got a lot of bodies to scan and maybe it'll stop them looking too closely."

"And now?" asked White.

"And now, we wait," said Cohen, "until Warden completes his mission and Smith signals that they're ready for the pick-up."

14

<Nice move> sent Marine X as Captain Warden heaved himself upright, leaning against the wall, <elegantly executed>

Warden ignored him and focused on his leg, which hurt a lot and wasn't moving quite properly. His neck and shoulders ached, as did his back and his other leg, but nothing seemed to be broken.

"You okay, sir?" asked Goodwin, hurrying over.

Warden nodded, although in truth he could have done with a week off, a massage and a decent meal.

"The Rupert?" he asked, looking around as boots banged across the foamcrete paths and gravel on the other side of the wall and shouts floated through the night.

"I mostly caught him," said Goodwin apologetically, "but he's not dead yet."

<Ware above> warned Marine X. Then there was the familiar thrumming of a railgun round and a new bout of frenzied shouting from the walkway that led to the station.

"We need to move," said Warden, shaking his head to clear the last of the daze.

<Situation update> he sent as he picked up his rifle and checked it was in good order.

<Activity on the walkway, lots> came the reply. There was a long pause then another rail gun round thrummed over the wall. <Move now>

Goodwin snatched at the Rupert and slung him over her shoulder. Warden backed away from the wall, rifle raised, searching for anything to shoot at.

<Clear, move fast> sent Marine X.

Warden gritted his teeth as Goodwin, one hand wrapped around the Rupert to stop him sliding off her shoulder, began to jog awkwardly across the open ground.

<Slow works as well> sent Marine X but neither Warden nor Goodwin had the time to respond.

As Warden and Goodwin slogged their way across the open ground, Marine X fired again and again. They had made it nearly halfway before one of the Deathless returned fire. The sound of the rifle was strangely loud against the backdrop of the jungle.

"Keep going," said Warden, staggering on as fast as he could go, "just go!"

Goodwin pounded on. The armour took most of the weight but it was still heavy going; carrying bodies across the ruined undergrowth of an alien jungle probably wasn't in the design brief.

<Keep moving, Captain> sent Marine X as Warden crashed down into a stream.

He lay there for a moment then heaved himself around to look back at the base. The station was only a hundred metres away, which was absurd given the amount of effort Warden had put in. The Deathless were firing from the wall, and Warden ducked into the stream, unable to overcome the fear of being shot despite the incoming rounds all going well over his head.

<Get up, Captain> sent Marine X, <can't stay there, this jungle is most unhealthy>

"Fuck," said Warden quietly with gritted teeth. Marine X was right but that didn't make it any easier. Ahead, over the low bank of the stream, his HUD picked out the shape of Marine Goodwin, still plugging away across the open ground with the Rupert on her back.

<Two vehicles coming your way> sent Marine X, <thirty seconds max>

Warden swore again and pushed himself to his feet, clambering out of the stream and staggering after Goodwin. He could hear something, some sort of engine, and suddenly there were lights blazing out across the mashed vegetation. Ahead of him, Goodwin was nearing the edge of the open ground where the valley began to slope up towards the jungle where Marine X was hidden.

<Ware monsters> sent Marine X but Warden wasn't sure he'd read that right. The vehicles were turning towards him; he could see the headlights reaching for him through the misty night.

"Shit," he said, unslinging his rifle and standing on his good leg.

<Get clear> he sent as he aimed at the first vehicle.

<Negative; ware monsters>

Warden ignored the message and squeezed the trigger, firing short bursts at the lead vehicle as it closed rapidly on his position. Was he hitting anything? He couldn't tell, he just kept shooting.

And then there was a sudden noise of stampeding cattle and the lead vehicle flipped into the air. It flew end-over-end before crashing down in a spray of mud and water in the middle of the stream, engines screaming.

In front of Warden, a huge millipede beast reared up, standing on its back legs to claw at the night sky. The second Deathless vehicle swerved wildly as the driver veered away from the enormous creature. It bounced across the wrecked ground and over the stream then turned on a hairpin to flee back towards the compound.

<Captain? You still alive?> sent Goodwin.

Warden looked around but all he could see was the side of the millipede-thing as it charged after the second vehicle. The ground rumbled as it rocketed past, then the Deathless troopers on the wall opened fire and the monster screamed. It changed direction again, thrashing around as it searched for the flies that bit and stung its armoured hide.

<Captain?>

<Here> managed Warden. He almost dropped his rifle as he

turned to continue his stumbling escape towards the safety of the jungle. Now that the millipede-thing had moved on, he could see the dim shape of Goodwin as she slogged up the slope ahead.

His HUD showed the route to the rendezvous point. Only two hundred metres away. He gritted his teeth, slung his rifle and put his head down, grinding his way down the path in half-metre steps.

Behind him, it sounded like the Deathless troopers were letting rip with every weapon in their arsenal. The monster roared and screamed and then a great boom sounded across the valley.

Warden turned to see the great animal rearing up again, this time against the walls of the compound. It towered over the walls as the Deathless fired at it again and again. Then there was a sudden flash of light as the millipede fell against one of the curved spikes that jutted out from the top of the wall.

The huge beast screamed in pain and flopped back down to the ground, stunned and staggering.

<Move> sent Marine X and Warden resumed his trudge, glancing over his shoulder every few steps to see what was going on behind him.

<Survivors from crashed vehicle> sent Marine X, <dealing>

There was a thrumming noise as a railgun round flew overhead. Another followed a few seconds later, then a third.

Then Goodwin arrived out of nowhere, grabbed Warden's arm and hoisted him up off his bad leg.

"Got to move now, Captain, only a hundred metres or so, but those buggers are getting ready to come after us, I'm sure of it."

Together they half-climbed, half-crawled up the slope of the valley towards the jungle.

"Almost there," encouraged Goodwin, "just a little further, then tea and biscuits."

Warden grunted at the quip, focussing on the hill in front of him and staying upright as Goodwin dragged him steadily to safety.

"Where's the Rupert?" he managed through gritted teeth.

"Ten has him," said Goodwin, "jammed him full of meds and he's out for the count. Got some waiting for you as well when we've covered the last twenty metres."

A shape appeared on the edge of the jungle in front of them.

"Get a fucking move on," said Marine X, waving an exasperated arm at them. "They're heading out and we've got places to be." Then he swore and dropped to his knee, raising his ridiculously long gun. "They're getting bolder, need to teach them another lesson," he muttered, squeezing the trigger.

Then he dropped the rail gun and jumped down the slope, grabbing Warden's other arm to drag him the last few metres.

As he moved, there was a loud crack and the tree he had been standing beside sprouted a ten-centimetre hole.

"Sniper," shouted Goodwin in alarm as they all bundled over the edge of the rise and thrashed their way back into the jungle. They jinked left, back towards their temporary camp, and another rail gun round smashed through the foliage behind them in a cloud of splinters and flying leaves.

"Too close," said Marine X as they dropped down behind one of the huge tree-like plants, "far too fucking close." He fished in his bag for a painkiller and rammed the needle into Warden's leg.

"Ah, that's done it," said Warden as the drugs took effect. He shook his head and looked around, able to really focus on his surroundings for the first time in what seemed like ages. He paused as more railgun rounds crashed through the trees a metre or so above their heads.

"Firing blind," muttered Marine X as they all crouched, "any word from Milton?"

Warden checked his HUD then shook his head.

<Milton, sit-rep> he sent, hoping she was within range.

<Still on the train, disembarking in the next few minutes> came the reply.

"Right, we need to get to the extraction point," said Warden, checking his HUD for directions, "that way, about four kilometres." They had set a pick-up point away from the compound to avoid enemy fire, but now that felt like an extravagance.

Warden grabbed his kit and slung the bag over his shoulder.

Marine X looked around for his rifle before remembering he'd dropped it at the edge of the jungle. "Shit," he said, slinging his pack over his wings, "guess we'll manage without a railgun."

Goodwin collected her own bag then looked at Marine X.

"You need a gun," she said, again demonstrating her supreme ability for stating the obvious.

"I need a weapon," countered Marine X, glancing at Captain Warden, "but I guess I'll make do with a pistol."

15

"Three minutes, Colour," Bailey said, counting down as the train approached the station.

"Noted. Get ready to move, everyone. Looks to me like we need to go off the south side," said Milton, "and make sure you stay out of sight." The reconnaissance shots showed the station buildings to be on the north side of the track, which made sense as the camps Captain Warden had been investigating were also in that direction and they hadn't seen anything to the south from orbit.

The station itself was at the top of a steep, almost cliff-like, slope covered in the dense jungle foliage that blanketed the area. The pylons supporting the maglev track were much taller at this point on the line, particularly on the south side, which was going to present some issues. They'd had a good view as they approached the hillside and the total drop was about a couple of hundred metres.

Power armour had all sorts of advantages and could climb tough slopes with relative ease, but jungle terrain added its own dangers and even the best suit wouldn't save you from a two hundred metre fall. Rolling down a steep slope in power armour would be almost as bad as a straight fall. Milton had wanted a nice, safe platform but there was no such luck.

On the plus side, they'd had nothing to do for a couple of hours except cling to the train for dear life so the whole team had been able to review the reconnaissance shots and talk about their next steps. They now had a plan that should see them disembarking without being spotted, injured or left too far from Captain Warden's position to make the rendezvous. Probably.

"Everyone ready?"

"Sniper team, standing ready," confirmed Bailey. She and Parker would be disembarking as the train approached the station, making use of their clones' wings to glide away to the west before circling back to find a perch in the jungle where they could take up overwatch positions.

"Ready, Colour," said Cooke.

"Ready," said Harrington.

"Ready as I'll ever be, boss," Watson said, her voice breaking a little.

"You okay, Watson?" Milton asked.

"Just a bit nervous about dangling off the side of a train, Colour."

Which seemed reasonable, in Milton's opinion. Unlike the snipers, the rest of the team couldn't launch from the train and flap away.

"We could jump off right before the train reaches the station and let the armour take the pounding," Harrington had suggested, but staying out of sight would mean disembarking while the train was doing more than seventy kilometres an hour. Nobody fancied hitting a tree at that speed if the jump went a little wrong, so they had swiftly binned the idea.

Instead, they were going to have to disembark stealthily at the station in such a way that they weren't spotted by the Deathless in the station, in the base or on the train. There wasn't another station on the next thousand kilometres of line, which suggested that the Deathless troops on the train would be disembarking here as well. Either that, or they were going halfway across the continent, and Milton didn't think her luck would be that good.

The best they'd come up with was to attach climbing cords and rappel off the side of the train, then reattach under the tracks, preferably to one of the support columns. That seemed achievable, not fancy, not noisy and, hopefully, survivable.

"It's no big deal," said Milton cheerfully, hoping to persuade Watson and the rest of the team that high-speed train-surfing was a normal part of a deployment, "Ten does this sort of thing all the time and he always gets away with it."

"Can't be trusted with a piano, though," quipped Harrington to a round of laughter, although Watson didn't seem too amused.

"Yes, Colour. I'll try to do what Ten would do," Watson said.

"Er, well, maybe not everything, eh? Don't want to end up calling you Eleven. Right, Bailey, Parker, the train is slowing down, you think you can make it at this speed?"

"Soon find out, Colour," said Parker as he raised himself up into a crouch and unfurled his wings. They snapped wide like a parachute and he was immediately lifted clear of the train. He banked away to the south and was quickly lost in the night.

"It's fine up here, no bother at all," said Parker a moment later. "I'm off to find a perch." At that, Bailey took to the air as well.

"Watch out for those gasbag creatures, I don't want you two getting electrocuted and eaten," said Milton as she adjusted her own position on the train.

"Colour, there's a firefight going on by the base. Looks like the captain has made his presence felt," Bailey said.

"Roger that. Continue as planned, find a perch and get us covering fire," ordered Milton.

The train was slowing to a stop. Captain Warden had said that the earlier train had been stationary for about a minute but surely this one, laden with troops, would need longer? They couldn't wait for the Deathless to clear the station. As soon as the train came to a stop, Milton gave the word.

"Go, go, go!" she ordered, dropping off the side of the carriage and into the night, her team following close behind.

Milton pulled up short as the rest of the team dropped below her. She turned to face the tracks and fired her grapnel then reeled herself in towards the track.

"Colour? Where are you?" Harrington asked.

"Making plans for Nigel. Get yourselves over to that pillar, I'll catch up." Milton hauled herself up, under the train. It took her only seconds to turn her plan into reality and then she detached her grapnel and wound the cable in before forward rappelling off the track into the air again.

She was glad it was so dark; the drop really didn't matter so much when she couldn't see the ground. If she didn't hurry, though, she'd still be attached to the train when it departed and that would be a thrill for all of about two minutes before it became seriously unpleasant and likely quite grisly.

The rest of the team had made it to the pillar and their lines had disappeared, so they must have detached their magnetic clamps and reeled them in. Milton brought herself right way up and began to swing her legs to generate a pendulum effect so she could get closer to the pillar.

"Colour, you don't have time, just use your grapnel," said Watson.

"Negative, I could hit one of you at this range," Milton replied.

"Good point, aim for the sound of Harrington's voice," said Watson.

"Hey!" said Harrington. "Sorry, Colour, we're all fine but you know these lines, they're great but too light to be able to throw them to you."

"Yeah, I know, Harrington. I'll be fine this way," Milton said, doing her best to keep the scepticism from her voice. She'd only thought of this plan at the last minute and hadn't had time to discuss it or warn the team. It might be helpful if it worked, but this bit was harder than she had imagined.

She felt the pendulum motion begin to change and it took a moment to realise it wasn't the wind blowing her about or her suddenly working out the best way to rock her body back and forth to generate a swing. It was the train moving away from the station.

"Fuck," she muttered, as the train began to accelerate. "Get climbing! I'm coming in fast!" she yelled.

"Roger that," said Harrington, calm as anything.

Milton prepped her grapnel and turned her night vision to max as the train reeled her in, slowly at first, but getting steadily faster.

With only seconds to go before she was mangled against the pillar, there wasn't time for more thought. She picked her target, aimed the grapnel and fired. As soon as the bolt bit home, she hit the quick release on her line and fell away, thumb jabbing desperately at the launcher control until the motor began to spin.

It whined loudly against the strain of her downward motion, reeling in the line as she swung toward the pillar that her team were climbing. For a moment she feared it would be heard by the Deathless over the noise of the train.

She reached the end of the arch with only a metre to spare between her and the foamcrete pillar. The launcher's motor screamed its objection but it held, another admirable demonstration of the quality of the Deathless kit. The sudden stop almost wrenched her arm from its socket, only the power armour saving her from a nasty injury.

Then she began to swing back the way she'd come, dropping away from the tower. She let the grapnel pay out some line.

"I'll be back!" she yelled, as the team receded from her view.

"We'll throw you a line, boss, see if you can grab it," said Harrington.

"Yeah, should be a doddle," Milton replied as she started the return trip.

She could see Harrington hanging on to a line with his left hand and spinning something around in his right. Was that a gun attached to the line? Oh, bloody hell.

He released his improvised weight just as she approached the pillar. It was a pretty good throw, the weapon arcing through the night sky to only just miss her. But Harrington was attached to the pillar on her left side and he'd thrown the weapon so it passed in front of her to the right. She couldn't grab the gun but she collided neatly with the line and managed to loop it around her left arm.

She swung back again, the line paying out behind her.

"Have you got it tight, Colour?" asked Watson.

"Yup, I've got it."

"We'll haul you in as quick as you can when you come back then. Is your arm okay?"

"Hurts like you wouldn't believe but nothing the med-suite can't handle."

"Now!" said Watson and Milton felt the line go taut in her hand. She dangled there for a moment as the Marines fought against the gravity that tried to drag her backwards, then they had her. She thumbed the switch on the grapnel and payed out more line as they dragged her slowly towards the pillar. She ended up a few metres below them, clutching the pillar for all she was worth and breathing heavily while the suit pumped painkillers and anti-inflammatories into her shoulder.

"That was exciting, Colour Sergeant. What was that little diversion in aid of, if you don't mind me asking?" Bailey enquired.

"I realised that we'd been a bit rude to our hosts, so I left them a little present to remember us by."

Bailey nodded and Harrington said, "Ooh, that's nice. When will they be opening it?"

"I'm sure they'll pick the right time," Milton replied, "but we need to get cracking. There's a firefight going on up there."

They began to clamber around the supporting pillars, heading to the north side of the line. The climbing gear built into the power armour suits simplified the exercise but the need for stealth slowed everything to a crawl. As they climbed, Milton checked in with the sniper team.

"Give me an update please, Bailey."

"We have a good solid perch, Colour. We have LOS to the train station and the base."

"What's going on at the base?"

"Looks like there are Deathless on the walls firing at something and troops in vehicles heading west from the base towards the jungle. Someone has been returning fire from the jungle and the Deathless have a sniper on their walls."

"If you can take him out, do so, but first tell me about the station."

"A full company of Deathless getting ready to move out, piling into vehicles like those large APCs we captured on New Bristol. I don't see them being able to actually get into the jungle with those, though, not unless they've got a road they can follow."

"Anything else I should know about?"

"I'm pretty sure you lost your bet with Ten," Bailey replied, "because there's another megafauna out here, thrashing about between the base and the edge of the valley."

"One of the gasbags?"

"Er, no. Looks more like a giant millipede, if you can believe it."

"Yeah, I already saw one of those, a couple of metres long."

"Yes, Colour, if at your school 'a couple' meant about a hundred and fifty."

Milton was silent for a moment as she focused on her climbing.

"So, we have a base full of Deathless troopers firing into the jungle, a sniper, some kind of special forces company-in-training between us and the captain and, to top it off, a millipede the size of a train."

"Oh no, Colour, it's much bigger than a train."

Milton took a moment to order more painkillers from her medsuite to dull the pain of a headache she could feel building behind her eyes.

"Right, sort out that sniper and anyone else who thinks he looks clever. Keep an eye out for this company of special forces recruits as well. If they're the best they've got and full of vim and vigour, I really don't want to tangle with them tonight. Oh yeah, and watch out for space monkeys, according to Ten."

"Roger, will do," said Bailey, ignoring the weird comments about 'space monkeys'.

<Captain> sent Milton in a private message as her team moved out, walking west under the canopy provided by the train platform and station, <we are at the train station, flanking west. A company of Deathless arrived on the same train from what looked like a special forces training camp. Otherwise, we're having a good day>

<Roger that. We have the prisoner. I have a light injury, Goodwin and Ten are fine. Get to us as quickly as you can. What's the status of that Deathless company?>

<Looks like they're moving out to chase you. Will you be able to stay ahead?>

<Possibly. Don't put yourselves at risk to hold them up, though. There's no way you can cope with a full company>

<Acknowledged. Will avoid engaging if possible>

<We have eyes on the enemy sniper on the wall. Permission to engage> sent Parker.

<Update first. We've made it to the rainforest. What's happening with the Deathless company from the train?>

<They're lining up to get into lightly armoured trucks, six in all> sent Parker. <They'll probably head out in maybe three minutes. It's a target rich environment>

<Sniper first, then officers and NCOs. Don't hang about too long before you change your roost. Understood?>

<Roger that, Colour. We can probably hit the truck engines as well; they look like normal vehicles. Should we engage them as well?>

<Only after the officers. And I repeat, don't hang about too long. They're bound to have snipers in that company. Over>

<Acknowledged, we'll check in when we're moving. Out>

Milton glanced at her team. They were making good progress through the rainforest, having found a tunnel that must have been punched through the foliage by a seriously large machine, probably a resource gathering vehicle of some sort. It didn't go in precisely the direction they wanted to travel but it was only off by a few degrees and it allowed them to maintain a good speed-marching pace.

Without the power armour, that would have been impossible. Even with the flattened plant life, their gear would have cut their speed. They would have to enter the pristine rainforest further ahead but, for now, the HUD showed they were gaining on Captain Warden.

"Colour, once Bailey starts taking out their officers, they're going to start moving much quicker. Do we need to stand and fight them off?"

"No, but we'll stop here and leave some deterrents for anyone who comes after us. Harrington, get it done for me, I have to check Bailey's progress."

She wondered if it was time for her present to be opened yet. Opening up the feed from Bailey and Parker, she surveyed the situation as she slowly walked away from the traps that Harrington was laying for the Deathless.

Milton watched as Parker flagged targets for Bailey, scanning back and forth with the range-finding scope on his rifle, picking out Deathless officers. Each figure was flagged with a yellow box and a number with the target count showing in the HUD for Bailey to work through.

Then he was done and the view flashed back to show the Deathless sniper on the wall. Milton switched to Bailey's feed, watching as the enemy's railgun swept gently across the jungle. The sniper was clearly completely oblivious to Milton's team, still focused on finding Warden and the kidnapped Deathless officer.

Parker gave the go instruction and Bailey squeezed the trigger. The helmet of the Deathless sniper snapped back as the round punched through it, but Bailey's viewpoint was moving before the Deathless had finished collapsing, swinging towards a target labelled '2' in the right of her scope.

A yellow box appeared around an officer on the wall, who was looking away from the sniper. Whoever they were, they hadn't yet registered what had happened further up the wall. Bailey squeezed again and the officer's head was removed from his shoulders.

Then they were on to the Deathless from the training camp. Milton had to fight the urge to puke as Bailey's rifle panned across the open area in front of the base, inducing momentary motion sickness.

Bailey's gun spat again, delivering a round through the armoured windshield of one of the transport trucks. It passed through the neck of the officer in the passenger seat and out into the back of the vehicle.

As Milton watched the view from Bailey's scope, she could see that Parker had opened fire as well. The targets were at the extreme range of his rifle's capabilities but Parker was an excellent shot and his efforts were already being felt.

Parker fired burst after burst into groups of Deathless as they ran for cover, looked around for the enemy gunmen or just stood around in shock. Between bursts, he marked priority targets for Bailey, who had changed clips twice already.

"Hurry it up," muttered Milton, tense despite her team's obvious impact on the enemy.

They were targeting the vehicles now. They had no protection against railgun rounds and Bailey quickly shot through their engine blocks, freezing the light transports in place.

Around the station there was chaos. Milton watched, waiting for the moment when the Deathless would scatter and run; special forces they might be, but these troops had clearly not yet seen action and were unprepared for the murderous fire laid down by the sniper team.

"Time to open the present, I think," she muttered to herself. She glanced at a pair of icons blinking on her HUD and activated them in sequence. The explosives on the maglev train detonated in the distance, somewhere beyond the valley, and the night sky lit up. That drew looks from the Deathless, wondering, no doubt, what the hell had gone wrong over there. With any luck, the track had been destroyed and the train had crashed off the track into the ground at high speed.

Then the device under the station exploded and any coherence the Deathless might have had was blown away. They stared as a large part of the station structure and building above the track crumpled and fell down the slope into the jungle.

Milton grinned with satisfaction. The damage wouldn't really affect the Deathless war effort but it was a pretty good hit for the effort and, more importantly, it was causing consternation amongst the troopers, who couldn't tell what had happened, where the enemy was or how many they faced. The Deathless scattered and ran, their resistance broken even as Bailey's rounds continued to fall amongst them.

Milton wondered for a moment if the grenade launchers might be brought into play but her HUD showed they were too far from the enemy even if the rainforest canopy wasn't blocking their line of fire.

<Parker, time for you to leave. Join us as soon as possible. We're moving out as soon as Harrington has finished with his booby traps>

<Roger that, Colour Sergeant. We'll break the last two engine blocks then pull out>

<Acknowledged>

Milton switched off the feeds and looked over to Harrington and the team. They had set up several lines of simple traps, covering a hundred metre radius. It would be hard for the Deathless to come near to their trail and not set off at least one, and one was all it would take to slow them down. The moment they lost someone to one of Harrington's traps, the doubt and fear would grow. Where was the next one? What if they couldn't see them? What if I let the man next to me go first and I hang back a little? Is the woman next to me hanging back? Hey! She's using me to check the path. Will I be next? What was that beneath my foot, was it a twig or a tripwire?

"Don't use all your supplies, Harrington, let's leave something further up the trail."

Harrington laughed, "Did you get back from a psychological warfare training week just before we shipped out here, Colour?"

"No, I simply remember the last time I did a barracks locker inspection and the shock you get after finding a few clean ones and then you stumble upon the next horror show," Milton replied. "Let's move out!"

<Pursuit disrupted, Captain> sent Milton, <on our way to the rendezvous>

<Good work but don't hang around> replied Warden. <We're almost at the dropship and I'm looking forward to my kippers>

16

Smith punched the controls and the dropship began to lift even before the doors had finished closing. The Deathless troopers kept firing as the ship climbed past the canopy and into the relative safety of the early morning sky.

"*Ascendant*, this is dropship four, come in," said Smith as the main engines fired and the ship rocketed forward, pulling away from the enemy base and moving beyond the range of their small arms. "Come in, *Ascendant*, this is dropship four," Smith repeated.

"Problems, Smith?" said Milton, dropping into the vacant co-pilot's chair.

"There's something funky going on, Colour," said Smith, concentrating on the distant mountains as the dropship climbed past a flock of gasbags.

"Funky?" said Milton, not liking the sound of this. "I thought the flight paths and rendezvous points were agreed before we left?"

"They were," said Smith as he wrestled the controls and threw the dropship across the jungle canopy, keeping it deliberately low, "but when Captain Warden's little jaunt went hot, the Deathless got suspicious and sent two warships to intercept and board *Ascendant*. When I came down to land, she was heading out to avoid an uneven fight."

He slowed the dropship and pulled up a little to skim it over a ridge. "I'd hoped she would be back by now."

"Hoped?" said Milton, really not liking where this conversation was going. "And what do we do if she isn't back?"

Smith spared her a glance that said everything. Without *Ascendant*, they were in serious trouble.

And then a message showed on the comms monitor.

<<*Ascendant* incoming. Flightpath by secure link. Rendezvous in seventeen minutes. One pass only>>

Then a data dump arrived and Milton flicked it onto the main monitor, updating their rendezvous plan. Even to her eyes, it looked like an aggressive course.

"Shit," murmured Smith as he glanced at it, confirming Milton's fears about the flight plan, "that's going to be tricky." He glanced at Milton and then back at the monitor. "Can anyone in your team fly? It would be really useful to have another set of eyes on these problems."

Milton snorted. "We're Marines. 'By Sea, By Land', remember? You deliver us and we'll fix it but we don't drive the planes."

"Then you'd better bloody learn," snapped Smith, "because I can't do this all by myself." He pushed the controls and heaved the dropship around a looming mountain peak, then dropped it into a long, thin canyon on the other side. A lamp glowed suddenly red, and a klaxon sounded.

"What's that?" said Milton, alarmed.

"It's the fucking missile lock warning," snarled Smith, heaving the dropship sharply up and out of the canyon, "so buckle up and check the monitors and try to work out what's bloody shooting at us!"

"Shooting?" said a happy, carefree voice from the doorway. "Are we home already?"

"Shut up, Ten," said Milton, in no mood for the penal Marine's jokes, "unless you can help fly this thing."

"Nope, sorry Colour, it's been years since I flew anything and my qualifications have lapsed."

Milton stared at him, mouth open. Then she shook her head. Of course Ten could fly, why was she even surprised by these things anymore?

"Then take a fucking seat and help Smith with the flight plan," she said, thoroughly hacked-off with the entire situation.

"Right ho!" said Ten, dropping into the navigator's chair and peering at the monitor. "This is a joke, right?" he said, his sense of humour rapidly evaporating as he scrutinized the flight plan and compared it with the location data on the other monitor.

Smith yelled something and flicked the dropship across to starboard, dropping suddenly back into the canyon. A rocket screamed overhead and struck a cliff. "Aargh!" said Smith as he hauled back on the controls to avoid following the missile into the rock. "Which way?" he yelled.

Marine X concentrated on the flight path, suddenly focused. He blinked, scanning the numbers and shaking his head. The UI on this ship wasn't anything he was used to and it took a few moments to work out how to push the flight path into the nav-computer. Then he punched the warning klaxon, just in case anybody hadn't already noticed the sudden manoeuvres and was still sufficiently alive to take precautions.

"Sixty degrees to port, come up to forty-five degrees and punch it with everything we've got," said Marine X, his voice calm and cool.

"That'll put us above the mountains," pointed out Smith, "and they're already shooting at us."

"Gotta fly higher than the mountains to reach the stars," said Ten, "and if we don't move soon, our only option will be to wipe out against a mountain and redeploy, which means failing the mission." He leaned over to rest a hand on Smith's shoulder and whisper in his ear. "Don't make me fail a mission, lad."

Smith shook off Ten's hand and muttered something about 'psycho Marines' then glanced at Milton. "You okay with this?"

"Live fast or die trying, Smith," said Milton through gritted teeth.

Smith looked at her and shook his head. "You're both fucking mad," he opined. Milton grinned at him, wide-eyed, and Smith shook his head. "Fuck it," he said, hands flying across the controls. The dropship shuddered as Smith pushed it around a mountain and flipped it up to aim well above the horizon.

"How's that for you?" yelled Smith, as the engines screamed and the dropship blasted across the sky.

"Come to port by another five degrees on my command," said Marine X calmly as he concentrated on the screens before him, "rockets to the left of us, railguns to the right," he muttered. "And now!"

Smith swung left, and a rocket blazed past, so close that he could almost read the message scrawled on the casing.

"And up another ten degrees, please," said Marine X, watching the nav computer's interpretation of *Ascendant*'s flight path and plotting the intercept course. It was going to be tight, very tight.

"What's that?" said Milton, frowning as she pointed at a monitor showing an external view of the world behind the dropship.

Smith glanced at the monitor but couldn't make out what she was pointing at. Marine X flicked at his screens until they showed the same image. He zoomed in and grunted.

"That looks like a fighter craft of some sort," he said quietly. "Strange, wouldn't have expected to find those on a planet like this." He looked at the dropship's trajectory again, trying to work out what they could do about the fighter. It was closing fast, and the unarmed dropship wasn't ideally equipped for countering enemy attacks.

"Goodwin," said Marine X as he flicked at the screens and tried to make the intercept course work, "are you available for a little improvised weapons duty?"

"It's a bit bloody bumpy back here, Ten," said Goodwin, as if Marine X could possibly have failed to notice. "What do you need?"

"Could you be a dear and pop back to the loading bay? Need you to open the rear doors and throw out anything explosive that comes to hand."

"Are you fucking joking?" yelled Goodwin, apparently not entirely happy with Ten's request.

"Right now, if you would be so kind. We're about to be shot down by a Deathless fighter and we need another minute or so to clear the atmosphere."

Goodwin closed the comms link, and there was a moment of quiet during which Ten could almost hear the tech yelling at him from the far end of the dropship.

"Come up another five degrees, Smith," said Marine X, his hands now very heavy as he operated the controls that were dangling above him as the dropship powered through the atmosphere.

"Five degrees," acknowledged Smith. The dropship tilted a little further as Goodwin shouted obscenities across the comms link.

Then the alerts sounded to indicate that the rear doors were opening. Marine X zoomed out on the rear camera and saw that the fighter was now very close, only hundreds of metres behind the dropship.

"He's an enthusiastic little fucker," said Marine X with no small degree of admiration in his voice, "getting very close, bravely doing his duty, determined to bring us down." He checked the interior loading bay camera and saw that Goodwin was wedged onto a bulkhead, still wearing her power armour and with a crate of grenades by her side. He frowned as he watched, not quite able to work out what she was doing and why she wasn't moving.

Something flashed at the front of the fighter and Smith shouted a contact warning. In the loading bay, bullets pinged off surfaces as Goodwin worked, hidden behind her bulkhead.

"Come on, hurry up," Ten muttered to himself. Then he blinked as the fuse warnings on the grenades all went live at the same time, flashing up proximity warnings on the HUDs of every nearby Marine.

Goodwin grabbed the crate and tipped out its contents, emptying three dozen grenades out the back of the dropship. They bounced across the steeply inclined floor and fell through the open doorway, hurtling towards the fighter.

Half a second later, the first exploded. Then another, then a whole load of them as the fighter flew right through their midst.

"Nice move," muttered Ten as he watched the fighter break away.

Goodwin tossed a second crate of grenades out but by now the fighter had peeled away and the second batch exploded harmlessly. Then Goodwin slammed her hand over a button, and the rear doors began to close.

"That's it," said Smith, "we're pulling free." The dropship, which had bumped and rumbled its way through the thick atmosphere of NewPet, finally began to fly more smoothly as the last wisps of air fell behind. The shutters had closed over the forward windows and now the monitors showed only the vastness of space, huge and empty.

"Come around ten degrees to port," said Marine X, his focus back on the nav-monitors, "and up another five degrees, then give it everything we've got."

"Attitude thrusters firing," said Smith, somewhat more relaxed now that the missile lock warning alerts had stopped screaming for attention, "pushing to one hundred per cent on the main engines in three, two, one." The acceleration kicked them again as the dropship surged forward, heading for its rendezvous with *Ascendant*.

"Is that *Ascendant*?" asked Milton, peering at one of the forward monitors and pointing at a black shape that drifted across the suddenly bright and full starscape.

Smith and Marine X looked at it for a moment then shared a glance.

"No," said Marine X quietly, "that looks like a Deathless warship, a big one."

"And we're going to get pretty close to it," said Smith as he checked the monitors, "about three hundred kilometres, I think." Not good. At that range, the unarmed dropship would have no hope of avoiding whatever ordnance the Deathless choose to deploy.

"So where the fuck is *Ascendant*?" asked Milton, not unreasonably.

They spent a frantic few minutes checking the monitors, tweaking their trajectory to hit the flight path *Ascendant* had sent and trying to make sure the sensors were all working before Smith spotted a likely candidate.

"There," he said, pointing at something dark moving fast towards them along *Ascendant*'s planned flight path, "there she is." He sat back with relief and looked at Marine X. "How are we looking?"

Marine X flicked at the nav-monitors and nodded to himself. "Need some minor adjustments, but we're looking good."

They sat silently for a few minutes, nothing to be done but watch the monitors and wait to see what happened next.

"How's the captain?" asked Milton to fill the time.

"Fine," said Marine X, "flesh wound. He lost a fair amount of blood but these Deathless clones are pretty tough. He'll be okay." He stretched, just remembering not to flick out his wings. "And the Rupert's still alive, so we got what we came for. Goodwin's going over the files she pinched at the moment."

He sat up as if just remembering something important. "If she didn't fall out the back of the dropship or get shot to pieces by that fighter. I'm going to check on her." And he heaved himself out of the seat and headed off to the loading bay.

"Nothing from *Ascendant*," muttered Smith, "she must be coming in hot and quiet."

"How long?"

"According to the flight plan," said Smith, flicking through the nav computer's screens, more relaxed now that the hands-on flying was done, "about six hundred and forty seconds."

"And how long till we shoot past that warship?" Milton looked at the main monitors where the dark bulk of the Deathless ship was helpfully circled in yellow, its trajectory picked-out in a dotted line.

Smith looked at her then back at the flight path. "About the same," he said in a strangled voice.

"And does *Ascendant* know about our little friend?"

Smith glanced at the monitors then looked at Milton, eyes darting around.

"*Ascendant*. Be advised. We have an enemy vessel in our vicinity. Coordinates attached," said Smith, triggering the secure comms system to convert his speech to text and send the enemy vessel's position and flight vector to *Ascendant*.

They waited for a response. Nothing.

"Then I guess all we can do is wait," said Milton, sitting back in her chair.

"Only five hundred and forty seconds," said Smith, setting a timer.

"Nine minutes and hope," murmured Milton, "story of my life."

17

"Where are they?" murmured Cohen, staring at the monitors as if he could uncover the enemy ships by willpower alone.

Space was big, and the two Deathless vessels had played their hand well. Combat between capital ships was a long, dull game of waiting followed by a short period of intense action and then, for one or more vessels, an eternity drifting through space as an expanding cloud of radioactive debris.

Now, Cohen assumed, the two Deathless warships waited, lurking near the planet, ready to charge in when *Ascendant* returned to collect the dropship. It was all getting a little bit dicey.

"Where are they?" Cohen murmured again, chewing his lip. Then a message flashed up on the comms screen.

<<Ascendant, this is dropship four, come in>>

Another message came in a few seconds later.

. . .

<<Come in, *Ascendant*, this is dropship four>>

"That's our cue," said White, "how do you want to do this, sir?"

Cohen paused, not absolutely convinced that he wanted to do it at all. He looked at the monitor, which now showed the dropship's location on the planet.

"Fast and hot, please, XO," said Cohen eventually, "but keep us quiet for as long as you can."

"Acknowledged," said White, settling into his chair. "Taking us to action stations, prepare for high-G manoeuvres." He flicked a couple of buttons, and a ship-wide broadcast went out in a computerised voice, deliberately tweaked to make it stand out from orders given by the bridge directly.

"Prepare for high-G manoeuvres. All personnel to assigned seating, immediately."

"And let's bring the weapons online, Mr MacCaibe," said White.

"Aye, sir," said MacCaibe as the action stations klaxon sounded half a second later, "firing solution available in twelve seconds."

"Helm, put us on the straight and narrow, prep for main engine burn as soon as Mr Jackson has a course."

"Acknowledged," said Midshipman Martin, "twenty-second low-power burn on attitudinal thrusters in three, two, one." There was a very small kick as the thrusters fired and the ship's spin slowed and stopped. "Manoeuvre complete."

"Navigation solution plotted. Course laid in and on screen," said Midshipman Jackson, flicking the series of points she had plotted to fulfil Cohen's orders across to the main viewers.

The course was conservative and safe, putting them comfortably into a neat orbit to rendezvous with the dropship. A simple, textbook flight plan.

"Thank you, Mr Jackson, but that's no good at all. We need to go in much harder, much faster," said Lieutenant Commander Cohen. "We need to be on top of the dropship before anyone knows we're there, then we need to burn our way out again before the dropship has come to a rest."

Jackson frowned and looked at his numbers. "We can burn longer at the start, sir, but then we would be moving far too fast for the dropship to dock safely. There won't be time to match velocities before we'll be well past them."

Cohen nodded and grinned. Jackson was right, of course. He knew his stuff but like all of them, he lacked real combat experience despite the training and the vast number of hours logged in the simulators.

"Let me suggest another way," said Cohen, leaning forward to describe his plan.

"That might work, sir," said the navigator his uncertainty obvious in his voice, "but the dropship would need to be carefully positioned. It's a precision job."

"Your concerns are noted, Midshipman. I have every confidence in Smith's abilities, so let's plot the course and send him the details."

"Are you sure about that, sir?" asked White with a frown, leaning in close so that only Cohen could hear. "What if the transmission is intercepted?"

"If we don't tell him where we're going, Mr White," replied Cohen, "they're really going to struggle to meet us at the rendezvous point."

White settled back in his seat, clearly still worried about the situation. That was fine by Cohen; he was more than a little worried himself.

"Course plotted, sir," said Jackson, flicking the new course onto the monitor. Cohen peered at it for a moment, nodding. It was aggressive, very aggressive, but it might just work, even if it did put great stress on the crew of *Ascendant*.

"Million to one shot," Cohen murmured. Then he stretched his neck and nodded again. "Send it to the dropship, Mr Jackson, and lay in the course."

"Acknowledged, sir, sending now," said Jackson, flicking controls. "Sent and laid in, ready to go."

"Then take us out, Ms Martin, quick as you can."

"Aye, sir," said Martin, hitting the high-G warning klaxon, "one hundred and sixty-second full-power burn in three, two, one."

"That never gets old," muttered White as the engines fired and they were all pressed firmly into their seats.

"At least these clones are engineered to take the Gs better than our Navy standard issue," said Cohen, frowning. "I wonder if that says something about the Deathless attitude to space combat?"

"Or maybe they're just over-engineered," pointed out White as they watched the numbers count slowly down to zero.

"Main burn complete," said Martin finally, "on target for rendezvous in eight hundred and fifty seconds." Her hands flashed across the console, and a timer appeared on the main monitor alongside the planned trajectory.

"Thank you, Ms Martin," said White, easing himself into a slightly more comfortable position. "What's the status of our weapons, Mr MacCaibe?"

"Ready to fire as soon as we have something to fire at, sir," said the weapons officer.

"Eyes open, people," said Cohen, "passive sensors only, but find me *Posvist* and any other Deathless vessel in the volume."

"Eight hundred seconds to rendezvous," said Martin. "No sign of the dropship."

"Incoming transmission from dropship four, sir," said Midshipman Wood. "There's a data package, pushing to monitors."

scendant. Be advised. We have an enemy vessel in our vicinity. Coordinates attached>>

. . .

Wood hummed to himself as he pushed the new information to the monitor so that it now showed the trajectory of dropship four and the presumed location of the enemy vessel alongside the charging flightpath of *Ascendant*.

There was a moment's quiet while the bridge crew reviewed the new information.

"Target that vessel," said Cohen eventually. "I want a full broadside of railgun and missile fire available on my command, Mr MacCaibe."

"Aye, sir, preparing now."

"We'll send them a 'vessel in distress' signal as soon as they give any sign of having seen us, Mr Wood."

"Ready and waiting, sir."

"Let's warn the docking bay crew that dropship four might come in a little warm," said White, "and have fire suppression systems and damage control teams standing ready, just in case."

"Six hundred seconds to rendezvous and closest approach to the enemy vessel," said Martin.

"We're rendezvousing at the closest approach point?" muttered White, shaking his head at such staggeringly bad luck.

"Ready countermeasures, Mr MacCaibe," said Cohen, "and give them everything we have at the first sign of enemy fire."

"Already queued up and ready to go, sir," said MacCaibe.

"Dropship four is moving at a fair clip, sir, but we'll need to brake aggressively to pick her up safely," said Martin as the main monitor showed the updated trajectories.

"No movement yet from the Deathless vessel," reported MacCaibe, who was peering at his screen with a frighteningly intense look on his face, "assuming it is a vessel."

"Mr Wood, send dropship four a message, give them our ETA and let them know this will be a hot and untidy pick-up."

"Aye, sir, sending now."

"Ms Martin, get ready to spin us around for the braking manoeuvre," said Cohen.

"Program laid in and ready, sir. Three hundred and seventy seconds to main engine burn for deceleration."

"Then let's do it, Midshipman."

"Aye, sir," said Martin, sounding the low-G manoeuvre klaxon, "minimal burn, attitudinal thrusters only, firing in three, two, one." There was a gentle nudge as the ship slowly spun until it faced back the way it came, following its engines. "Manoeuvre successful, ready for deceleration burn."

"Thank you, Ms Martin. Anything from that vessel or Soyuz?"

"Soyuz is behind NewPet, sir. Deathless vessel is just sitting there, no obvious signs of life."

"Sixty seconds to main engine burn," said Martin.

"Incoming message, sir," said Wood, "can't tell where it's coming from." He flicked it up onto the main monitor.

<<*Varpulis*. Enter orbit around New Petropavlovsk-Kamchatsky. Surrender immediately>>

"Predictable," muttered White, "but at least they're still talking."

"Send this reply, Mr Wood," said Cohen, clearing his throat. "'Acknowledged. Entering orbit in two hundred seconds.' Let's see what they make of that."

"You think they'll fall for it?" asked White quietly. Cohen shrugged because it didn't really matter. Their trajectory was locked in, they had to collect the dropship four and they were out of options.

"Thirty seconds to main engine burn." Martin waited a little longer then sounded the high-G manoeuvre klaxon. "Main engines firing on full power for one hundred and thirty seconds in three, two, one."

"Anything from that Deathless vessel, Mr MacCaibe?" asked Cohen through gritted teeth as the deceleration rammed them into their chairs and pressed heavily on their lungs.

"Nothing, sir, and no sign of the other warship."

Cohen pondered that, looking for meaning as the counter ticked steadily down.

"Dropship is slightly off course," said Martin, frowning even as the deceleration tried to flatten her features, "I think we can adjust but it's going to be bumpy."

"Do it, Midshipman," said Cohen, "and let's warn dropship four."

"Sending now, sir," said Wood.

"Attitudinal thrusters firing now," said Martin. There was an indiscernible change in pressure for the briefest time as the huge ship twisted slightly.

"Manoeuvre successful," reported Martin, her voice a little tense. "Ten seconds left on the main burn."

"Sound the combat alarm, everyone remain calm," said Cohen, so hyped that he could barely follow his own advice. "Grab us a dropship, Midshipman."

"Bay doors opening," said White, "and for what we are about to receive, may the Admiralty be forever grateful."

"Firing attitudinal thrusters," said Martin as her hands flew over the controls. The ship shook and twisted as it bore down on dropship four. All eyes were on the monitors as the dropship suddenly appeared on the monitor and rushed towards them.

"That's a bit bloody quick," said White, then the dropship's engines fired and the rate of approach fell as she accelerated.

There was a brief moment when the dropship was so close to *Ascendant* that every scratch on her hull was visible to the bridge crew. Then it was gone, and there was the most awful screeching of metal scraping against metal followed by a long, drawn-out rumbling crash.

"Bay doors closing," said White quietly.

"Attitudinal thrusters firing, four-second rotation manoeuvre, main engine burn in six seconds," said Martin.

<<*Varpulis*. Heave-to and prepare to be boarded>> came the translated orders from the Deathless ship.

"Fire everything, Mr MacCaibe," said Cohen.

"Aye, sir," said MacCaibe grimly, punching controls on his

console, "rail guns firing, random spread, four-second burst. Missiles away, counter-measures deployed."

"Main engines firing now," said Martin, "one hundred and fifty seconds, full power."

"Keep firing the rail guns, Mr MacCaibe, we don't need to hold onto the ammunition."

"Firing again, sustained burst," said MacCaibe. "No incoming fire yet, three seconds till delta-v renders weapons ineffective."

"Active sensors, find *Posvist*, please," said Cohen.

"Sensors online," said Jackson, "scanning."

"Firing paused, out of effective range," said MacCaibe, "railgun ammunition depleted by forty-two per cent, six hours to replenishment, auto-manufacture beginning now."

There was a pause, just a few seconds long when nothing happened.

"That went about as well as could have been hoped," said Cohen, "thank you, ladies and gentlemen." There was a murmur of quiet celebration, muted slightly by the continuing acceleration.

"Ten seconds left on the main engine burn," said Martin before she counted them down to zero.

"Excellent," said Cohen, standing up from his chair. "Let's see what we caught, shall we?"

Then Jackson gave a strangled cry.

"*Posvist*," he said, horror in his voice. There was a flash on the forward-facing monitors as something huge and dark flashed across them. Kinetic rounds ripped into *Ascendant*. The ship shuddered and shook.

Then the hull-breach alarms sounded.

18

"Hull breaches across all decks," said Midshipman MacCaibe, "primary weapons bank inoperative, ammo-fabs offline."

"Forward sensor array offline," said Jackson, voice shaking, "starboard sensor array damaged and only fifty per cent operational, all other sensors functioning correctly."

"Focus on the hull breaches," said Cohen, more loudly than he had meant, "what's our status?"

"Interior doors are closed, atmospheric pressure is stable," said White as he reviewed the monitors, "multiple punctures to the hull but no explosive concussion detected." He paused to change the view on his screens. "No radiation leaks, no obvious damage to the power plant or distribution system."

"Get the repair teams out," said Cohen. "I want a full assessment inside an hour and details of everything that's been damaged. And get me a list of casualties."

∾

"All hail the conquering heroes," muttered Goodwin to herself as she peered out through one of the holes in the hull. The stars stared back at her from the cold vacuum of space. Then she sighed and removed the inner panel, flicking away insulation and shattered components to clear the area.

Whatever had hit them – and Goodwin hadn't yet found a projectile – had punched a seventy-millimetre hole in the hull and decompressed the room beyond. This one had been empty but she had already fixed holes in two rooms with frozen corpses.

She shook her head. The hole in the outer hull was ringed with torn metal where the projectile had struck. The angle was awkward but the plasma cutter attached to the arm of her engineer power armour suit made short work of the metal and it fell quickly away.

Goodwin fitted a slab of armour plating over the hole and welded it in place. Then she sprayed insulating foam across the whole area, filling the gap between the outer and inner hulls before replacing the inner plate with a new panel.

"Almost as good as new," she muttered. On the other side of the room, a matching hole showed where the projectile had travelled further into the ship. Goodwin inspected the ruined panels but couldn't see any damage to critical systems. She slapped a lightweight internal patch across the wall, welded it in place then packed up her kit.

<Room four fixed and ready for re-pressurisation> she sent.

<Acknowledged. Area clear, re-pressurising now> came the response from engineering control as the HUD display listing breaches that to be sealed and damage to be repaired was updated again.

There was a hiss as air bled back into the room and in moments it was back to normal.

<Pressure holding, looks good> sent Goodwin. Then she checked her slate and moved on to the next room on the list.

"That's the last of the hull breaches sealed," said White as he reviewed the updates on his slate. It had been two hours since the attack and *Ascendant* was a hive of frantic activity as repairs were made and casualties triaged and patched up.

"What news on the primary weapons bank?" asked Cohen as he reviewed the casualty list again. It was bad – thirty Marines and seventeen crew – and with the deployment bay offline after the attack, there was no way to redeploy them.

"It's shredded," said White, looking at the pictures of the damage. "Looks like it took several strikes, at least one of which went through the primary fire controller. They're trying to rebuild it from spares but it's not looking good at the moment."

Cohen and White were in the meeting room behind the bridge. Monitors all around the room showed status reports and damage assessments. The encounter with *Posvist* had been short but brutal, and *Ascendant* was going to need some serious work to fix everything properly. Right now, all they could do was patch the holes and get as many systems as possible back online.

"The good news is that the personality backup systems are fully operational, as are the engines, life support and navigation systems. The secondary weapons banks and the counter-measure launchers escaped damage, but the ammo-fabs are going to be offline for a few hours while the manufactories churn out the necessary components. Given all the damage, they're running non-stop."

Cohen grunted, staring at his slate.

"How did we miss *Posvist*?" he asked quietly, replaying the video and sensor readings captured by the forward arrays. "Why didn't we see her coming up on us?"

White said nothing for a moment then sighed. "It was a bluff. All that 'prepare to be boarded' and 'heave-to for inspection by *Posvist*' stuff. They were playing us. They knew all along, ever since Warden's fuck-up at the base, that we weren't what we claimed."

"So why go easy on us? They must have fired their engines for that attack run well before we got there, did they see us coming?"

"Or did they intercept our comms? Yeah, I worried about that. We're using their kit, after all. Have we been hacked or do they just have the encryption keys? Maybe they simply snagged our comms and plucked the trajectory from dropship four."

Cohen looked up from his slate and swore. Then he cleared his throat, his decision made. "Right. Get the techs to run over the entire ship, check it for bugs, backdoors and anything that might be a listening device or an intercept. Then have the fabs make new comms kit, new nav-computers, new AI processors, new helm. Everything, internal and external. Every single piece of Deathless comms or processing tech is to be systematically stripped out and replaced, got it?"

"That'll take forever," said White, frowning. "Is it really necessary?"

"Hah! You said it yourself." Cohen grimly replied. "They knew we were coming. They've known everything since we left Soyuz. Every bit of intelligence we've shared over their kit, they've known. We have to assume we're utterly compromised, so our only option is to rebuild our systems from the ground up. Start with navigation, helm, life support and engine management, then move on to comms, weapons control, atmosphere management, fabs. Everything."

White nodded, realising that Lieutenant Commander Cohen's assessment was correct and that he was quite serious about the changes.

"Aye, sir," he said, "at least these are our slates."

"No! Dump the slates as well, and no mention of this across the wires or in a slate until we've cleaned the ship and we're certain we're secure, got it?"

"Got it," said White, slightly shaken by Cohen's vehemence.

"Only the paranoid survive," muttered Cohen, shaking his head.

19

The Rupert was tied to a medical gurney in one of the meeting rooms. Captain Warden, Marine X and Colour Milton watched the monitors as the med-techs finished checking his wounds and his restraints. He was hooked up to a drip that would keep him incapacitated but cogent; docile, but awake enough to answer questions.

"How do you want to play this, sir?" asked Milton as the med-techs left the room.

"Believe it or not, this will be my first interrogation of an alien prisoner, Colour Sergeant, so I think we'll play it by ear." Warden paused to look around at his team. "Anything else?"

Milton and Marine X both shook their heads. Warden found it surprisingly disconcerting that Marine X hadn't done something like this before. His unusual career history might be a patchwork of secrets classified way beyond Warden's pay grade, but this was the first time he could remember the Penal Marine failing to offer an opinion based on previous experience.

"Right," said Warden, squaring his shoulders, "let's get to it."

Limping slightly from the wound in his leg, Warden led Milton into the meeting room leaving Marine X to watch from next door. The head of the gurney had been raised so that the Deathless Rupert now faced into the room rather than staring at the ceiling. His eyes tracked Warden and Milton as they came in.

"Let's see how well this works," muttered Warden, flicking at his slate to activate the translation features. The techs had been furiously training the app in every spare moment but there were still gaps in its vocabulary and the output had already been shown to be less convincing than they had hoped when they had dealt with Soyuz.

"I am Captain Warden and this is Colour Sergeant Milton. Who are you?"

There was a pause as the machine worked then it spat out a sentence in what sounded to Warden like fluent Deathless.

The Rupert blinked in surprise then answered slowly.

"Corporal Uladimov Vyacheslav Savelievich, second class. Where am we?"

"This is the British Commonwealth Royal Navy vessel, *Ascendant*, in orbit around New Petropavlovsk-Kamchatsky. You are a prisoner of war."

The Rupert coughed, obviously surprised to learn that he was anything of the sort.

"What war? No war here."

"We don't think you are a corporal, second class," said Warden, ignoring the question, "you wear an officer's clone, and the attendee list for your retreat shows you as 'General Guryev Zakharovich'. We want to know why your troops invaded the peaceful colony of New Bristol."

"Never heard of it," said the Rupert. "Is above clearance level of humble corporal."

Warden turned off the translation device and glanced at Milton. "You think he's a corporal?" asked Warden in a low voice. Milton glanced at the Rupert then shook her head. "No, neither do I. Bring over the palm-reader." He flicked the translation device back on.

"We want to understand, General, but if you won't help us, we'll just get the information another way." The Rupert stiffened at the perceived threat and drew away from Milton as she stalked forward with the palm-reader. She grabbed his wrist, but the Rupert made a fist and refused to let it go.

"I could break his fingers, sir," offered Milton, only half-joking. The Rupert tensed as Warden's slate translated Milton's words.

"No need, Colour, I'll just increase his meds," said Warden, poking at his slate, "and we'll wait till he passes out to get a reading." The slate translated that, and the Rupert snarled. For a moment it looked like he might resist, then his fingers uncurled, and Milton was able to press his palm against the reader.

"Well, well," said Warden, peering at the results, "welcome aboard, General. I should apologise for the rough treatment at the base and your subsequent condition. We've done what we can and your wounds will heal, but I'm afraid your colleagues on the planet were rather more capable than we had expected."

"What do you want, Captain?" asked the Deathless general. "And what is this 'war' you talk about?"

"You really don't know? Your people attacked one of our planets, New Bristol, and began killing our civilians. My troops stopped the invasion then we captured one of your warships, destroyed two others and came here looking for answers. You're going to help us get those answers."

The Rupert snorted derisively. "You know nothing. I am soldier, not politician or leader. I have never heard of this planet you speak of or your people. I cannot answer your questions even if I wanted to. Kill me or send me back. I cannot help you."

"Why do your people make war, General? What is it you need from us, from our planet, that you cannot get elsewhere? What are your plans? Why are you training so many troops on New Petropavlovsk-Kamchatsky? Where are they all being sent?"

Warden rattled through the questions but Zakharovich remained silent, staring at Warden, unblinking, as the interview rolled on. After ten minutes of veiled threats, enticements and questions were all met with stoic silence from the prisoner, Warden switched off the translator and turned away.

"This isn't going anywhere," he said. "Any ideas?" Milton glanced at the Rupert then shook her head. "Right, well, we've got better things to do with our time talk to an uncommunicative prisoner. Get him locked away somewhere safe and make sure he's comfortable and secure." Milton nodded and flicked at her slate to summon the med-techs.

Warden watched, somewhat depressed about the vast effort they had expended to acquire a general whose knowledge was either too limited to be of use, or whose discipline was too great for him to be chatty. Then his slate pinged and a message from Goodwin appeared.

<Hand print and DNA accepted. File decrypted. You need to see this>

Warden and Milton slipped into the crowded briefing room to join Cohen, White and a host of other officers all eager to learn what Goodwin and Cornwell had found when the general's palm print and DNA had given them access to the encrypted file.

"The prisoner is General Guryev Zakharovich, not quite the most senior soldier in the system but pretty important," began Cornwell after Cohen had cleared his throat to silence the room. "He hasn't answered any of our questions but his palm print and DNA have unlocked the encrypted files that Captain Warden and Colour Milton took from Soyuz." There was a buzz of excited anticipation in the room.

"The contents aren't as explosively interesting as we had hoped," said Goodwin. She flicked at her slate to pull images onto the room's main monitor. "They don't give us any of the reasons behind the Deathless' actions, so we still don't know why they're here, why they attacked us or where they're shipping their troops."

"What we do know," said Cornwell, "is that although NewPet is an important part of their ground-troop training programme, it isn't the only such centre. Mention is made of 'Training Base 7', which we think is their name for the NewPet system's features as a whole, and that obviously suggests that there are at least another six training bases somewhere."

"Training Base 7 also isn't the only facility in the system," went on Goodwin, pulling up a manifest and punching it across to the monitor, "but it is the only collection of ground-based troop-training centres. The files don't tell us how many troops are being trained or how the programmes are organized but they have suggested somewhere we can go to look for more answers."

A picture of a large moon flashed onto the screen. Like NewPet, it was heavily wooded and studded with large mountain ranges that marched across medium-sized continents set in large blue seas.

"This base," said Cornwell as the view zoomed down from moon-sized to focus on an area only a few kilometres across, "seems to be some sort of command centre. It's heavily defended, as you can see from these shots, and appears to be the system's principle communication depot. If they have a wormhole link to their home planet, that's where it'll be."

Cohen cleared his throat again. "How do you know all this, Midshipman? Was there a file listing top-secret bases?"

"No, sir, but the moon's name and the station's designation appear in the meta-data for many of the files. The Deathless seem to have a file format that allows their top-secret documents to be tracked, so we can see how the transmission was routed and from which base or space station they came. That allows us to infer the existence of other places beyond the system but the names are meaningless without more contextual information.

"Importantly, though, it also shows that every single file in the data package that originated outside the system entered through the comms point on this moon, which strongly suggests it is their one and only wormhole endpoint," Cornwell concluded.

Cohen nodded thoughtfully. "Good work, Midshipman. What else do we know?"

"Unlike the officer's retreat on NewPet, this base is properly defended. Walls, guards, towers, all the normal things, plus some sort of ground-to-air defences."

"Do we have any recon shots of our own, or are we relying on Deathless files again?" asked Cohen, wary of being fooled into trusting the Deathless data or systems again.

"I'm afraid it's all Deathless data, sir," said Goodwin apologetically, "and the moon is too far away for our sensors to do more than confirm its existence."

"Well, Captain," said Lieutenant Commander Cohen as he looked at Warden, "it sounds like we have another job for you. Fancy taking a closer look?"

Warden caught Milton's eye briefly before looking at Cohen. "I think we might be able to help with that, if you can get us into position."

"Excellent," said Cohen, rubbing his hands together and sitting forward on his chair to look at White. "Have we switched out the nav-computer yet?"

"Let me check," said White, flicking through the checklist on his slate. "No, there's probably another couple of hours to go before we're ready to do that."

"Good. In that case, there's one last thing the nav-computer needs to do for us before it goes the way of all flesh."

"Okay," said White, frowning at Cohen's vagueness, "I'll send a note to the techs."

"Thank you, Mr White. I suggest we reconvene in, say, eight hours, by which time we should have some idea of the amount of work left to do to secure *Ascendant* and return her to full combat readiness." He paused to look around the room. "That'll be all for now, folks."

20

"I can't believe you've found us another base on another jungle-planet to assault," said Warden once the meeting room had emptied and the team had dispersed to carry out their assigned tasks. He pored over the limited collection of images they had retrieved from the encrypted files, looking for anything that might constitute good news. "Does it at least have a pool-side bar?"

Cohen snorted and shook his head. He and White were reviewing the trajectory that would take *Ascendant* halfway across the system and into orbit around the moon of the second planet.

"How hard do you want to hit this place?" asked XO White, pushing a list of ordnance and weapon systems to the main monitor. "I mean, we could take out their satellites and any probes they might have in the upper atmosphere. Maybe make them think we had a much larger force?"

Warden looked up from his slate and glanced over the weapons list. The forward weapons bank was still offline, not that it would have done them much good against a planet-side base, and the other options were somewhat limited.

"How do you feel about an orbital bombardment?" he asked

Cohen, not entirely sure that it was something he himself was comfortable with.

The lieutenant commander shook his head. "Tricky, very tricky. Apart from the fact that we don't have any appropriate ordinance," he wagged a finger at the list on the screen, "it pushes right up against our rules of engagement. It would need to be very finely directed, and we'd need to be dead certain it was a purely military target. If there's any possibility of civilian casualties…"

"But you're okay with missiles?" asked Warden, raising an eyebrow.

"Strangely yes, although they would probably burn up in the atmosphere before they did any harm to anything on the surface."

Warden nodded, somehow relieved that orbital bombardment wasn't really an option. He had seen what such weapons could do to a city; he had no wish to visit that on anyone else, even an enemy.

"The goal is to get to the ground before they blow us out of the sky," said Warden, restating the problem in an attempt to elicit new ideas, "and without giving them so much notice of our arrival that they're fully prepared with reinforcements on the way by the time we knock on their front door."

"And we need to make sure you have enough time to get back to *Ascendant* before *Posvist* and her evil twin turn up to put the boot in," said White, voicing the fear that cast its noxious shadow across the whole enterprise.

"That at least, I think, we can deal with," said Cohen, flicking away at his slate until he could push something up onto a monitor. "We load this trajectory into our hacked Deathless nav-computer, wait for it to bounce the information off to our friends on Soyuz, then we rip out the machine, replace it with our own and load the real course."

"Nice," said White, nodding appreciatively. "We send them on a wild-goose chase by feeding them false information. Do you think they'll fall for it, Sir?"

"Who knows?" shrugged Cohen. "But it's got to be worth a try. If we've found all their bugs – and that's a big 'if' – then the worst-case scenario is that we find the planet held against us, but we'll still surprise them."

"And if not? If they still have a bug on-board?" asked Warden.

"Then they'll probably be waiting for us," said Cohen darkly, "and things might get a bit sticky."

~

Ascendant powered on. Patching the systems damaged by *Posvist*'s attack took hours; ripping out the comms infrastructure and sweeping the ship for bugs took much longer and nearly three days had passed before Cohen pronounced himself happy.

"I'd prefer to spend another week checking things over and re-working the tier two service hardware to make sure there aren't any bugs or backups hanging around in the system," said Cohen, "but time is pressing, and we've already waited long enough that they could have brought new forces into the system or moved things around."

The Marines were certainly bored with waiting. As soon as the cloning bay had come back online, they had redeployed the casualties from the *Posvist*'s attack, and now, back at full strength, they were ready for the next action and eager to head to the moon's surface.

"We're going in hard and fast," Warden said when he briefed his officers. "Brown, you'll take the majority of A Troop in drop pods, into the southwest quadrant of the base. Hayes, your pods will drop B Troop outside the wall, again in the southwest. Lewis and C Troop will arrive in the dropships. A Troop will secure the southwest quadrant, and B Troop will breach the wall to join them, creating our exfiltration path. A and B troops will then storm the base, take down any opposition with maximum aggression, grab everything they can find that looks like intelligence before exfiltrating through the breach. C Troop will secure the dropship landing zone, provide overwatch and cover the retreat."

He paused to look around at his team.

"This has to be done quickly. We'll be using every pod in *Ascendant*'s inventory and we get only one shot at this. We don't know what sort of opposition we face or how long it will take them to organise a meaningful defence. We go in, we grab anything that isn't nailed down, the techs take anything they can find that looks interesting, then we're out. Fifteen minutes tops, if it goes well. If not, we'll give it another ten to find the intel we need, then pull out. Lieutenant Commander Cohen can't give us longer than that."

He paused again. "Questions?"

"What's the priority, sir? Intelligence or destroying the base and eliminating personnel?" asked Lieutenant Linda Hayes, who would be leading B Troop.

"I'll be leading the team to gather intelligence," said Warden, "with Bailey and Parker on overwatch to identify likely targets for us to investigate. The priority for the rest of A Troop is to sweep the southern quadrant and eliminate the opposition. B Troop needs to get breaching charges in place on the wall and then assist A Troop. The breach can be made as soon as the Deathless rumble us. After that, both A and B Troops should focus on taking out any Deathless between my team and the wall to secure our retreat but make sure everyone knows that they should take any opportunity to grab intel. Make sure your techs have drones up, keep the HUD updates coming. Standard operating procedures, basically."

There was a little shuffling; then Lieutenant Hayes cleared her throat.

"Will Marine X be on this mission, sir?"

Warden rolled his eyes and ignored the question. "If there's nothing else, get your squads ready. We're eight hours out."

~

<Four hundred seconds to drop>

The message flashed across the HUDs of the Marines as they sat in their drop pods. *Ascendant* hurtled in at a huge speed, bearing down on the Deathless moon base like a badly thrown Roman candle.

Warden sat in a four-body pod with Milton, Goodwin and Harrington, who would be supporting Goodwin's data exfiltration work.

<Main engine deceleration burn, full-power, in one hundred and fifty seconds>

Ascendant's command messages were being relayed from the bridge to Warden's officers. The Marines were only getting timing updates, although Warden suspected that Goodwin and Harrington were both listening to the command channel.

<Full-power burn for one hundred and sixty seconds in three, two, one>

There was a brutal kick from the main engines as *Ascendant* began her final approach to the moon base.

<No sign of *Posvist* or any other Deathless vessel>

A rare piece of good news.

<End of main engine burn in three, two, one. Thrusters firing for attitude correction>

Getting the pointy end to face forward, as Warden always thought of it. The main weapons bank, at the front of the ship, had been one of the last systems to come back online but it was now, Cohen assured him, one hundred per cent operational.

<Reorientation complete>

<Forty-five seconds to pod deployment>

<Orbital weapons platforms identified. Targeting>

<Incoming messages, translating>

<Thirty seconds to pod deployment>

<Firing railguns, firing missiles>

The flow of messages was both reassuring and alarming. It was good to see Cohen's team working so smoothly, but a quiet, easy entry would have been even better.

<Incoming fire, deploying counter-measures>

<Attitudinal thrusters firing in preparation for pod deployment>

<Five seconds to pod deployment. Good luck>

Then there was a bang, and suddenly the pod was free of *Ascendant* and on its one-way journey to the Deathless base.

21

The pod shuddered as it slammed through the soupy atmosphere of the moon the Marines had designated 'Puzzlewood', after the weird trees in the forest they were now hurtling toward. The drop pods were little more than guided bullets with brutally simple deceleration systems intended merely to bring the craft to an abrupt stop right before they impacted the target site. The ride was not comfortable.

Warden watched the feed from the hardened cameras on the outside of the pod as they fell towards the Deathless base. A neat 'X' glowed to show the target landing point, well within the perimeter. The pods had little in the way of guidance features and nothing that was accessible to the Marines, relying instead on the accuracy of the initial launch.

They should miss buildings and other obstructions, but they were still dropping directly into a hot zone, a bold and risky tactic that would expose them to immediate fire if the enemy were on the ball.

"Fifteen seconds to impact," intoned the pod's onboard computer.

Warden was sharing the pod with Milton, Goodwin and Harrington, the first three members of the team he would be operating with on the mission. Marine X, Parker and Bailey were in a separate pod aiming to land outside the base so they could find a suitable sniping perch. Chief Science Office Mueller had reported that the megaflora on the moon were even taller than those on NewPet, so they hoped to find a good, high spot to work from.

There was a great roar as the pod's engines fired, pressing the occupants firmly into their seats.

"Brace for impact in five seconds. Inertial dampeners do not exist," intoned the strangely philosophical onboard computer.

Great, thought Warden, *even the drop pod has a sense of humour.*

Then the engines stopped, and the parachutes deployed, snapping out to take away the last of the speed before the pod slammed into the ground with bone-crunching force. As drop pod deployments went, it was pretty smooth, thought Warden, since he hadn't bitten off his tongue or heard the alarming sound of metal twisting and shearing.

Warden was first out of his seat. He slammed his fist against a large red button, under which some joker had written, 'Inflight Entertainment', and the side panel of the pod blew open, falling to the ground with a thump to form an exit ramp.

Warden shouldered his rifle and leapt through the doorway into the compound as the last swathes of parachute rustled back into the pod's nose, clearing the way for the disembarking troops.

He scanned the compound, checking for immediate threats, then looked for falling pods; they should all have hit the ground at about the same time. Lieutenant Colonel Atticus had once been killed by a late-arriving pod, and Warden had no intention of going the same way.

"Come on," he said, waving an arm, "get moving, people." Milton, Goodwin and Harrington emerged from the pod, weapons raised, and began to move out. Warden shuddered, glad to be clear of the pod, which was a potential death trap if it came under fire.

The base compound was eerily quiet. There were a few final thumps of landing drop pods from outside the base walls, and then only the sound of the Marines deploying. The temperature and humidity were oppressive, and the thick atmosphere made everything sound strange.

"Nobody around," muttered Warden, frowning as he scanned the open ground.

The Deathless must have noticed their arrival. The pods had parachutes but, since the purpose was a speedy arrival, they screamed through the atmosphere until the rockets fired to slow their descent so that the parachutes could usefully deploy. At night, they looked like a meteor shower but they sounded like a jet with a damaged engine, and they often made a booming noise like a dropped shipping container when they landed.

Warden headed across the compound and Milton, Goodwin and Harrington were quick to follow, all seeking cover against a sturdy-looking building to the north. Not knowing where to look, they planned simply to crash the most likely building then go from there. Goodwin worked on the lock while Warden checked-in with the rest of the team.

<Command team is down> he sent, <at the first building. Troop leaders check in>

<A Troop down, sir, all on target. Securing the southwest quadrant now> sent Lieutenant Luke Brown. He'd been brought in by General Bonneville to take over Warden's troop when he was promoted.

<B Troop landing was clean. Approaching the south-west wall and preparing to breach> confirmed Lieutenant Hayes.

<C Troop present and correct, securing exfiltration route. We have good LOS to the base and are setting up overwatch for B Troop assault> sent Lieutenant Felicity Lewis.

<Roger that, troop leaders. Let's try and keep it quiet as long as we can. Wait until the Deathless sound the alarm before letting rip>

Behind him, the door to the building opened, and Harrington slipped inside, suppressed pistol ready.

<Bailey, Parker, Ten, we're going into the flagged building. Let me know when you're in position>

<Roger that, Captain> acknowledged Parker,

Warden slung his rifle, drew his own pistol and followed the team into the building.

~

Ten scanned the treeline, picked a likely target and sprinted towards it. He pulled his grapnel launcher and sighted on the trunk, as high up as he could see. The grapnel bolt bit home and the indicator on the barrel went green. After giving the line a good tug to check it was secure, he thumbed the motor's switch and began to ascend.

Bailey and Parker followed suit. The trees didn't offer much cover, having an unusual pattern of leaf growth where thin, vine-like shoots wrapped around thick branches that sprouted from the trunk-like needles. As they were about to go into a full-on attack, though, these details really didn't matter to Ten.

He climbed further through the branches until he had a good perch and a clear view of the compound. Their pod had been one of the first launched, along with C Troop's dropship, to ensure they had time to get into position before Captain Warden and his small team arrived in the compound, and A Troop landed to clear the exfiltration route.

Ten sighted down his railgun at the tower closest to the captain. It was manned by four Deathless troopers. The tower itself was fifty metres high, about the height of Nelson's column. He chuckled to himself, imagining what old Horatio would have thought of all this; he'd probably have been thrilled at the prospect of taking *Ascendant* into battle against overwhelming odds.

The guard tower was topped by a square room, each wall with thick, and no doubt bulletproof, windows. The roof was a shallow pyramid, with a communications antenna protruding from the peak. A narrow balcony wrapped around the tower above the windows, creating a firing point that the guards could use in the event of an attack.

Inside the tower, the guards all looked very agitated, pointing towards something within the compound. It was odds on that they had seen or heard the drop pods of A Troop landing.

Ten twisted to face Bailey and Parker and said, "England expects," before he unfurled his wings and dove towards the base. He shot across the open ground, flapping his wings for height before gliding the rest of the way to the guard tower.

"Bailey, Parker, Ten, we're going inside the flagged building. Let me know when you're in position," Captain Warden announced. Ten let Parker deal with it so he could concentrate on the task at hand.

"Roger that, Captain," Parker acknowledged, "we have our first perch, and Ten is approaching the tower now. I'll update once we have overwatch. Over."

Marine X alighted on the roof, angling his wings to form billowing air brakes as he approached, slowing him to walking speed so he could drop neatly onto the tower. He took a few paces forward, grabbed the antenna and he was in control again.

Ten worked quickly, attaching a line from his waist to the base of the antenna. Then he ran off the roof, jumping face first over the balcony and swinging back to the wall as he dropped. His feet hit the wall under the balcony, and his knees protested about the impact, though he wasn't sure why since they were brand new, unlike his real knees, which were safely in storage back home. Or at least somewhere, closer to home. He had a sudden horrible thought that he couldn't actually remember where he'd left his body. Was it in one of the bases or in a storage unit at his home?

With the ease born of regular practice, he flipped himself over and payed out more rope, dropping to just above the window. He crouched, upside-down, and reached out to slap something sticky onto the glass in two places. Quickly, he pushed himself left along the wall, then pushed out as hard as he could, swinging away from the tower.

As he swung away, he activated an icon on his HUD and the charges on the window detonated. That definitely got the attention of the guards inside, who had apparently been so distressed by the arrival of the drop pods that they had completely failed to notice him landing on the roof or running down the side of their guard tower.

Ten let go of the belaying device, and it clamped down on the line, leaving both his hands free as he came around the tower towards the gaping hole in the window, feet first. He drew two pistols, and they coughed simultaneously as he burst into the room through the remains of the window.

He landed unceremoniously on his arse and slid across the floor. His guns spat, once at the face of the guard on the far left, once at the neck on the far right, then he followed up with two more headshots on the middle pair of guards as he rose to a crouch before giving them all another double-tap, just for good measure.

"Bailey, Parker, all clear for you to join me," he said as he moved to the window the guards had been looking out of.

"Roger that, incoming," Parker acknowledged.

Ten casually reloaded his pistols as he looked out of the window, working out which building the captain had entered. It didn't look like much but going in was the right thing to do, even if it wasn't the building they needed. Then he unslung his railgun and leaned it up against the wall before placing more charges around the windows.

Bailey and Parker arrived on the roof just as he was finishing.

"Hold there for a mo'," he said, hunkering down in the corner of the room. Then he detonated the rest of the charges in a series of pops that neatly destroyed the remaining windows. "Clear."

The two Marines dropped down to the balcony and climbed down the ladders into the guard room.

"Bailey, take the north tower," said Ten as the sniper unslung her rifle. "I'll deal with the one near B Troop if they haven't done so already. Can't let them get involved."

"Roger," said Bailey, moving to the north wall as Ten began rifling through the armoured cabinets on the west and east walls of the tower. Each contained a variety of heavy weapons, rifles, grenades and worst of all, railguns. If any of the guards were trained snipers, they could cause some serious damage.

Bailey aimed through the blown-out window as Parker began targeting for her.

"Lieutenant Lewis, the guard towers are equipped with heavy weapons, including grenade launchers and railguns. Repeat, the guard towers contain railguns. Recommend immediate counter-sniper measures. We have taken this tower and are eliminating the guards in the adjacent towers, flagged on the HUD."

"Understood, Ten. I appreciate the heads up. We'll get them dealt with immediately," Lieutenant Lewis responded.

Ten was already shooting, taking down two guards with one round before the others could react. His felt his eyebrow, or rather the brow ridge of the harpy clone, which didn't really have eyebrows as such, rise in surprise. That almost never worked; the odds of two of your enemies being so neatly lined up and the round going so straight that it would pass through two armoured heads was slim at best. It was so rare he hadn't achieved it more than a dozen times in his entire career.

The third guard turned to look for where the enemy fire was coming from. He had left himself exposed, and that did him no favours, he went down a mere second after the other two.

The fourth guard thought he was smarter and had dived for cover, grabbing a rifle on the way.

Good for you, son, thought Ten as he aimed. *Maybe next time you'll remember what railguns can do.*

He squeezed the trigger, his chosen target a spot fifty centimetres below the window, just in line with the barrel of the rifle that poked up from below it. He followed with second and third shots at close but different locations. The rifle disappeared from view and a second of scanning back and forth with his scope brought him a glimpse of a bloodied corpse through the massive holes the railgun rounds had made in the wall.

Ten scanned across the visible buildings, checking for snipers, his HUD letting him see through the night as if it were noon on a bright day. Then, satisfied there were none, he moved to the nearest gun cabinet. Bingo. It was like a toy chest in here. He grabbed a couple more magazines for the railgun, reloaded his gun then distributed some of the contents around the room, passing spare magazines to Bailey and Parker. The downside of a flying clone was the weight restriction, which limited their use of ammunition and prohibited heavier options like grenade launchers.

Here, though, they could use ammunition like it was going out of fashion, dramatically increasing their combat effectiveness.

"Right, let's see if we can't work out which building the captain should be looking at," said Ten as he looked out of the eastern window holes again, "because I'm pretty sure it's not the one labelled 'Virtual Reality Training Facility', is it?"

22

"What the fuck?" Warden breathed as he followed the team down the corridor and into the first room in the building. It was a sizeable warehouse-style space, with heavily insulated walls and a foamcrete floor. In itself, that wasn't too surprising, but the Deathless wandering around in it were another matter.

<Looks like they're in a virtual reality training session, Captain> Harrington broadcast to the team. <Might be a sound-proof room>

That made sense. The Deathless were spread out all over the otherwise empty space, some crouching, some jogging, all holding brightly coloured weapons of some kind. Presumably, the offensive colour scheme indicated that they were training replicas rather than live firearms.

<Yes. It doesn't look like we'll find anything useful here> Warden said as he watched the troops going through the motions, aiming and firing as their weapons made loud bangs and recoiled realistically. It was hard to tell quite how well they were doing, as he couldn't see the simulated enemy they were firing at. He wondered what models they were using for their enemy – Deathless in a different uniform or perhaps they were now training against Royal Marine avatars?

<So...> Harrington sent, waving his pistol meaningfully.

Warden glanced at Milton. She returned an exaggerated shrug.

<Okay, let's take them, quick and clean> Warden responded.

Harrington nodded and quietly padded up to his first target, clamping a hand over his mouth and swiftly pushing his F-S dagger up through the neck into the brain.

Milton was on the move too, also using her dagger – silence and stab then gently ease the victim to the ground. Goodwin was using her pistol, applied to the back of the skull and catching the corpses as they fell. Warden waded in, opting for his dagger. It was grim work but over in less than a minute.

They were almost rumbled when one of the Deathless tripped over a fallen comrade – it looked like the VR simulation wasn't programmed to account for obstructions in what was supposed to be a near-empty room, aside from the other players.

"Find an officer or NCO, we want their ID cards to open doors," Warden ordered as he cleaned his knife.

<Captain, I don't think you'll find much in that building> sent Marine X. <The HUD is translating the signage, and it says it's a VR training area>

<The translation is working then. We just found a section in here going through a training exercise. They're down. Any better idea where we should head next?>

<There's a covered walkway on the first floor of your building. I think that will take you into a good target but get in position and we'll update, sir> Ten replied.

<Roger that, moving to the first floor>

Harrington and Milton had both found cards by the time he'd finished his conversation with Marine X, so they moved immediately up the metal staircase in the corridor outside.

They gave the first floor a cursory check, but it was quiet, only empty observation and control rooms for the simulation space downstairs and some toilet facilities.

The covered walkway was a fully enclosed tunnel that ran the twenty metres to the next building, presumably a way to avoid the local weather. The analysis done by the science team on *Ascendant* suggested the conditions here on the jungle moon could get rough, so it made sense the Deathless would want to keep inside whenever possible.

The walkway was dark, but there were lights on the ceiling. Warden waved a hand experimentally into the passage, and the first light came on. He ducked back out of sight.

<Any joy, Ten?>

"Goodwin, can you hack those lights and keep them off? I don't want to be exposed out there if we can avoid it," Warden whispered as an aside.

<I had to move along the wall a bit to get a line of sight on one of the signs. It reads 'Command Operations Centre', so I think you're golden and that's the one you want to head for>

<Excellent news> Warden replied.

"Got the lights off, sir, we're clear," Goodwin said. "Permission to deploy micro-drones, sir?"

Warden nodded at her, motioning down the corridor.

<The lights are down in the corridor and we're heading in> he sent to Marine X. In the background, the whisper-quiet whirring of tiny rotor blades faded into the distance.

<Understood, sir. It's all very quiet here. Do you want me to have a shufty around some of the other buildings?>

<Yes. Feel free to leave some surprises for our semi-immortal friends but focus on intelligence gathering> Warden confirmed.

<Yes, sir. I'll be as quiet as a mouse until you tell me otherwise. Over> Ten confirmed.

Warden turned back to the team. "Ready?" he asked, and they all gave affirmative hand signals. It was a redundant question, of course. They were ready but you needed to maintain the habit, in case you had someone fresh out of training in your squad, or someone had been injured and wasn't responsive.

He tapped Harrington on the shoulder lightly, and the commando specialist moved off down the corridor, suppressed pistol at the ready. Goodwin's drones had mapped the open space beyond already, sending the floorplan to their HUD maps.

They came out of the walkway onto a balcony overlooking an atrium. On the ground floor, there was a reception desk, thankfully unmanned at this time. There were seating areas, and an archway led off to a cafeteria which was mercifully as dark inside as the sky was outside.

<Where to, sir?> asked Harrington.

Warden pondered for a second and then turned around. He grinned as he found exactly what he was looking for and he motioned for Milton to look too. It was a large building, and its size stood out even on such a large base. The architecture reminded him of a hotel or conference centre. As with many such buildings, someone had put a nice big floorplan on the wall to direct visitors to the correct room.

They scanned it with their HUDs and waited while the information was absorbed and the legend was translated. Then their HUDs generated a neat, augmented reality overlay with floorplans and room labels.

<Second floor, Colour Milton, that big room> sent Warden.

Milton nodded. The label said 'War Room', which sounded ominously interesting. Warden turned left and led the team towards the staircase. He opened a double door and began to move up the stairs, much to the surprise of the Deathless Rupert who was coming up from below.

Colour Milton acted first. Moving swiftly forward, she clamped her power armoured fingers over the throat of the unfortunate officer, barrelling him backwards and to the left. Her dagger came up once, twice, three times and he gurgled his last. She lowered the body quietly to the floor, wiped her dagger on his uniform and sheathed it. Then she picked up the body by the waistband and collar and jogged down the stairs to the ground floor, where she stowed the corpse under the first flight in the unused shadowed area beneath the stairs.

Warden continued up to the second floor, cursing his carelessness. They weren't going to remain unnoticed forever but longer was definitely better. He moved up the steps as quickly as he could without making too much of a racket. Even though the boots of his power armour suit had advanced composite soles that gave superb shock absorption, there was still a world of difference between a light step and stomping around as if your shoes were made of lead.

On the second floor, they found an empty corridor and another map. Warden scanned it while the team covered him and watched the corridors, then they followed the directions in their HUDs to the war room. It occupied a substantial portion of the second floor, somewhat more than half of the area on this level was devoted to it. The other end appeared to be offices and administrative areas.

<Captain. We've gone hot out here. You might want to get a move on> Parker sent.

<A bit more detail, Parker?>

<The southwest quadrant is a war zone, looks like a couple of mess halls emptied out. There's a railgun or two on the other side of the base. They're probably in the guard towers we can't see because they're on the other side of the buildings. They're causing problems. B Troop have breached the wall, but they were already over it before the real shooting started>

<Hayes. Parker sees railguns on the guard towers on the eastern side> Warden sent as they crept towards a large pair of wooden double doors that bore a brass plaque with the legend 'War Room'. It was a rather old-fashioned style, and he guessed senior staff liked their creature comforts in the Deathless forces as well.

<Yes, sir. They're hampering us>

<Marine X, if you can assist with those, do so. Lieutenants Hayes and Brown, I suggest getting some serious fire directed at those guard towers in case Ten is engaged. If you can get a targeting laser on them, get C Troop to send them a bunker buster> Warden ordered.

<Roger that, sir> Brown confirmed.

<Negative, sir, I'm too far away> sent Marine X. <Advise immediate action to be taken by A and B Troop>

That sealed it; if Ten couldn't make it in time, Hayes and Brown would have to deal with the towers another way.

Warden left them to it. Callous though it might seem, looking after his junior officers was not the mission priority. They were here to get the data to help the fight the Deathless across a battlefront potentially much larger than New Bristol. All their lives were somewhat less important than the hundreds of millions of citizens that might be at risk.

From the map alone, he knew the war room was huge, far too big for a four-person team to control properly, but they didn't have time to pull anyone else in. The situation outside could deteriorate at any moment, and *Ascendant* couldn't afford for them to hang about. Warden motioned the team to make their move. Milton and Goodwin pulled the doors open gently and he and moved in with Harrington.

An enormous circular table took up the entire centre of the room, and a holographic 3D representation of a dozen or so local star systems seemed to float above it. Various lines and symbols hung in the air between the systems, indicating strategic movement of fleets and troops, Warden imagined. Each wall was festooned with view screens, and they too displayed lists, some of which might have been the destinations they'd seen on the space station's departure gates.

A dozen Deathless Ruperts in sharp-looking uniforms peered at the displays, pounded at keyboards or shouted into communicators. Warden knew he needed to get a handle on the Deathless rank insignia, but it was a safe bet that some of these dignitaries were admirals and generals. There was space around the table for plenty more, but it looked like their planning session had petered out.

There were only a handful of other Deathless in the room, presumably junior officers and NCOs not involved in the planning but hanging around to make a good impression.

Don't go home before the boss, Warden thought wryly.

A frowning Rupert clone in a what was presumably a junior officer's uniform crossed the room to intercept them asking something in their Russian-based language. Warden tapped the side of his head with the barrel of his pistol as if there was something wrong with his audio feed. He didn't much like the tone this person was using.

And then, finally, a klaxon sounded as someone on the base raised the alarm.

The effect was predictably electric. The hapless officer's eyes went wide as he finally noticed the pistol, apparently having been unfazed by the Marines' power armour. The Rupert spat out another angry line at Warden and gesticulated to the door. He had no idea what the man was saying and couldn't be bothered to get the HUD to try the live translation the Puzzle Palace had concocted.

He recognised the tone, though. A green officer, unused to command and incapable of giving orders properly. Instead, the man was immediately throwing his toys out of the pram and issuing demands like a toddler given too much sugar. Warden cocked his head and wondered if this young idiot was actually trying to order him to go and find out what the klaxon was all about.

What an absolute arse he must be. Finally, something seemed to click in the Rupert's mind. Possibly it was the splatters of blood on his armour from their work in the VR training room, maybe just that he hadn't taken off his helmet or saluted or possibly even the fact he was wandering around an officers' area with a drawn weapon. Either way, he reached for his pistol in a way that suggested he hadn't done the drill necessary to draw a weapon quickly and smoothly.

"*Prosti, tovarisch*, not today," Warden said as he punched him hard in the face with his left gauntlet. The officer's head snapped back in a spray of blood, and he staggered backwards, falling over a trestle table covered with glasses and coffee cups and sending everything flying. That was one for the video album, thought Warden.

And then one of the senior officers at the conference table took notice of the commotion. He stood up and shouted.

"*Gospoda, vy ne mozhete srazhat'sya zdes'! Eto voyennaya komnata.*"

All eyes turned to the intruders, and more of the officers stood up.

"Prisoners, sir?" Harrington asked.

"Fuck no, slates and data only. I'm not carrying one of these moody bastards again. Goodwin, do we need any of them alive to access their slates?"

"No, sir, we should be able to crack it now that we've had more access to their systems," said Goodwin, "that said, it wouldn't hurt to have a couple of open slates; I have a way to keep them unlocked," she said, holding up a small device.

Warden nodded and walked up to the general, or whatever he was (he really did need an *I Spy* book of Deathless uniforms). He picked up the data slate by the man's plate and said, "I just need your signature on this, if you don't mind, sir," as he slapped the man's hand on the screen. It unlocked, and he passed the slate to Goodwin.

"Will that do?"

"All done, sir," said Goodwin, pocketing her hacking device and slipping the slate into her bag.

"Good," said Warden, and he shot the general in the head, "that's for New Bristol, and for wherever else you arseholes are."

The room exploded as the officers burst into action, reaching for weapons, yelling for guards or just diving for cover.

"Move," shouted Warden, firing his pistol until he emptied the magazine then unslinging his rifle. The Marines opened fire, their weapons shattering the peace of the war room as they worked their way through the officers.

In moments, it was all over. The air stank and the floor was littered with shell casings and corpses. Warden slammed a new magazine into his rifle as he stalked across the room, checking behind obstructions for targets they might have missed.

Goodwin grabbed a couple more slates and slapped their owner's hands on them before they finally expired and the device's security would no longer accept their authorisation.

Nothing moved as the Marines efficiently padded quietly around the great room.

"Clear," said Harrington from the far side of the room.

"Clear," echoed Milton.

"Harrington, watch the door. Milton, help Goodwin grab the slates," Warden ordered as he began rifling through the pockets of the officers, taking ID cards, data chips, personal slates and a small amount of actual paperwork.

It was all fodder for the intelligence section back at the Puzzle Palace. After a quick trip to a cloning bay, these officers would be back, and they would come back angry. The more they could learn about the enemy, the better. It also didn't hurt to take personal knick-knacks to vex them further. That thought sparked another one, and Warden checked the mission clock; time was tight, but they still had spare.

He cast his eyes around the room until he found what he was looking for. He jogged over to a rack of flags on poles near the door, pulled out his Deathless knife and thumbed the vibro control. A few quick cuts and his prizes came free.

There was a glass display case next to the flag poles, and he stuck the knife in that experimentally as well. It didn't so much punch through as shatter the glass into tiny fragments from the vibration. That might be useful in an entry situation.

He grabbed a few more mementoes from the case and hurried back to Harrington.

"Got some pressies for you, hang on," said Warden, opening the small pack on the Marine's back and dropping the loot into it.

Goodwin and Milton had grabbed every data slate they could find and installed several of Sierra's hacking boxes. The tech specialist pulled out her own slate, setting it to grab every file it could find.

"How much longer do you need, Goodwin?" he asked a little testily.

"There's a lot of data, Captain. We'll need about, er," she paused, calculating, "about twenty minutes to grab everything, but if we leave now we'll still get more while we're in range of the boxes." She looked at him across her slate.

Warden glanced at the timer in his HUD. From outside the conference room, the sounds of the firefight were now clearly audible. Warden shook his head. Twenty minutes was too long.

"No, that'll do, we've already burned more time than we had allowed. Let's move, ladies and gentlemen," he ordered, setting a route on his HUD to guide them back to the extraction point. Harrington and Milton began circling back to Warden's position as Goodwin flicked at her slate.

"Move, Goodwin, we're leaving," Warden shouted. The tech

nodded and finally slipped her slate into her bag. She shrugged her rifle from her shoulder as she jogged around the room.

And then, as she passed one of the Deathless, he raised himself onto his elbow and emptied his pistol into Goodwin's back. The tech cried out and stumbled, knocked forward by the impact of the bullets.

Harrington turned on his heel and loosed a burst of fire into the face of the Deathless officer, turning his head to bloody mush.

"Grab her," shouted Warden as Milton and Harrington moved towards Goodwin. The tech was on her knees, one hand on the floor, the other on her arse.

"Get up, Marine," shouted Milton, heaving Goodwin up with no regard for her injuries. "Where are you hit?"

Goodwin grumbled something through gritted teeth in reply as she was pulled her to her feet and bodily dragged through the door by Milton and Harrington. Warden grabbed her rifle and slung it across his back, determined to leave behind nothing that might give the Deathless information.

They stumbled together down the corridor towards the lifts, carrying a cursing Goodwin between them.

23

"Permission for Marine X to use performance-enhancing stimulants in the performance of his duties, sir?" Ten muttered to himself as he used his HUD to order his med-suite furnish him with a shot of combat drugs. "Why yes, you may absolutely do that, Marine X, and while you're at it, maybe you'd like to take an energy booster drink with a healthy dose of caffeine? Why thank you, sir, I'd just love to suck down a violently green concoction that makes my eyes water and my mouth feel like a sweaty retro-hipster has been living in it. Nothing like sipping from a tube on my webbing rather than a good old-fashioned cup." He could probably get by, but if the relatively green Lieutenants Hayes and Brown didn't get it right, a lot of Marines could take a railgun round to the head before they got the situation under control.

Resisting the urge to preemptively puke, he sought out the water tube that protruded from his webbing and ordered the HUD to inject the water supply with an energy cocktail, courtesy of Mueller.

Was this version still a virulent green that looked like a cross between a pressed juice from a trendy tearoom and an energy drink strong enough to keep a university student dancing until seven in the morning? Ten didn't know, and he had long since stopped looking when he'd realised the stuff resembled pond water. It was better not to know. The combination of sugar, caffeine and what tasted like heavily salted grass clippings, was more than enough to make the experience unpleasantly memorable.

It was undeniably effective, though. In a winged clone, you could either drink the stuff or stick to gliding. It was better to drink than try to get off the ground with your wings and wake up the following morning unable to move from the strain it had placed on your muscles.

<Parker, I'm moving to the wall, per the Captain's orders to help out the kiddies with their sniper problem. Are you two copacetic?>

<Copa-what-the-fuck?>

Fucking kids, thought Ten, shaking his head.

<Are you okay on your own while Daddy takes care of some bad guys?> he sent as he shot his grapnel up to the highest roof he could hit.

<Oh yes, Daddy, we'll be fine. Will you bring us back a present?>

<Only if you do your homework. I want to see ten kills before I get back from work. Over> replied Ten as the grapnel motor reeled in the line and he more or less ran up the side of a building. He clambered over the edge of the roof, releasing his grapnel as he did so and ended up on the highest nearby roof, which just so happened to be above the captain's team.

A present, eh? What do you bring the sniper team that has everything it needs? A double-barrelled railgun? No, that would be silly. Under what circumstances would you need two shots at once? he thought to himself as he worked.

He found a ventilation duct and ripped off the grill. He lowered a small package inside, tied it to the remains of the grill and attached a detonator.

Then he sprinted towards the east side of the building, lobbing a couple of other packages over the side to his left and right as he approached the edge. It wasn't effective, but he didn't need any extra weight for this next bit.

He leapt forward off the roof and immediately extended his

Ascendant

wings, allowing the air to catch them before he flapped to gain altitude. Below his feet, the base pulled away as he rose through the air. It was easier than he remembered, but despite the assistance of his med-suite, it was still a huge effort to get sufficient lift to achieve a rapid gain in altitude.

Observing the battlefield below him, he picked out the towers that were causing a problem for A and B Troops. He flagged them in his HUD and sent a broadcast, <Enemy railgun positions visualised. Flagged in tactical map. Moving to take out first target, Lieutenant Brown>

<Roger that, Marine X. Much appreciated. We have two Marines down trying to get a laser to bear on the towers> Brown responded.

<Recommend flanking the south tower with a drone while they concentrate on you, sir. Heading for north tower now> Ten responded, thankful that it was a HUD message and the lieutenant couldn't later whine about his exasperated tone.

<Acknowledged> came the terse reply. Ten imagined the young officer was cursing, angry that he needed a Penal Marine to suggest solutions to his problems.

He dropped into a steeply banked dive, coming around to glide north to south along the east wall of the base. As he dropped he pulled his railgun around and put three rounds through the windows of the north tower. Then he hit the walkway atop the wall hard and at speed, skipped a couple of paces and fell forward into a diving roll to absorb the impact.

He came up into a kneel and he found he had misjudged the landing, ending two metres short of the door. Cursing he shouldered the railgun and squeezed the trigger, sending two rounds in quick succession through the lock. He rose and dashed forward, dropping the railgun and drawing his pistols.

He wrenched the door open and dived forward into a roll that finished in the centre of the room. There were three Deathless left standing, one sprawled against a wall opposite the door, bleeding out. The guards were raising guns towards him, and he executed a neat three-sixty spin as he unfurled his wings, sweeping them from their feet. Ten felt and heard something snap with an unpleasant sound, but the enemy all lost their footing.

He was rising to his feet as his rotation ended, the barrels of his weapons extended in front of him. He was pretty sure he looked like an avenging angel, though if his wing was broken, it probably didn't look that impressive. He was still turning as the weapons in his hands dispatched the uninjured guards with neat precision.

When he stopped, he felt a little sick. Shit. All that rolling combined with the revolting energy drink cocktail was not agreeing with him. He ordered his med-suite to dispense an anti-emetic then turned to the Deathless guard, whom he must have hit when he breached the door. They were still coughing up blood, so he put it out of its misery with a double tap to the head.

Ten furled his wings, which confirmed that one was broken. He added a painkiller to his bloodstream and resolved to stick to walking for a while. Perhaps he'd need a new clone and could finally get one of the ogres to play with. That was well worth the discomfort in his estimation.

There was no way he could get airborne again with his wing as fucked as it was, so he went out and grabbed his railgun, reloading as he returned to the room. The next tower was directly along the wall to the south and seemed to still be intact. *What the bloody hell are the kiddies playing at?*

He sighed. Daddy would have to fix this one as well, it seemed. Sometimes they really tired him out. He looked down at the weapon in his hands. Yes, sometimes the new commandos were a bit like having a bunch of kids running around screaming their heads off, and that was wearisome. But then, sometimes, there were railguns. Railguns and improvisation were a heady combination for Ten.

Walking over to a gun cabinet he grabbed a roll of all-purpose tape and a second railgun. Double-barrelled railgun indeed. *What purpose could it possibly have?* he wondered as he calmly but swiftly taped the two weapons together. As he worked, he kept an eye on the tower to the south, tagging the guards in this HUD. Whistling softly to himself, he tore off the last strip of tape and checked his newly modified weapon.

He rested the barrels on the frame of the shattered window. The wonderful thing about railguns, other than the insane speed the rounds travelled at and the consequently colossal amount of damage they inflicted, was the comparatively spare frames they required, which meant the two triggers were very close to each other.

Extending both the stocks as far as he could, he grabbed a cushion that the sniper had been resting his arms on and shoved it between his shoulder and the railgun's butts. This might sting a little, but it should just about work.

Ten braced himself and took a grip in each hand, then began firing, two rounds at a time. The recoil was insane. The rounds were small, but their velocity was huge. A small mass, moving at a very high velocity had significant advantages, but if there was more energy going out the front of the weapon, there was more coming out the back as well. *Bring on the wormhole guns*, he chuckled to himself.

He was shooting as fast as he could bear. The twin rounds weren't nearly as accurate, but they utterly demolished the cover behind which the targets were hiding. At least a couple of Deathless troopers took direct hits as the south tower was torn apart by the railgun rounds that smashed through the walls and windows, turning chunks of foamcrete into deadly shrapnel.

After he'd emptied both magazines, he fell to the floor and roared in pain. Fucking hell that hurt. His shoulder felt like it had been hit with a wrecking ball. He dispensed more painkillers from his medsuite and rolled over, crawling towards the gun cabinet to grab a new weapon.

His experiment over, he loaded and shouldered the weapon, yelling again as he realised instinct had overridden his intention. Bollocks. He swapped to his left shoulder, struggled to his feet and pointed the weapon out of the window towards the shattered tower. Two guards were staring at him over the broken windows and bringing rifles to bear. The rounds they sent his way began to shatter against the wall below him, and in response, his weapon bucked in his hands as he fired it cack-handed.

He fired three times then ducked before their rounds could find their mark in his head. Ten had barely slumped to the floor before the explosions detonated. He patted the grenade launcher with his left hand. "Good girl."

A few seconds later, he gritted his teeth and risked sticking his head up to take a look. The south tower was gone, or more accurately, the roof had collapsed, the walls supporting them reduced to a small pile of rubble.

<Targets destroyed, Lieutenants Brown and Hayes. Anything else I can do for you?>

The captain cut in at that point. <Brown, Goodwin is wounded, we have the intel we need, but we need cover while we exfiltrate>

<On our way, Captain> Lieutenant Brown broadcast.

Ten checked his HUD and saw the icons for A Troop and B Troop start moving as one. The rate of fire increased dramatically as the Marines moved more quickly, freed from the threat of the railguns. Their aggression was restrained, but there were almost two troops of commandos in power armour down there with C Troop defending their rear. They moved by teams, smashing enemy positions with grenades or simply leaping over their cover and engaging them in close quarters.

Ten checked the location of the captain and his team. Still on the top floor of the operations building.

<Need a hand, sir?> he sent privately.

<We're a bit stuck, the lobby is full of Deathless, and we need a way out. The stairwell is blocked>

<Roger that, en route. Get to the south side if you can> Ten responded.

He moved to the gun cabinet and made his preparation, keeping an eye on his HUD as he did so, waiting until Captain Warden had got to the south side of the building. As soon as the captain's team had reached the south side of the building, he detonated the mines he had left all over the base.

The one in the vent blew out the windows on the north end of the operations building. A series of explosions detonated around the base at various points. *That ought to cause a few of them to need a change of trousers.*

<A little warning next time, Ten>

<Sorry, Captain. On my way to your location>

He moved to the west side of the guard tower and picked up the first weapon he'd set out there, emptying the magazine of the launcher as he sprayed grenades widely across the northern end of the compound. He followed up with a second grenade launcher and then emptied a few magazines of railgun ammunition in the general direction as well. If there was anyone over there, they'd have their heads down for a while. Assuming they still had them, of course.

Now all he needed to do was get to the captain. He slit the tape binding the two railguns and took his own back, then added the other to the pile he'd made in the corner, before taking a few extra grenades and some spare magazines. Then he looked out the window again and checked the mission timer on his HUD.

He sighed. This was not going to be fun. He climbed the ladder in the corner and walked out onto the wrap-around balcony at the top of the tower, then clambered up onto the thin wall that protected it, balancing precariously for a few seconds before he unfurled his wings. Pain shot down his broken left wing, but he gritted his teeth and ignored it, diving off the tower towards the captain's position.

It wasn't graceful, and he almost passed out from the agonising pain. The left wing tip wouldn't properly extend so he had to compensate by leaning his body, but the rush of air against the broken limb wrenched it uncontrollably. It might be a limb added to a basic human frame, but it still had a blood supply and nervous system, and it registered pain just as any other limb would.

His barely-controlled fall carried him towards the south side of the operations building, and he thought he was dealing with the lopsided nature of his wing remarkably well, right up until some bastard began shooting at him. A squad of Deathless troops were pinned down by the advancing Marines, hiding behind a squat enclosure of foamcrete that served as storage for several large, wheeled, rubbish bins. One of them was facing him directly and had fired at him with a combat shotgun.

Pellets shredded the membranes of his right wing, and he plummetted toward the ground, desperately trying to stabilise his fall with one broken wing and one shot to pieces as he scrabbled for something in his webbing. With just metres to spare, he pulled the trigger, holding the launcher with both hands and thumbing the motor switch as the grapnel bit home in a rooftop ahead of him.

It tugged him back skyward, directly towards the Deathless squad, and he snatched a random grenade from his webbing, hurling it towards them. His feet touched the ground at the bottom of his arc, even as the grapnel was pulling in the line and he ran a few faltering steps until it wrenched him up again. The flashbang he'd thrown detonated, and he detached the grapnel bolt, launching himself at the squad of Deathless troops.

Landing with an agonising crunch that brought him to one knee, he forced himself up and forward, straight at the trooper with the shotgun. He threw out his right hand to grab the top of the barrel and push it flat against his enemy's chest, even as his left hand closed over the Deathless trooper's trigger hand. He thrust his thumb into the trigger guard, pushing the trooper's finger down with the trigger.

The shot rang out and took the head off the soldier to Ten's right. He wrenched at the shotgun, ramming the butt into its owner's face, once, twice until he let it go. Ten flung it away and drew his vibroknife, jamming it into the soldier's chin with a snarl then snapping a kick to his left as one of the troopers turned to face him. He lobbed the knife at the trooper behind him, and it plunged into his shoulder. Despite the safety having turned off the vibro function, it was still a heavy combat knife, and it wasn't the first time Ten had thrown one.

He pulled his pistols, and turned to his right, as the last trooper came at him with his own knife. Ten's suppressed weapons discharged in the soldier's face and he dropped to the floor. Five down or injured. Done. Good job that flashbang had disoriented them or they might have given him trouble.

Wait a minute, weren't there six?

He swayed to his right, even as a huge blade slammed down into the ground to his side. Ten screamed as he lost half a metre of his broken left wing entirely, sliced away by the glowing blade. It was just like the sword he'd looted, only working reliably and wielded by an ogre class clone.

Ten turned to face the uninjured final opponent, dancing a few steps back to stay out of reach of the sword. The troopers he had he had kicked in the face and thrown the knife at were recovering and going for their rifles. Ten dropped a pistol and scrambled over a foamcrete planter that protected the walkway from the passing vehicles, desperately seeking cover from the gargantuan fencer.

In any other circumstances, he'd have felt quite secure behind a three-metre long foamcrete planter with a few tonnes of soil and some massive bushes in it. But the ogre's vibro-sword was at least two metres long, and the hugely muscular Deathless clone swung it down in a vicious arc.

The blade sliced through shrubs, soil and the foamcrete planter as if they were nothing more than cheap bio-plastic. Ten scrabbled backwards, and the tip of the sword slammed into the road surface between his feet. The ogre pulled it out, and only the impact of bullets from Ten's pistol held him back.

The Deathless swordsman dropped to a crouch behind the remains of the planter, which was great cover from bullets but bloody useless against a vibro-sword. His magazine empty, Ten decided to try something else.

He dropped the pistol and pulled out his second vibro-knife, thumbing it on as he rose to his feet, screaming a challenge.

"Fucking come on then! Let's be having you, you big beautiful bastard! I'll be wearing one of you sooner or later! Come on!" he yelled at the top of his lungs.

The ogre rose up from behind the planter, with a huge and menacing grin on its face. Whether or not the Deathless had a working translation system, it understood the challenge, and it stomped one heavy foot onto the planter, then the other.

"Yeah, that's right, you climb up on that and roar impressively. You want to fight? You want to fight me?" Ten screamed at it, nodding encouragingly and waving his knife. The ogre roared back at him, presumably an acceptance of the challenge.

"Well, I fucking don't, you gullible twat," Ten giggled happily, pressing the detonator in his left hand as he hurled himself back to the road. The grenade he'd pressed into the soil as he went over the planter exploded beneath the ogre. Ten expected him to disappear in a shower of blood and guts.

Instead, there was a dull bang, and a streak of fire shot up the ogre's legs. Soil exploded upward, and the distinctive thunderclap of the flashbang echoed across the plaza. The ogre staggered back, falling on his arse on the remains of the planter. Ten swore and struggled to his feet, rushing forward, as the ogre snarled and rose up to meet him, swinging the huge blade one-handed from Ten's left, ignoring the flames on his legs.

Ten saw the blade coming in a fearsome arc, but instead of trying to leap back, he barrelled into the surprised ogre, grappling it around the chest. The small, winged, clone tackled the giant ogre, causing it to stagger back. The Deathless trooper dropped its useless sword, but it was too late.

Ten wrapped his legs around the Deathless warrior's chest and squeezed, hanging on tight, then he slammed his head forward to bring his scaly forehead straight into the bridge of the ogre's nose. It shattered in a gout of blood, and the ogre roared, horribly loud in Ten's ears.

But now the vibro-knife hummed and sizzled as Ten plunged it into the chest of the ogre, again and again, stabbing in a frenzied attack until the Deathless trooper finally toppled backwards.

The Penal Marine staggered upright and hopped painfully back from the corpse. Then he reached down and grabbed the sword, heaving the ridiculous blade awkwardly onto his shoulder. He stalked over to the terrified soldier he had kicked in the face and the one he'd thrown his knife at. They cowered in fear as he stood over them, sword still resting on his shoulder.

Ten leaned down and grinned at them, covered in blood and muck, eyes wild. He reached out his hand and the soldiers whimpered.

"That's mine, sonny," hissed Ten through bloody teeth, "and I need it back, so you'll want this morphine." He jammed a tube against the soldier's chest, and it hissed as it delivered its load of drugs through the skin. Then he gripped the knife buried in the trooper's shoulder and pulled it free. The soldier fainted.

Ten looked at the other soldier and saw him glance at a discarded rifle.

"Don't," warned Ten, shaking his head expressively. The Deathless trooper seemed to understand, drawing his hands together and sitting as still as he could.

Ten walked back to the ogre, dragging his new sword behind him, and picked up his guns. He slammed home another round of painkillers and looked around, trying to remember why he was here.

<Ten. We're in a bit of a jam here. How are you doing?>

24

Warden stared out of the window as Ten rounded the corner of a building. Behind him, Harrington and Milton were laying down covering fire and throwing flashbangs down the corridor towards the staircase. The lobby was full of Deathless troops, both trying to reach the top floor and get up out of the stairs.

What they didn't realise was that some of Goodwin's micro-drones were still active, so each time they tried to rush out of the staircase, Milton and Harrington could see them coming. It was like shooting fish in a barrel but it wouldn't last, not least because their ammunition was running low.

The courtyard below wasn't much better. Warden couldn't get too close to the windows because every once in a while the Deathless below would take a shot at them. They were struggling to hold back the advance of A and B Troops, who Warden could see pushing forward to capture the space around the operations building. It was not going fast enough.

"Too long," he muttered to himself, shaking his head as he watched another Deathless trooper make an attempt on the stairs, "it's all taking far too long."

Then Ten appeared, looking a total mess, coming around the

corner behind some of B Troop. His wings were bleeding ruins, his face and chest were covered in blood and dust and he didn't look at all happy. Warden was sure that wouldn't last; Ten might not be looking his best, but he was in his element.

Marine X propped the largest sword Warden had ever seen against the wall the Marines were hiding behind, and snatched a grenade launcher from a protesting colleague. Warden sniggered.

"What's so funny?" Milton asked over her shoulder.

"Ten just arrived," Warden said as he smashed the windows out completely with a few rounds from his pistol. Then he pointed it into the courtyard without aiming and emptied the rest of the magazine. He wasn't going to hit anything, but he didn't need the weight and it might distract the Deathless troopers.

"Goodwin, get your drone out there, I want to see what's happening without getting my head blown off," he ordered.

"Yes, sir," Goodwin responded, throwing the large combat drone out of the window and wincing as she did. They'd given her a plethora of antibiotics and painkillers, but she had indeed been shot and wasn't moving well, even if she had mostly stopped whining.

"Where are you hit? Where are you hit, Goodwin?" Milton had demanded as they half-dragged, half-carried the staggering tech along the corridor. The colour sergeant performed a basic first-aid check as they went, a simple enough exercise with a conscious patient.

"They shot me!" Goodwin had mumbled in surprise as Warden's quickly-rigged booby trap went off at the top of the stairwell.

"Yes, I know that. Where did they shoot you, Goodwin?" Milton asked insistently.

"In the arse! They shot me in my arse!" Goodwin said, apparently incredulous at the thought of it.

"The cheeky bastards," Harrington said.

"Oh for fuck's sake," said Milton and motioned Harrington to stop for a moment while she used her HUD to call up an override on Goodwin's med-suite via and dispense more painkillers and stimulants. She took a quick look and determined it was most likely a flesh wound, a very fleshy wound actually, that had penetrated a joint on the power armour, slipping between some of the armour plates and into Goodwin's left buttock.

"Well, you've been injured now, Goodwin, so you'll have to bring up the rear while we get out of here," Harrington said.

Goodwin wasn't so out of it that she didn't notice the dreadful pun. "Hey! Stop that, I've been shot, it's not funny."

"First time?" Milton had asked sympathetically.

"Yeah."

"Well, it won't be your last if you don't stop pissing about. It's only a flesh wound, Marine," the Colour Sergeant had responded, with substantially less sympathy than the tech had expected.

"Yeah, if you whine about it too much, you'll be the butt of loads of jokes in the company, Goodwin," quipped Harrington.

"Stop it!" Goodwin complained.

"Find us a way out of here, and I'll not only stop, I'll buy you a beer."

"That's a bloody miraculous offer right there, Goodwin. If you can get Harrington to stand his round, nobody is going to have time to make jokes about you getting shot in the buttocks," said Milton.

Ten's commandeered grenade launcher popped repeatedly as he emptied the magazine as fast as he could. There was a pause for a magazine change, then it began to pop again, just as the first barrage of grenades detonated. Warden could tell it was Ten because he'd never known any other Marine to fire a hand-held grenade launcher on full-auto with such aplomb.

He brought up the overhead view from Goodwin's combat drone and saw the Deathless cowering, heads down behind whatever cover they could find. Ten was saying something to Brown and pointing towards the building. Brown was apparently arguing with him. Ten turned towards the troops around him and shouted at them, pointing at the building and they began to let rip. Brown seemed to be protesting.

The Deathless, meanwhile, were keeping their heads down after the incredible barrage of grenade fire. Quite a few were mangled beyond repair.

Ten cracked his neck and Warden could almost hear the noise, almost as if he were stood right beside him. Then he grabbed the sword and shouted again at the commandos near him. He leapt over the low wall in front of him with a painful-looking pump of his mangled wings, and charged.

The Penal Marine ran directly at the Deathless, his ridiculous over-sized sword held high above his head as he screamed like a banshee. The sword began to glow as he reached the first group of Deathless troops and he pumped his shredded wings again to leap over their cover. He let rip another blood-curdling scream – whether of rage or agony from his wounds, Warden couldn't tell.

He twisted in mid-air and kept turning as he landed, swinging the sword in a wide arc and slicing through three Deathless in one blow. Warden winced at that then switched back to his main feed.

"Let's get out there and help, shall we?" he said to Milton, turning toward the shattered window. He kicked the ruined frame its setting, sending it tumbling to the courtyard below. Then he unslung the combat shotgun he'd been carrying as a backup and blasted the suspended ceiling, bringing it down in a cloud of dust.

He clipped his grapnel launcher to his waist then fired it through the hole in the ceiling so that the grapnel buried itself in the foamcrete floor above.

Warden grinned briefly at Milton, grabbed his shotgun and walked out of the hole where the window had been. The line payed out behind him as he rappelled head first down the side of the building, shotgun held before him.

Ten rushed another group of Deathless lizardmen as they began to rise from cover. Warden pulled the trigger repeatedly, and one of them went down. The rest tried to bring their weapons to bear, torn between the sword-wielding maniac on one side and the gun-toting horror running down the wall on the other. They weren't fast enough. Ten disembowelled or dismembered all four of them before Warden even hit the ground.

<Milton, get Goodwin and the intelligence package out the moment we're inside> sent Warden.

<Roger that, Captain> she replied.

He turned back to the building and charged. The Deathless troopers on the ground floor laid down a barrage of fire and Warden ground his teeth, blasting away as he ran. He knew Ten was close behind, using his power armoured captain as cover.

And then a roar erupted behind him. A Troop were following the lead set by their captain and Ten, charging the enemy position and yelling for all they were worth.

<Goodwin, have you got all the data you need?> Ten broadcast.

<At 98% of available data> she replied.

<Tell me when you hit 100%>

<Roger>

Warden didn't have time to think about that as low-calibre rounds pinged off his armour. He vaulted through a shattered window and slammed his foot into the face of a Deathless trooper.

Despite the onslaught of small arms fire, Warden strode into the room firing his shotgun in rapid bursts, not bothering to deal with anyone he missed. He simply pressed forward; the mission data was all that mattered, and Goodwin needed time to complete the exfiltration.

Ten came in behind him and went right, dancing amongst the enemy troopers and lashing out with his sword. The Penal Marine moved continuously, even as bullets sprayed everywhere. The tattered remnants of his wings were spread out by his sides and twirled around in a manner that Milton would later describe as 'like an extremely angry fairy ballerina who's had way too much coffee' although not to Ten's face.

In moments, it was all over. The rest of A Troop were in the building, mopping up what little resistance the Deathless still had to offer after Captain Warden and Ten's onslaught.

<Done, that's all the data, Ten> Goodwin broadcast.

<We should leave now, Captain, while they're confused> Ten sent privately.

Warden really wanted to know what the Penal Marine had up his sleeve, but he knew better than to waste time asking questions. Cohen wouldn't thank them if they fell further behind schedule.

<Fall back to the RV> he ordered on a broadcast channel, triggering the display of the exfiltration route to appear on the HUDs of the Marines.

Ten was ahead of him, having stuck to the edges of the massacre in the lobby of the operations building. He was sprinting away, following A Troop and still carrying that ludicrous sword despite his injuries.

Warden was the last to leave the building, chasing out Milton and Goodwin as the tech stumbled down the steps and into the open compound. The moment he was clear, Ten popped up from behind a wall almost a hundred metres away. The harpy clones had a fair turn of speed, but Marine X must be on combat drugs to keep going with the wounds he was carrying.

Ten grinned and tapped his wrist suggestively. Warden sprinted as hard as he could, and a second later there was a devastating explosion on the north side of the base. The shockwave blew him from his feet and sent him tumbling end-over-end. Half the troop was blown over, but by the time Warden had cleared his head enough to notice, all he could see was Ten, and grinning like a Cheshire cat, as if all his birthdays had come at once.

Warden looked around as he stood up. There was hardly anything left in the north end of the base. Half the operations building had collapsed and the night sky was now lit by the flames that rose from the shattered ruins. Whatever Ten had used, it packed a punch.

The Deathless seemed similarly stunned, their resistance shattered. Those that could were backing away or nursing their wounds, no longer at all interested in fighting.

Warden checked his HUD for casualties and saw that Bailey and Parker were still in position and apparently, still shooting things.

He ordered them to get out immediately and they dove off the wall, gliding back towards C Troop. Behind them, the guard tower blew itself apart in a series of explosions, mere seconds after the snipers were clear.

Warden made notes in his HUD as he watched his troops retreat. He would need to discuss Lieutenant Brown's performance with Lieutenant Colonel Atticus. Whatever his problem with Ten, it should not have needed a heavily injured Marine to lead the charge, secure the success of their mission, and help Goodwin to safety, which had been the only important objective by that point. It was their first time working together, but that was no excuse.

He surveyed the Deathless base one last time and then turned to the assembled Marines. "Let's get going. I'm gasping for a cup of tea."

EPILOGUE

The conference room of HMS *Iron Duke* was crowded and Captain Warden, the last person to arrive, had to shuffle around the table to find space next to Lieutenant Colonel Atticus and Governor Denmead. When he finally squeezed past the throng and took his seat, he was only mildly surprised when a familiar voice whispered in his ear.

"Morning, Captain," said Marine X quietly, "are you ready for the bad news?"

Warden sighed and half-turned in his chair.

"Should you really be in here, Marine? This briefing is supposed to be restricted."

Then Vice Admiral Staines cleared his throat, and Marine X's opportunity to explain was snuffed out.

"Good morning, thank you for coming," he said, looking around the room at the attendees, his face unexpectedly grim and serious. "Thank you to our colleagues joining us by wormhole transmission," he finished, gesturing to the view screens lining the walls from which General Bonneville and a number of other military dignitaries looked on.

"I know you've all been looking forward to a little downtime after *Ascendant*'s mission to NewPet, but I'm afraid, given the information retrieved by Captain Warden, that you'll have to put your plans on hold for a little while longer," said Staines.

A ripple of disquiet passed through the offices until Staines held up his hand for silence.

"Settle down," he said, in a largely reassuring tone. "We've all seen a lot of action over the last few weeks, some more than others, admittedly, but we can't go back to our day jobs just yet." He paused to poke at his data slate until new images were pushed to the holographic display that hovered over the conference table.

"The purpose of this briefing is to bring everyone up to speed on the developments since *Ascendant* left to reconnoitre the Deathless facilities in the NewPet system. A great deal of data was recovered at various stages of the mission, and it is now being analysed by the combined brainpower of the Commonwealth's military intelligence agencies," he paused to allow the wave of tittering to calm down.

"If you have all quite finished with your amusement at a joke that has to be at least a millennium old," Staines admonished sternly, "we'll move on.

"You've all seen these images from *Ascendant*, of course," he said, zooming in to show an image of a large structure in orbit. "This is the Deathless space station Soyuz, in orbit around the planet NewPet. Captain Warden visited the station and confirmed that it is a staging point through which the extensive troop training facilities on NewPet itself are funnelling tens of thousands of well-trained and well-equipped troops to destinations unknown.

"Having established that the Deathless are shipping troops to more than one location – which of course means they aren't just attacking New Bristol – it was clear that the mission of *Ascendant* should be extended in the hopes that we might identify the targets. Further excursions, conducted on the planet itself, established details of the Deathless training facilities and methods, as well as supplying the majority of the information gathered over the mission as a whole. However, those details are best discussed in further briefings and are not what I wish to focus on today," said Staines, clearing his throat.

"We have now received the decrypted intelligence in full, and the first results of the analysis are troubling, to say the least. This star chart," he said as the projection changed to a view of the Milky Way with a large three-dimensional section broken into volumes distinguished by colour, "shows the extent of space currently claimed by the Commonwealth and other Sol governments."

Another blob appeared, further out from most of the Sol space but almost as large as the Commonwealth itself. The edge of the area touched the volume of space in which the solar system of New Bristol could be found. Warden had to resist an urge to whistle. Behind him, Ten whispered, "Wow."

"As I'm sure you can guess, this region is the area that the gathered intelligence shows as being claimed by the Deathless government already." Staines flicked at his data slate again, and a new volume was marked, with shipping routes all leading from NewPet. "These are the systems to which NewPet has been sending ships."

A murmur of horror went around the room. If the data was correct, the Deathless were not just attacking Commonwealth space, but planets and systems claimed by other Sol governments as well. Simultaneously.

"Those aren't just colony planets, are they?" Lieutenant Commander Cohen asked.

"No, they are not. As well as invading the indicated first stage colony worlds, the Deathless are also occupying systems that Sol governments have, to date at least, deemed unsuitable for colonisation," Staines confirmed.

"Does anyone have a theory as to why?" Governor Denmead asked.

"The prevailing opinion is that they require vast resources for economic growth and are strip-mining asteroid belts and uninhabitable planets to gather the materials they need," Staines said.

"But, if they aren't building colonies, why would they need to mine systems on an interstellar scale? Surely they're not building a Dyson sphere?" Denmead joked, the very idea being universally considered a laughable waste of time.

"Actually, that's exactly the scenario that our intelligence analysts say is our best case, Governor. If that is what they're doing, their expansion would have a theoretical limit, and they would be concentrating on building up one system to an unprecedented level. Other data have suggested this is, unfortunately, not the case," Staines continued.

He flagged another system, well outside the boundaries of Sol space and a significant distance from the known volume of Deathless control. "Now we come to this system, as yet unnamed but designated U-235 for the time being, due to the likelihood of it exploding into something unforgettably nasty. This is the information that has caused the most alarm."

"More alarming than a multi-system interstellar invasion plan?" asked Lieutenant Colonel Atticus.

"Yes, very much so. U-235 contains a shipyard and only a shipyard. It has no colony, as far as we can tell, no troop training facilities and its planets are likely uninhabitable. What we do know is that it contains vast wealth in metallic elements, far beyond what is found in the average solar system. This may explain why they've gone so far out of their existing space to build these facilities. The boffins estimate that the production capabilities at U-235 equal or exceed those of the Commonwealth," Staines concluded, allowing time for that information to sink in.

Warden stared at the highlighted system in a mixture of awe and horror. Ten leaned forward and whispered in his ear, "Told you it was bad news."

Warden frowned. It didn't sound like Ten was being his usual cynical self, it sounded like he had known already. Oh dear. He should probably mention it to Lieutenant Colonel Atticus and get Goodwin to sweep their systems for signs that Ten had breached them for some reason. He wouldn't put it past the Penal Marine to nose around the Commonwealth's classified databases out of idle curiosity.

"On the off chance that any of you missed your courses on the importance of economic power to the conduct of long-term or large-scale military endeavours, let me put it in simple terms. If correct, our analysis of this system, which has been entirely dedicated to the production of ships that we assume are military in nature, can out-produce the combined capabilities of the Commonwealth shipyards across all our systems," Staines said to further horrified mutterings.

"In short, ladies and gentlemen, it appears they have not only the means and the population to start a war against us, the Deathless have the capability to launch attacks against all the other Sol governments at the same time. They've also been preparing for decades and we are already hopelessly outmatched. Have a think about that, and let me know your questions," he finished.

There was another pause while everyone absorbed this.

"Given all this, Vice Admiral, what is the Admiralty planning to do next?" asked Governor Denmead, one of the few civilians in the conference room. "I mean, if the Deathless are almost as numerous and widespread as the entire Commonwealth and they have been on a military footing for some time, we are in a rather worrying position."

"You are quite correct, Governor, both in your estimate of the scale of the problem and your assessment of the concern being displayed by the Commonwealth government on Earth. They are, to put it bluntly, panicked, and I think you'll agree they have good reason. A number of measures are being put in place. New fleets are being commissioned as we speak, recruitment is being stepped up, the colonies are being informed of the existence of a new threat, and intelligence is being passed through channels to other Sol governments," Staines said.

"What about the other systems they've already attacked?" Governor Denmead asked.

"The Admiralty currently plans to launch missions to each of our colony worlds that may have been attacked, and strike back. They will use New Bristol as a staging post for those fleets, which will mean that we will regularly have more ships here to defend the system."

"Does the Admiralty even have enough ships to defend the frontier, Vice Admiral Staines? I mean, without wishing to be rude, we haven't come close to anything on this scale for a very long time," said Atticus.

There was a pause, and it was clear Staines was uncomfortable with the question.

"No, we don't have enough ships," he admitted. "We're bringing everything we can out of mothballs and placing new production orders. Old capital ships are the priority, but anything that can be pressed into service will be seized and made available. Former personnel are being re-activated to provide crews, and they'll be used for lower priority patrols. We're also reactivating retired Royal Marine Space Commandos and other military personnel across the Commonwealth," Staines said.

"That's all reassuring, sir and I'm glad to hear they're taking the situation seriously. Do we have new orders yet?" Warden asked.

"Yes, Captain. We're being sent all the ships the Admiralty can spare to defend New Bristol, as well as ships to form a strike and reconnaissance fleet under the command of Admiral Morgan." There was an audible groan from Ten behind him, causing the Vice Admiral to honour him with a frown. There was an awkward silence and Warden wondered why Ten had reacted poorly to news of Admiral Morgan's imminent arrival. He coughed politely and posed his next question.

"So I'm guessing we'll be going back out to investigate the shipyard?"

"General Bonneville and I are still discussing the details, but yes, you and Lieutenant Commander Cohen will be part of the fleet we select to investigate U-235. Your company of commandos will join *Ascendant* for boarding actions and ground missions, though we anticipate this will be a largely Naval affair," Staines said.

"Thank you, sir," said Warden. Then he turned to Cohen with a malicious grin. "Looks like it's over to you for the next one, Lieutenant Commander Cohen."

THANK YOU FOR READING

Thank you for reading Ascendant, Book Three in the Royal Marine Space Commando series. We hope you enjoyed the book and that you're looking forward to the next entry in the series, Gunboat.

It would help us immensely if you would leave a review on Amazon or Goodreads, or even tell a friend you think would enjoy the series, about the books.

In Book 4, we'll follow Lieutenant Commander Cohen's career more closely, as the mission to explore U-235 launches and the Royal Navy must find a way to survive the threat posed by the Deathless fleet. Captain Warden and his company of Royal Marine Space Commandos will be aboard to handle all the bits the Senior Service don't do.

Can our young officers repeat the success of their first mission? Stay tuned to find out what happens!

SUBSCRIBE AND GET A FREE BOOK

Want to know when the next book is coming and what it's called?

Would you like to hear about how we write the books?

Maybe you'd like the free book, Ten Tales: Journey to the West?

You can get all this and more at imaginarybrother.com/journeytothewest where you can sign up to the newsletter for our publishing company, Imaginary Brother.

When you join, we'll send you a free copy of Journey to the West, direct to your inbox*.

There will be more short stories about Ten and his many and varied adventures, including more exclusive ones, just for our newsletter readers as a thank you for their support.

Happy reading,
    Jon Evans & James Evans

We hope you'll stay on our mailing list but if you choose not to, you can follow us on Facebook or visit our website instead.

imaginarybrother.com

* We use Bookfunnel to send out our free books. It's painless but if you need help, they'll guide you through so you can get reading.

facebook.com/ImaginaryBrotherPublishing

ALSO BY JAMES EVANS AND JON EVANS

Also by James Evans

James is writing the Vensille Saga, an epic fantasy tale that began with A Gathering of Fools and continues with A Gathering of Princes, due for release later this year.

A Gathering of Fools

Marrinek has fought his last war.

Once an officer in the Imperial Army, he has been betrayed, captured and named traitor. His future now holds only imprisonment and death - but that doesn't stop him dreaming of revenge.

Krant lives a clerk's life of paperwork and boredom until a chance meeting with an Imperial courier rips his world apart and sets him on a new course. Sent abroad with only the mysterious Gavelis for company, Krant faces an impossible task with no hope of success.

For two years, Adrava has hidden from her husband's enemies. But her refuge is no longer safe and she must venture forth to seek justice at the end of a blade.

In Vensille they gather, fools seeking shelter from a storm that threatens to drown the city in blood and fire.

A Gathering of Princes

War threatens the city of Vensille.

An unseen enemy strikes at the city and Duke Rhenveldt struggles to maintain control.

As the danger grows, Marrinek forms a desperate plan to save his household and the twins.

Adrava and Floost must embark on a dangerous journey, deep into the

Empire. Can they evade capture long enough to return to Vensille?

Far across the Empire, Tentalus marches west with his armies, bringing death and battle with him. Rumours of betrayal and conspiracy grow. Will the traitors spring their final trap before the Emperor can uncover their schemes?

And in the forests of Sclareme, an ancient horror awakens from its long slumber. Pursued and hunted, can Mirelle and her crew escape to bring a warning to Vensille?

Can anything save Vensille?

Also by Jon Evans

Jon is concentrating on the Royal Marine Commando series for the time being but is also writing a fantasy series. The Edrin Loft Mysteries follow the adventures of Edrin Loft, Watch Captain of the Thieftakers Watch House.

You can read the first book Thieftaker now.

Thieftaker

Why was the murder of a local merchant so vicious?

Mere days after he takes charge of the Old Gate Watch House, Captain Edrin Loft must solve a crime so shocking that even veteran Sergeant Aliria Gurnt finds it stomach turning. With no witnesses or apparent motive for the crime, finding the culprit seems an impossible task.

But Loft has new scientific methods to apply to crime fighting. His first successful investigation caused a political scandal that embarrassed the Watch. Promotion to his own command was the solution. Known as The Thieftakers, they are the dregs of the Kalider City Watch, destined to spend the rest of their careers hunting criminals in the worst neighbourhoods. After all, what fuss could he cause running down thieves and murderers in the slums?

Old Gate and this murder might be the perfect combination of place and crime to test his theories. The Thieftakers are the best Kalider has at tracking criminals, and Loft must teach them investigative skills to match.

Can he validate his theories and turn the Thieftakers into the first detectives in Kalider?

ABOUT THE AUTHORS JAMES EVANS

James has published the first two books of his Vensille Saga and is working on the third, A Gathering of Arms, as well as a number of other projects. At the same time, he is working on follow-up books in the RMSC series with his brother Jon.

You can join James's mailing list to keep track of the upcoming releases, visit his website or follow him on social media.

jamesevansbooks.co.uk

facebook.com/JamesEvansBooks
twitter.com/JamesEvansBooks
amazon.com/author/james-evans
goodreads.com/james-evans
bookbub.com/authors/james-evans-d81a33f8-688b-4567-a2c5-109cd13300fa

ABOUT THE AUTHORS JON EVANS

Jon is a new sci-fi author & fantasy author, whose first book, Thief-taker is awaiting its sequel. He lives and works in Cardiff. He has some other projects waiting in the wings, once the RMSC series takes shape.

You can follow Jon's Facebook page where you'll be able to find out more about the first trilogy of the RMSC series and the upcoming sequel, Gunboat.

If you join the mailing list on the website, you'll get updates about how the new books are coming as well as information about new releases and the odd insight into the life of an author.

jonevansbooks.com

- facebook.com/jonevansauthor
- amazon.com/author/jonevansbooks
- goodreads.com/jonevans
- bookbub.com/authors/jon-evans
- instagram.com/jonevansauthor

Printed in Poland
by Amazon Fulfillment
Poland Sp. z o.o., Wrocław